Rough

Simon Dinsdale

Dedication.

To my fantastic children, Emma, Katie & Nick who's support never wavered.

Acknowledgements. The author is indebted to his wonderful editor Dea Parkin and her staff at Fiction Feedback for their hard work and encouragement. Richard Foreman and Tara at Sharpe books for their support.

Also by Simon Dinsdale
Dark Shadow
Vengeance Day

1

Colin Parr took a swig of whisky before counting the pile of cash. He made a meticulous note of the total and packed it all into his black leather shoulder bag. Parr was a burly man; in his sixties, with a full head of wiry grey hair and a grizzly beard. It was a hot sultry night and the sweat ran from his brow. He poured a fresh shot, settling down to relish the memory of his pleasurable evening.

A sharp rap on the door startled him and he looked at his watch with a frown. Two o'clock in the morning. He crossed the sleazy room in his underwear, scratching his hairy belly as a louder knock rattled the frame. Parr cracked it open an inch, ready to snarl at whoever thought it a good idea to bother him.

The door crashed in, its edge colliding with his big toe, knee and forehead, sending him staggering backwards, hopping on one leg.

'What the hell,' he bellowed and put a hand to his head, which came away bloodied.

A figure in a hoody dressed all in black followed and kicked him hard in the groin. Parr groaned and staggered against the wall as he clutched at his injured testicles, but didn't fall. With a snarl of anger, he clenched his fists and steadied himself to retaliate. His attacker stepped in and thrust a small handheld device into the big man's stomach. The stun gun emitted a loud crackling sound as the electrical charge pulsed through him. Parr let out a high-pitched squeal as he fell, paralysed and unable to stop his assailant from pulling his arms behind his back to snap handcuffs on.

Through tears of pain, Parr watched as two lengths of rope were pulled from a backpack. Then he was dragged across the floor.

His mind worked. Who was this fool to think he could be treated this way? And how was he going to get out of this? Fury replaced outrage. No one treated him like this and got away with it. Someone would pay dearly.

The carpet scraped and stung his body as his muscles responded. He frantically kicked out to free himself. Three more brutally effective kicks between his legs stifled his efforts and left him retching in agony. Then he was hauled into the small bathroom.

'What do you want?' he panted.

His assailant said nothing while tying Parr's feet together with a rope that was wrapped around his wrists and pulled tight. His heels were touching his fingertips, bowing his body painfully back, leaving him rocking on his belly.

'The money. Is that it? It's in the bag. Take it,' Parr gasped.

'You can't buy yourself out of this,' a harsh voice replied.

'You have no idea who you're messing with.'

'Oh, yes I do.'

Parr's shoulders were soon cramping and burning with pain. He desperately wanted to ease his position, but any movement made it worse. A second rope was tied about his ankles and this time looped about his neck, yanking his head back towards his heels, digging into the soft flesh of his throat.

His tormentor removed the handcuffs and sat down on the toilet, holding a Stanley knife and glaring at him.

Their eyes met and Parr's flared with shock as he recognised the face opposite him. Then a frisson of fear coursed through his gut as he realised his predicament was more dangerous than he'd imagined.

'Come on. Take the cash. There's enough there to set you up and we'll be quits. What do you say?'

'Don't worry. We'll be even in a minute.'

The implication confirmed his worst fears. This couldn't possibly be real. He tried to scream for help, but only managed a croak.

'I'll do anything. Let me put it right. Please,' he panted, desperation taking over.

The look of utter contempt and loathing turned on Parr chilled him.

'There's nothing you can do. Except die.'

Parr snarled and spat abuse. 'You won't get away with this. I've still got friends.'

'You're on your own now.' And suddenly there was no one in his line of sight.

'Please, don't do this, I'm begging—'

He felt the rope securing his wrists to his ankles go slack for a moment then release, and the noose snapped tight to cut off his entreaty. His legs inexorably extended, pulling the rope round his neck tighter and tighter, cutting off the oxygen and blood flow to his brain.

Parr's vision blurred and slowly closed into a tunnel. His killer sat back down and stared into his eyes as the darkness took him.

2

A cloud of exhaust overpowered the sweet scent of freshly cut grass as the mower clattered past the open windows. This did not distract the woman at the head of the table, who was in full flow.

It was a blazing hot Friday morning. Assistant Chief Constable Caroline Wix was concerned about the declining performance of the force. She wanted to know what the fourteen senior police officers in front of her were proposing to do about it.

Detective Superintendent Christian Dane was one of them. He was having difficulty concentrating and, judging by the looks of the others, he wasn't alone.

Dane shifted in his seat. His shirt clung to the small of his back and his backside was damp with sweat as he caught his boss's eye. Detective Chief Superintendent Garfield Greenidge, known to all as Sobers, gently shook his head and rolled his eyes.

Dane's mobile rang, making him jump and interrupting Wix, who turned to glare at him.

'Why isn't that thing switched off?' she demanded.

'I'm the on-call senior investigating officer, ma'am. Sorry, but I'll have to take this.' He walked out, trying not to smile at his good fortune. He stood next to an open window to catch the faint breeze and answered the call.

'Hi, sir, it's Bob Soanes here.'

'Hello. How are you enjoying being a uniform sergeant?' Dane replied.

'Loads of fun, but if you've got any vacancies…'

'I'd love to have you back, but there's nothing at the moment. What can I do for you?'

'We're at the Florida Motel, which is on the A12. The management here found the body of a guest tied up in his room. My inspector thinks it's self-inflicted, and he trussed himself up to strangle himself for sexual gratification. They'd locked the door from the inside and the manager smashed the window to gain entry.'

'Why aren't you happy?'

'It doesn't look right. I don't see how he could have tied himself in that way, and he didn't have a safety release. They always have one.'

'Have you identified him?'

'He booked in under the name of Smith. But the car belongs to a Colin Parr with an address in Billericay. I'm sure he's ex-Detective Chief Superintendent Parr.'

Dane knew these types of deaths were not uncommon, but the victim being a former senior police officer could make it problematic. If the press got wind of the circumstances, there would be negative, salacious headlines. He needed to take charge and properly investigate the incident.

'Put the inspector on the line, please.'

'Inspector Green here.'

'This is Detective Superintendent Dane. I'm on my way down to join you. Stop what you're doing and seal the room.'

'You don't need to do that. This is a suicide or an accident, there's nothing suspicious about it.'

'Do as I ask. I'll be with you in about twenty minutes.'

He turned round as his colleagues filed out of the meeting followed by Sobers and Wix, who joined him. Dane explained the situation and who Soanes thought the victim was.

'Did you know Parr?' Wix asked.

'Yes, he worked in Basildon when I was there. He retired a good few years ago.'

She nodded. 'Okay, keep me informed, but before you go I want to see you both in my office.'

Caroline Wix had arrived from the Met three months before on promotion and was fiercely ambitious. She was in her late thirties, tall and willowy with blonde hair swept back in a bun because she was in uniform today. She wore just enough makeup to accentuate her sharp features and looked the epitome of efficiency. The effect was marred somewhat by her reedy voice and hectoring manner. Her predecessor had secured a promotion to Deputy Chief Constable of Hertfordshire Constabulary. Dane missed him because things had changed drastically since he'd gone.

Wix sat behind her desk and Dane stood beside Sobers, feeling like a naughty schoolboy and wondering what was wrong now.

'What's going on with the central team?' Wix asked, glaring at Dane. 'I understand you've not properly supported the DCI.'

'Debbie Evans experienced some issues and reported sick on Monday. We're looking after her. I've taken charge of her team while she's away,' Dane replied.

'It was your duty to ensure this sort of thing didn't happen. Why have you failed her?'

'I accept full responsibility and I'm addressing the situation.'

'That's not good enough—'

'Hang on,' Sobers broke in. 'Debbie chose not to tell either of us about her problems. She intended to work through them herself, and now accepts she should've sought our help. So don't lay this all on Mr Dane because that isn't right.'

'Thank you, Sobers.'

'And that is something else I take exception to, calling your superiors by a nickname,' Wix snapped.

'What are you talking about?' Sobers growled.

'His referring to you as Sobers all the time. It's inappropriate and demeaning.'

Sobers turned to Dane. 'You should go and attend the incident, Christian. We'll speak later.'

Dane lingered in the corridor for a moment, listening to the distinctive Barbadian accent as they argued. Sobers and Dane were long-standing friends and colleagues. He became Dane's boss after the incompetence of the previous incumbent led to near-disastrous consequences for Dane and his family. Sobers was a brilliant detective and a good leader who vigorously supported his SIOs. This attitude brought him into frequent conflict with Wix.

*

As Dane drove away from headquarters, he reflected on the week he'd just experienced. He was the senior officer in charge of the force's major investigation teams. A unit that, until the previous Monday morning, enjoyed an excellent reputation. Then

Detective Chief Inspector Debbie Evans, who was leading the central team, reported sick with stress.

Debbie had become a senior investigating officer six months earlier. Despite being new to detective work, she enthusiastically accepted the post as the next part of her development. Dane had spoken to her regularly since her appointment and she always came across as positive and enthusiastic. She'd mentioned no problems, so to hear of her collapse with stress was a surprise.

Dane and Sobers had visited her and found her curled up on the sofa in floods of tears. She complained that the inspector and sergeants in her squad openly doubted and criticised her decisions in front of the other officers. She'd assumed it was a test, or an initiation, and once they saw she could do the job, they'd lay off. But of course it wasn't, and they hadn't, and she could no longer cope.

Dane knew this must have been going on for some time and chastised himself for missing the signs, taking the failure personally. Sobers agreed he should take over Debbie's responsibilities.

He'd found an office in disarray and spent the week trying to put it straight. Detective Inspector Mason was the second in command of the team. An experienced officer, whose performance had so far failed to impress Dane. He wondered how Mason would fare with this new investigation.

Dane was so engrossed in his thoughts he nearly missed the entrance to the motel. It was on the London-bound carriageway of the A12 and effectively camouflaged by overhanging foliage. A metal post which must have once held the motel's sign stood forlornly next to the slip road that twisted to the left and into the car park. There was space for about fifty vehicles in front of two, two-storey buildings. Dane parked and studied his surroundings. The place looked like every American motel he had seen at the movies. Ten doors on the ground floor of each building opened onto the car park. Bedrooms, Dane surmised. Above them was an outside landing with another ten doors. These were accessed by an external staircase at the end of each block. A single-storey building which must be the reception connected them. The place looked shabby, with peeling paint and weeds sprouting through the concrete walkways and drainpipes.

Why would anyone want to spend a night in this dump? Dane wondered. He spotted Sergeant Soanes standing with a uniform inspector on the external landing outside a first-floor room and walked up to meet them.

'Good afternoon, sir, I'm Inspector Green. There's really no need for you to be here,' he said, glaring pointedly at Soanes.

'Why don't you run through what's happened?' Dane replied.

Green pointed to a slim, dark-skinned man, who was leaning against the railings puffing nervously on a cigarette.

'This is Mr Roux. He's the manager and he booked the deceased in yesterday evening. He paid for one night, so should've checked out by half ten this morning. There was no sign of him by then.' Green gestured to Roux. 'Tell the superintendent what happened.'

'The cleaners couldn't get in, so I unlocked the door using my pass key. But something blocked it, so I broke the window.' He pointed to smashed glass scattered across the landing. 'The chair was wedged under the handle. I climbed in and found him.'

Green butted in. 'He's trussed up, hand and foot, with a noose around his neck. There's a stack of porn magazines lying on the bed and his clothes are in there. It's a classic case of that auto-erotica thing, strangling yourself to get a hard-on.'

'Bob, what are your concerns?' Dane asked.

'He couldn't have tied himself up like that. The rope goes directly from his feet around his throat, so it was impossible to escape if something went wrong. The people who do this always have a way out in an emergency.'

'There might have been someone else in there with him who panicked and left him when he died,' Green said.

'That's a possibility. But why didn't they release the ropes, or raise the alarm?' Dane replied.

'And block the door,' Soanes added.

'But if there was another person how did they get out?' Green asked.

'You position the chair just inside the door and tipped back against it. Then you squeeze through the door and pull it closed behind you. As you do so the back of the chair will drop down under the handle,' Dane replied then turned to Roux. 'Did this guest have anyone with him?'

'No, he was alone.'

'Has he been here before?'

Roux hesitated. 'He's stayed with us once or twice. I thought he was a commercial traveller.' Dane didn't believe him, but let it run for now.

A white van arrived and Pauline Rose, the forensic crime scene manager, joined them.

Dane briefed her, then called Mason's mobile phone. There was no reply, so he rang the incident office and Detective Sergeant Reece Lewin answered.

'Where's Mr Mason?' Dane asked.

'Not sure, boss, he went out earlier and I haven't seen him since.'

'I want you and four officers to come to the Florida Motel. We have a potential murder here and work to do. Get someone to find the DI and tell him to ring me.'

'Yes, sir.'

Once dressed in protective forensic suits, with blue plastic booties over their shoes, Dane peered in.

'Who moved the chair?'

'I did,' Green said.

'I took a snap of it on my phone,' Soanes put in.

Dane studied the picture of the wooden chair tipped back against the inside of the door. The top of the chair back was stuck under the doorknob, preventing it from being opened. The cramped room was sleazy, with a cheap, stained carpet, a double bed with cabinets on each side, and a table. There was no television or telephone. A tweed sports jacket and a pile of clothes were on the floor beside a pair of black leather brogues with socks stuffed in them. There were pornographic magazines with explicit pictures of young girls on the unmade bed.

The tiny bathroom contained a shower cubicle, toilet, hand basin, and the corpse face down on the floor. A length of rope, secured around the neck and attached to the ankles, pulled the head back, arching the body backwards like a bow. The eyes bulged and a swollen, purple tongue protruded through blue lips.

The perpetrator had used a separate rope to tie the victim's hands behind his back and bloodied lacerations encircled both wrists.

'That rope did not cause those injuries,' Dane muttered, and glanced at Roux, who was watching him. 'Did he have any luggage with him?'

'I don't think so. He might have gone to his car for a suitcase after he signed in.'

'Bob, have you checked his vehicle?'

'I looked in it, but saw nothing of interest, and it's locked,' Soanes replied.

'Where're his keys, then?' Dane felt the pockets of the jacket but only found a black leather wallet. 'How did he pay?'

'One hundred pounds in cash,' Roux said.

'How many other guests did you have last night?'

'Ten. They've all left.'

Dane considered what he'd seen. He agreed with Bob Soanes's assessment. The death was suspicious.

'Okay. This is now a crime scene. Mr Roux, your hotel is closed until my forensic department has finished their work.'

Green looked shocked as Dane turned to him. 'Put a marked vehicle on the approach road. No one is to enter, and the officers are to start a log.'

'How long will this take?' Roux asked anxiously.

Dane referred that to Pauline, who considered what she would have to do. 'Three days maximum.'

Two cars arrived containing Reece Lewin and the detective constables. Dane gathered them together for a briefing before tasking Lewin to go to Parr's home.

'Make sure no one injured or at risk is in there and if there's no reply, get in and search the house. Did you locate the DI?' Dane said.

'No, he isn't answering his mobile and I can't find Ian Lockhart, either. Reg is waiting at the office with everyone else.'

Dane was annoyed. The first few hours of any murder investigation were crucial. If they did the right things during the golden hour, the chances of catching the persons responsible increased. To have his detective inspector and a sergeant missing seriously hampered his ability to achieve that.

He would deal with that later. In the meantime, he wanted another look around. Dane stood in the doorway for a few moments. He considered each crime scene to be like a good book. Read it properly and the story will unfold. Examine it carefully and they would miss nothing.

This was going to be an unusual case, and not just because of the killer's modus operandi. Unlike every other murder victim he'd investigated, he knew this one.

Parr was renowned for being an unpleasant bully and Dane had crossed swords with him early in his service. Parr tried to damage him personally for a reason Dane never discovered. But he had no problem investigating his death and bringing whoever was responsible to justice.

Dane gazed around him, fixing the scene in his memory.

The duvet lay half off the bed, exposing a smattering of semen stains and a larger bloodstain in the middle of the bottom sheet. A mobile phone was on the table with the hotel door key next to it. In the bathroom, he crouched down beside the corpse. Dane could recognise Parr despite the distorted features.

He had attended hundreds of crime scenes and seen the very worst humans could do to each other, especially in anger. There was an overt cruelty to this murder, and Dane wondered if the killer had set up this scene deliberately to fool the police into believing it was an accident.

A surprising number of men kill themselves by practising auto-erotica asphyxia. Dane understood why the inspector jumped to that conclusion. But it would be obvious to any competent investigator that this wasn't self-inflicted. Bob Soanes had done well to spot it. It took courage to go over the head of a senior officer, and Dane made a mental note to congratulate him on his actions.

He stood and winced as his knees cracked, and walked onto the balcony, deep in thought. Who was responsible, and why? How did they travel to the motel and leave afterwards? Why the bizarre method? Dane had seen nothing like this before. Could it be a message? All questions Dane needed answering.

After finishing in the room, Dane went to the reception where a couple of officers were busy examining the hotel register.

One of them showed him the slim volume. 'This won't be much use to us, I'm afraid. Everyone is called either Smith or Jones and the addresses are all suspect as well.'

'Is Mr Roux cooperating?' Dane replied.

'Yes, but he's not happy.'

'Where is he?'

'In his office.' The officer pointed over his shoulder with his thumb.

Dane found him speaking on the phone in French. Roux finished his call and glanced up.

'That was my area manager. He wants to know when we can reopen.'

'Not until we've completed the forensic examination. We also need details of all your employees, please. Have you got any CCTV here?'

'Yes, there's a camera covering the reception and the car park.'

'Does it record?'

'It should do. It's on time lapse and records for forty-eight hours before starting again.'

'I'll need the tapes.'

'There's only one, and it's never come out of the machine.' Roux opened a small cabinet beside his desk where an ancient video recorder sat. He ejected the cassette, but it only came halfway out of the slot. Before Dane could stop him, Roux yanked it out, snapping the tape.

Dane put the tape in an evidence bag and handed it to the officers in reception as Reece Lewin rang him.

'The house is empty, but we've found something you need to see.'

3

Dane drove through the sprawling estate of expensive detached properties on the outskirts of Billericay. The area had become popular with well paid professionals who commuted to London from the nearby railway station. A lot of police officers lived in the area and Dane himself had recently viewed a house nearby.

Reece Lewin was in his early thirties and the least experienced sergeant on the team. Dane hadn't worked with him before, but he'd made a good impression. Debbie Evans described him as capable, although lacking in self-confidence. Dane found Lewin waiting outside a detached house at the end of a tight cul-de-sac.

'What've you got, then?' Dane asked after he'd locked his car.

'This is Colin Parr's house. According to the neighbours, he lived here with his wife Joyce until about eight years ago when they moved to their home in France. Since then, they've rented this place out. At the beginning of this year, he returned alone, and no one's seen her at all.'

'Good work. So, what is it I need to see?'

'We found the house insecure when we arrived. Come on in and I'll show you what we've discovered.'

The lack of furniture struck Dane: only a battered settee and a card table with a portable TV perched on top were evident in the spacious sitting room. Three of the bedrooms held no creature comforts, while the fourth contained a sofa bed with a single filthy pillow and sleeping bag. A couple of pairs of trousers and some shirts hung in the wardrobe with underwear and casual wear in a chest of drawers.

'He's not brought much back from France,' Dane said.

'The best bit is up here,' Lewin replied, pointing to a ladder on the landing, and led the way up.

Parr had converted the loft into an office with white walls and three bright fluorescent strip lights, giving the space a stark, antiseptic feel. A computer and printer sat on a desk against the far wall, with a leather BMW fob with the car and house keys lying next to it. Bookcases containing hundreds of photo albums, DVDs and CD ROMs lined the rest of the room. Someone had searched in here and pulled several of the albums out of line or scattered them on the floor. One lay open, and Dane saw it contained indecent pictures of children. There must be thousands of images in these albums, and how many more on the computer and disks? he wondered.

'Let's leave everything as it is. Pauline and her SOCOs can go through here when they've finished at the motel. Is there any reference to his wife or an address in France?'

'No, nothing obvious, but we've not searched for papers,' Lewin replied.

'We'll worry about that later. Wait until the scene guard is in place, then come back to the office.'

Dane returned to the incident room where he found Reg Phelan waiting for him. He was tall, scruffy and skinny, in his mid-forties, and had been a detective sergeant for many years. Dane knew he had talent and, with the right encouragement, could do a good job.

'Have you heard from the DI?'

Phelan shook his head. 'He's not called in. I left a message on his answerphone about an hour ago.'

'What about Ian Lockhart?'

'He'll be here shortly.'

'Where's he been?'

'Doctor's appointment.'

Pauline Rose rang to inform him the post-mortem would be at six. Dane spoke to Sobers and briefed him before his final call to Wix.

'You took your time,' she snapped.

'I can confirm the victim is retired Detective Chief Superintendent Parr.' He described the scene and what they'd discovered in the loft.

'This will cause a splash when the story gets out. I'd better form a Gold group to oversee this and manage the consequences. Be at headquarters at eight tomorrow for the initial meeting,' Wix said.

'Can we make that ten, please? I must brief my team first.'

'Can't your inspector do that?'

'No, that's my responsibility. There'll be people out on enquiries this evening. I want to know what they might have discovered before I come to you.'

'Okay, don't be late.'

Dane heard a knock and looked up to find Detective Sergeant Ian Lockhart at the door. He waved him in.

'Where've you been?' Dane said.

'At the dentist, which is why I switched my phone off. I came back as soon as I received the message.'

Dane didn't believe a word but decided he had more pressing matters to deal with.

'Get an update from Reg, then organise the house-to-house enquiries. I want every building within line of sight of the front of the victim's home visited. Interview all the occupants and ask if they knew Parr and when they last saw him. Have they seen any visitors or anything suspicious. You got all that?'

'Yes, but I'm the office manager. The other sergeants do this sort of thing.'

'I set the duties, and this line of enquiry will be your responsibility during this investigation. I'll expect a report on how many houses there are and any returns in the briefing tomorrow. Now, where is DI Mason?'

'He's gone sick.'

'What's wrong with him?'

'No idea, but he said he'll be back in the morning.'

Dane dismissed Lockhart and caught a whiff of peppermint mixed with booze.

'Dentist, eh,' he muttered.

Lockhart was in his fifties, overweight, overbearing and nearing retirement. He had not left the office once in the previous week, which was why Dane gave him the task he had. The sergeant and Pete Mason were close friends and enjoyed a beer together in the nearby pub after work.

Dane stood and gazed into the main office. The major investigation team occupied the whole of the second floor of a new police building. It comprised a spacious open plan space with seven groups of four desks, each with a computer for use by the detectives. Two glass-walled offices lined the outside wall, one for Dane and the other for Mason. The room buzzed with activity as the team got down to their tasks.

*

Dr Hume, the forensic pathologist, was a rotund man who enjoyed telling awful jokes as he worked. He was already regaling everyone when Dane arrived at the mortuary. The cadaver lay face down on the metal table, cocooned in a large plastic sheet. Pauline and her team had lifted the corpse while it was still tied up, and it presented a macabre spectacle.

They removed the sheet and Hume pointed to the deep lacerations and heavy bruising encircling each wrist. 'Those injuries are consistent with restraint by handcuffs.'

'We found none in the room,' Dane remarked.

'They squeezed them tight, and his struggles made the edges dig into the skin, causing the deeper cuts. I'd estimate they were on for several minutes before they applied the ropes. When they cut the rope from wrist to ankle, the victim couldn't hold his legs in that position as they straightened, so he strangled himself. A cruel way to kill someone.'

'It's barbaric. Have you seen anything like it before?'

'No, thank goodness.' They turned the body over and Hume pointed to abrasions on the stomach and chest, just visible through the post-mortem lividity. 'These are carpet burns from where they dragged him into the bathroom. Let's open him up.'

The dissection took another three hours before they sat together in the mortician's office to discuss the findings.

'He died from strangulation caused by the rope between his ankles and neck. In addition, there's severe bruising to his testicles. Someone kicked him several times, crushing one testis. There are also two tiny burn marks on his belly, probably inflicted by an electric stun gun.'

'Parr was a big man. It would have taken some strength to subdue him,' Dane replied.

'The damage to his private parts happened after they secured him, and he couldn't defend himself. That suggests anger or

16

something personal to me. I'll send my report through tomorrow,' Hume said.

Dane sat down with Pauline, and they spent some time reviewing the long list of forensic exhibits recovered from the motel room and body.

'The bed sheet is our best chance for a quick result. They'll get DNA from the blood and semen stains,' Pauline said.

'I agree. Get it all up to the lab today if possible.'

'Will do. They should have something for us by Monday.'

It was late when Dane parked in the driveway of his new home. He let himself in through the front door and the powerful smell of paint hit him. Dust sheets, tools, tins and ladders littered the wide hallway. After hanging up his jacket, he ran his fingers along the wall. He'd been up late the previous evening adding a final coat. He took a moment to inspect his handiwork before going into the sitting room. He found his partner, Vicky, sound asleep on the couch.

Chief Superintendent Vicky Needham commanded the police in Cambridge. They'd met the year before when they discovered a victim of the killer Dane was hunting. They shared a mutual attraction, and soon started a relationship. It had been an eventful time and they'd faced terrible danger together.

The previous November, a small group of renegade Irish republicans had fired mortars at the Remembrance Parade in London. Dane disrupted that attack, but a number of terrorists escaped.

They seized Vicky with Dane's mother and daughter, holding them hostage at his parents' home. It had nearly ended in disaster.

The events of that weekend cemented their relationship and soon after, Dane sold his house in Benfleet and Vicky did the same with her Cambridge home. They bought this nice four-bedroom detached house outside Chelmsford together. It needed restoring, and they'd done most of the work themselves. The project had become a labour of love, but their professional commitments put them behind schedule. Dane had planned to complete the last room that weekend, but those plans now lay dashed.

Dane watched her for a few moments, marvelling that this intelligent and beautiful Chinese lady would want to spend her life with him. Her birth mother had abandoned her as a newborn close to Victoria Harbour in Hong Kong, where a British couple discovered and adopted her.

Vicky had recently started her senior command training at the police staff college in the West Midlands, an intensive twelve-month course that should lead to her eventual promotion to Assistant Chief Constable. They'd hoped she'd make it home for weekends, but the pressures on her were heavy and he'd not seen her for a couple of weeks. Dane woke her gently with a kiss and, as he made them both a mug of tea, told her all about the new investigation.

She smiled as he apologised for having to leave her alone over the weekend.

'Don't worry. I intend to sleep a lot and then do some work of my own, so I won't be much company. Try and make Sunday lunch at least.'

*

Dane left Vicky sleeping the following morning and drove to his favourite café for breakfast. He had patronised the place for years and Tony, the owner, had become a friend and useful source of information. Once he'd finished his meal Tony joined him for a chat.

'Not seen you for a while. Has Vicky got you on a healthy diet or something?' Tony said.

'Nothing as drastic as that. She's away on a course and I've been busy. What do you know about the Florida Motel? Up on the A12.'

Tony frowned. 'I thought it closed down ages ago.'

'It's still operating.' Dane described the case.

'I remember Parr. He used to come in here expecting everything for free,' Tony said.

'I'm surprised you let him get away with that.'

'I was new to the trade and thought you had to look after the law. Then a few other coppers, including you, started coming in and paying for their grub. So I told him, no more freebies.'

'Did he cause you any trouble after that?'

18

'Nah. He was just a bully who didn't like being faced down.' Tony picked up a paper and turned to the football pages. 'And now he's dead. Good riddance, I say. I'll see if I can find out about the motel.'

'That'll be great, thanks.' Dane promised that he and Vicky would be in again soon and left.

The morning briefing went as planned, except for Mason arriving ten minutes late. Word of what they'd found in the victim's attic had swept through the office. The house-to-house team had spoken to a few residents, and they intended to visit more that day, but so far no one had seen or heard anything.

'The priority is to trace his wife and inform her. She's believed to be living in France. Who's next up as the family liaison officer?' Dane said.

'Tom Jones,' Phelan replied.

Dane glanced at the young dark-haired detective, who smiled when he realised he was getting the job.

'Are you okay taking this?'

'Yes, boss.'

'Good, get on and find her.'

Once they all had their assignments for the day, Dane covered one last matter.

'The details of what we've discovered in Parr's house are to stay within these walls. It's likely to be related to his murder, so I don't want any loose talk. I can't emphasise enough how important that is. Okay?'

Everyone nodded in agreement and the meeting broke up as Dane called Mason aside.

'What happened to you yesterday?'

'I felt awful. It might have been something I ate,' Mason replied.

'If you go sick, you tell me. I also expect you to be here for work on time. All the others made it, and most of them were out late last night. If they can get here, so must we.'

'Yeah, sorry.'

Mason shambled back to his office and closed the door behind him. He was a thirty-four-year police veteran and infamous for his string of failed marriages. He looked down at heel, and no amount of peppermint could disguise the smell of booze that emanated from every pore.

*

Dane drove to police headquarters and joined Sobers for the first gold meeting. Wix had invited representatives from a variety of departments and organisations. She opened by explaining in excruciating detail how they would manage the consequences of the crime together. Dane recounted the discovery of the body and what his investigators would work on during the coming week.

'Do you think there is a connection between Parr's murder and what's in the loft?' Wix asked.

'We found Parr's keys in his house. The killer must have brought them, and it's a safe bet to assume they searched through the albums. So, yes, I do think there's a connection.'

Wix nodded and Dane continued.

'We need to discover why Parr visited that motel regularly when he only lived a few miles away. So I'd like your authority to call out the high-tech team to examine the computer. We've got to establish what's on it,' Dane said.

'Can't it wait till Monday? Calling them out will incur considerable expense.'

'We need to study it in place to make sure it's safe to move. Its contents could prove vital to the inquiry and might help us identify the killer.'

Wix remained silent as she scribbled notes. 'Okay, call out whoever you need on my authority. We'll meet again at ten on Monday morning for an update. If there's anything urgent that needs my attention over the weekend, ring me. Dane, Mr Greenidge, come up to my office.'

Once they took their seats, she turned to Dane. 'You do not have an open cheque book on this case. I've agreed to you calling out those specialists because they're needed. But keep a close eye on what you spend because I'll be checking.'

Dane sighed. Money was always tight, but he didn't need reminding of the fact every few seconds.

'I appreciate I have to watch the pennies.'

'Good, so long as you're clear on that. Now, the chief officers agreed yesterday that a journalist is to be embedded in your team. She's doing a series of articles on different aspects of police work and wants to follow an SIO through a case. She'll be arriving at your office on Monday and will shadow you for the next few weeks. We've granted her full access to everything. This initiative is important because it'll address public concerns about the service.'

Dane stared at Wix, stunned by this bombshell. 'You have got to be joking.'

'No, I'm not. You're to assist her with whatever she needs.'

'Why me?'

'Why not you? You're the senior investigator, and this case will be an interesting one for her to follow. It shouldn't take too long for you to clear it up, and then she'll move on. She has excellent credentials, and this will show the force in a better light,' Wix said.

'Are you sure it's a good idea to put her on the central team? There are some issues in that office, as you know.'

'You can work round that.'

Dane was sure she was doing this to unsettle him and provoke an angry reaction. His actions during the attack on the Remembrance Parade had caught the attention of many editors. Much of the subsequent comment about him had been inaccurate and often insulting. Dane didn't like, or trust, the media. He took a deep breath before replying.

'Those vultures have done their best to ruin my life and career. Before you send her to me, tell her I won't be answering questions to do with my family or my past.'

'I'll make sure she's aware of that. But she is to be informed about everything else.'

'Who is she?'

'Her name is Jane Mitchell.'

'She can't publish anything about this current case until it's complete. She knows that, doesn't she?'

Wix slammed her pen down on her desk. 'Of course she knows. We're not amateurs. No matter how good you think you are, there are others around who know better. So do as you're told, for once.'

'I will, as long as you understand I'm doing it under protest.'

'Noted.'

Dane calmed down as he walked up the stairs with Sobers. 'Did they tell you about this?'

'Not that they were plonking her on you. Look, welcome her with a smile. Keep it civil and professional and leave her in no doubt about what she can and can't do. You've got no choice.'

'Okay. But it's a bad idea. What was all that about with her yesterday?'

Sobers shook his head. 'Wix thinks I need protecting from you nasty white boys. She's never heard of Garfield Sobers or Gordon Greenidge and doesn't understand why everyone calls me Sobers. I gave her a potted history of Caribbean cricket and pointed out that my parents, my wife, my children and all my friends, including you, call me that. It's not a problem. She can continue to address me as Mr Greenidge.'

'I bet she loved that.'

When they reached their office on the fourth floor, Sobers slumped into his chair and puffed out his cheeks.

'Wix doesn't like you at all. You know that, don't you? What have you done to her?'

'I haven't got a clue.'

4

Detective Inspector Ian Harding, the head of the High-tech Crime Unit, appeared at Parr's house on Sunday morning in a foul mood. He was a short man with a tendency to lord it over anyone who wasn't as competent as he was with computers. His team's responsibility was to examine all electronic devices seized during police investigations.

'It's a computer. What do you expect me to do with it here?' he complained to Dane. 'I'll unplug it and it'll go in the queue until one of my team has time to copy the hard drive and then we'll view it. There's no rush.'

Dane let him finish his little tirade. 'This equipment and what it contains are now your top priority.'

'No, it's not how we do things.'

'This isn't a debate. You've been seconded to my investigation, and this machine is to be examined at once.' Harding's face reddened. 'That's an order, Inspector, so wind your neck in and get on with your job. I'm concerned there might be a program designed to wipe the memory clean if we push the wrong button and I need to see what's stored on it.'

'It's unlikely we'll find that sort of security here,' Harding replied pompously. He returned a few minutes later, looking sheepish. 'I'm sorry, sir, you were right to be cautious. It is protected and it'll erase everything if I touch anything else.'

'What have you done?'

'I tried to access it, but I'm not a complete amateur. I'll bring an expert here tomorrow. You must make sure no one accidentally touches it.'

'Why can't your man come today?'

'He lives in Sweden, but he should be able to catch the early flight to Stansted and be here about lunchtime. He's expensive. He charges three grand a day.'

'What! Who is he, Bill Gates?'

'He probably knows more about computers than Mr Gates. He's licensed by the Home Office to do this, and it's got to be him.'

'How long will it take for him to find out what's in there?'

'I won't know that until he sees it. But he's the best there is.'

'Okay, do it. In the meantime, you catalogue all the DVDs and CD-ROMs and start reviewing what's on them.'

'I can't do all that on my own,' he yelped.

'Then call your team out to help you. But make certain you're able to give me a summary at the briefing later this afternoon,' Dane said, and rang Wix to tell her about the latest development.

She demanded to speak to Harding, who convinced her they needed to use the expert.

There was nothing else Dane could do at the house, so he drove to the motel and joined Reece Lewin. The sergeant confirmed all the names and addresses in the register were false.

'We asked the manager why that was, but he claimed he knew nothing about it.'

Dane refused to believe that, so confronted Roux. 'What kind of clientele do you attract here?'

'We're popular with couples having affairs, both men and women. Many of my guests only need a room for a few hours. If I didn't allow that, I'd soon go broke.'

'By the look of those registers, you only cater to people who want to remain anonymous.'

'My area manager expects me to keep the footfall ticking over. So, if a Mr and Mrs Smith book in, I won't turn them away, because that's not good for my business. I'm not concerned about what they get up to, as long as they don't wreck the place.'

'Sounds like you're running a brothel.'

'No. You can't say that.'

'How often did the victim stay here?'

'Two, perhaps three times a month.'

'Was he always alone?'

'He was when I saw him.'

'How long would he be here?'

'Only for the night. He'd usually arrive late evening and be out first thing in the morning.'

'Did he have visitors?'

Roux looked away and shrugged.

'You're not being truthful with me, are you? That's not a good idea right now,' Dane warned.

'Many of the guests bring friends in with them. It's difficult to see the accommodation blocks from the reception area. But as I've already told you, if they don't cause trouble, I'm happy to take their money.'

'Do you or your staff provide company for them?'

'No, this is a respectable establishment.'

'That's the last thing this is. And believe me when I tell you I will discover what's been going on here.'

Dane left Roux looking sullen and returned to Lewin in the reception, who apprised him that the CCTV cameras were both pointing to the sky and covered nothing, and the tape was useless. The solitary chef/barman hadn't turned up for work since the murder. He lived in a small room at the rear of the motel and had a criminal record for assault and possession of drugs. The local intelligence officers were extremely interested to discover he'd been living there.

'What's his name?' Dane asked.

'Kenneth Richard Johns, better known as Kenny. His job was to prepare the so-called continental breakfast and run the bar in the evenings. We've got people looking for him. He shouldn't be too hard to track down.'

'Do they provide any other meals?'

'No; which, given the state of the kitchen, is just as well. The place is running with cockroaches and all sorts of other creepy-crawlies. There's no food in there and almost no booze in the bar and no one's pulled in to enquire about a room since we've arrived.'

'Makes you wonder how they have so many people staying here, doesn't it?'

Dane left them to drive home for lunch with Vicky before she had to leave. They chatted over baked peppers stuffed with goat's cheese and topped with pine nuts. 'You must have been slaving over that hot stove for hours,' he mumbled, shovelling the delicious food into his mouth.

'Not quite, but it's better for you than a bar of chocolate.'

'That it is. By the way, Tony sends his love and wants to know when you're going to pop in.'

'How about we go next Sunday? I could do with one of his brekkies.'

Dane smiled as he looked at her. She was petite and extremely fit but loved her food. 'He'll like that.'

'It's not a free pass for you to overdo his full English,' she joked.

'I'll be good and eat a few carrots. What've you got on this week?'

'Equal opportunities and ethics.' She grimaced.

'I'll stick with the gory stuff,' he replied, and told her what he'd been doing.

'What an awful way to die! He must have seriously upset someone for them to do that to him.'

'Yeah, it's not a method you encounter every day, thank God. And I've got this bloody journalist coming tomorrow.'

'Let her do her thing. I doubt she'll come straight out and quiz you about your past.'

Dane knew she was talking sense and agreed he might have become a bit paranoid, but still didn't like the idea. When she left, he waved until her car disappeared round the bend in the lane. Preparing to leave himself, he felt miserable. He loved Vicky and was missing her more and more. The course was important to her but still had months to go. Absence makes the heart grow fonder, he thought as he locked up.

*

Dane watched the crowd of detectives as they took their seats for the evening briefing. They were all chatting among themselves and came over as a tight-knit group. They were working hard with an enthusiasm that impressed him.

Reece Lewin brought everybody up to date with the enquiries being conducted at the motel. Pauline told him her team had finished at the motel and were ready to return the property to Roux. They would concentrate on the Parr house once the computer whizz had done his stuff. Lockhart reported the house-to-house sweep was complete, but no one had been able to provide any useful information.

'I want to see the folders after the meeting,' Dane said. 'Ladies and gentlemen, thank you all for the hard work you've put in over the weekend. We'll all be back here for nine o'clock sharp tomorrow. Have a good evening and catch up on some rest.'

There was a scraping of chairs and the murmur of conversation as they stood and headed for home. Half an hour later Dane was still waiting for the house-to-house folders, so went to Lockhart's desk. As he did so, he heard voices from Mason's office and the chink of glass on glass.

Mason had not impressed Dane over the last two days. The inspector occasionally emerged from his office and made a show of examining some documents or talking to the sergeants. But he avoided Dane and wasn't doing much actual work. He took no part in the team briefings and wore the same clothes every day. Mason looked up as Dane walked in. Lockhart was sitting there and they both had a glass in their hands, a half-empty bottle of Scotch between them.

'Oh, hi, boss. Ian and I were just having a wee dram. Will you join us?' Mason said.

'No, thank you. Sergeant, where are those files I asked for?'

'On my desk.'

'Then go and get them and put them in my office. Leave the glass.'

Lockhart looked surprised but did as he was told, and Dane closed the door behind him.

'Perhaps I didn't make myself clear the last time we spoke. This is not some nineteen seventies CID office where we close the day with a snort. So, pour that back in the bottle and take it home with you when you leave.'

'We're not doing any harm. It's a tradition,' Mason said.

'Not anymore, it isn't. No one else is swilling booze while they're working, and you won't see me doing it either. You're both setting a poor example, and it stops. No drinking on duty, by you or anyone on this team, understand?'

'Yes, sir.'

'I'm concerned that your work is being affected by drink. Is that a fair assessment?'

'No, it isn't. I enjoy a drop of Scotch, always have done, but I know when to stop and I don't like what you're implying.'

'Which is what?'

'That I'm a drunk and can't do my job because of it. I've been doing this for a lot longer than you, mate,' Mason snapped.

'I doubt you're aware of how much you're drinking. Sort yourself out or I'll refer you to occupational health.'

'There's no need for that.'

'Then cut out the booze and seek help before it's forced on you.'

'Okay, I'll ease up, but please don't send me to the welfare people. It'll be the death knell for my career.'

'Make sure you do. I won't accept it in here. Now, how are we set for staff for the coming week?'

Mason blustered for a few seconds before Dane realised he hadn't completed the duty rotas.

'This is basic stuff, Pete, and you should have sorted it out hours ago. Get it done before you go home,' Dane ordered and walked out to find Lockhart putting a pile of folders on his desk. He gave the sergeant the same warning about drinking on duty and sent him on his way.

Dane sat down and puffed his cheeks out. No wonder Debbie reported sick, he thought as he picked up the top file.

There were thirty dwellings within line of sight from Parr's home. Each folder represented one address, and the officers should have spoken to everyone who lived there. It took minutes for him to learn this hadn't happened. There were houses with teenage children who no one had interviewed and seventeen were incomplete.

Dane was about to bellow for Lockhart and Mason when the last sheet caught his eye. It was from the house opposite the Parr residence where an elderly lady lived alone. She recounted being disturbed in the early hours of Friday morning and getting up to make a cup of tea. While she was sitting by her front window, she watched a dark figure leave Parr's house and jog down the street and out of her sight. She knew Parr was living there and had noticed he received the occasional visitor, so thought nothing of it until the officers had asked her.

Dane researched HOLMES but found no record of the woman's information beyond her brief statement. He called Mason and Lockhart in.

'Sergeant, you told me earlier the house-to-house enquiries were complete?'

'That's right. And the DI checked them,' Lockhart replied, defensively.

Dane looked at Mason. 'You've signed these off?'

'Er, yes I have.'

'Did you read them?'

'I had a flick through. I trust Ian.'

'Well, that was a big mistake.' Dane picked up the folders and passed them to Lockhart. 'These enquiries aren't even halfway completed. There are family members no one has spoken to. That's unacceptable, gentlemen.'

'Why do we need to talk to kids? Their parents have told us they saw nothing,' Lockhart said.

'Your instructions were explicit, and I haven't changed them. So why have you decided not to carry them out?'

Lockhart didn't reply, but glanced at Mason for support, which wasn't forthcoming.

'Take these files and do the job properly,' Dane said.

'Yes, sir.'

'Why has nothing been done about Mrs Wallace's information?'

'She's a dotty old bird in her nineties. I doubt she can even see across the road.'

'I haven't seen that one,' Mason admitted.

'It's a good thing I did, isn't it? What she saw might be critical to this investigation.' Dane stared at them for a few moments. 'I'm less than impressed with the pair of you. You're supposed to be senior detectives, showing the younger officers how to do things. If this is the example you've been setting, I fear for the future of some of our people. Buck your ideas up or you'll find yourselves out on your ears.'

They both nodded and shuffled out. When Dane left an hour later, he spotted them both deep in conversation in the garden of the nearby pub. They each had a pint glass of beer and a short beside them.

*

Dane was back at his desk by seven thirty the next morning, preparing for the briefing. At eight the journalist arrived, laden down with a computer case, handbag and a bulging supermarket bag for life crammed full of ring binders and notebooks. She plonked them all down inside the door and gave him a beaming smile before leaning over his desk to shake hands.

'Hi, I'm Jane Mitchell. I think you're expecting me.'

'How do you do? I'm Christian Dane.'

She was in her thirties, attractive, tall and slim, with brown hair worn in a single plait that fell to her waist. Her bright blue eyes sparkled with excitement.

'I'm delighted to meet you. Thank you so much for agreeing to all this.'

'What is it you hope to achieve while you're here?'

'I'd love to watch you and your officers at work. To understand how a major investigation unit works and follow you from the discovery of the body to the final verdict at trial.

'We can help you with that. What are you going to be producing once you're finished?'

'I've been planning this project for ages and the original idea was to do a series of magazine articles looking at the various aspects of police work. I soon realised if I'm to do the subject justice that wouldn't be enough. I persuaded a publisher to spring for a nice fat advance and went for a book. So far, I've spent time with a terrific crowd of uniform patrol officers in Sussex, a dog section in Hull, a traffic squad in Wales, and now you. After here, I hope to do the same with a divisional CID team and a firearms unit. That should take me to the end of this year and then I'll have to sit down and put it all on paper.'

'What've you been told you'll have access to while you're here?'

'Ms Wix made it clear I can see everything.'

'There are some things that you can't know.' He held his hand up as she protested. 'If I'm not able to share something with you,

30

I'll say so.'

'Such as?' she retorted.

'I'm thinking of a situation where I might have to deploy covert resources or deal with personal information pertaining to the victim or their family. It doesn't happen often, but when it does, most of my officers aren't told, so it won't just be you. I should also tell you I'll not answer questions about my past in the army or what happened to me last year.'

'What a shame. I was hoping for an exclusive.'

Dane frowned, and Jane's eyes sparkled as she smiled. 'I'm joking. Until Ms Wix told me where to report to, I had no idea I'd even meet you, much less work with you. If I do drop the odd probing question in, please understand it'll be my journalistic instinct kicking in and nothing personal.' She gave him another disarming smile.

'So long as you understand the rude rebuff is also a force of habit,' Dane replied, and couldn't help but return her smile.

'Fair enough. I'm a supporter of the police and I think you all do a great job. Sometimes things don't go as smoothly as they should and some officers are corrupt, but that's life. I promise you I'll always be fair.'

'Let's start by telling you about my current investigation.'

Jane sat opposite him, took out her notebook and listened intently as he told her the circumstances of the Parr murder and what she could expect in the coming days. She made copious notes and asked incisive questions. He answered them all without feeling he was being interrogated, and her obvious enthusiasm was refreshing.

As they spoke, the team gathered in the main office. Dane took his place at the conference table and noticed there was no sign of Mason.

'Have you seen the DI?' he asked Lockhart.

'No, I've not heard from him this morning.'

There was a sudden commotion at the door, accompanied by raised voices and an obvious struggle. Lockhart stood and ran towards the noise. Dane followed as the row got louder and saw a uniform officer wrestling with Mason as Lockhart tried to separate them.

'What's going on?' Dane questioned.

'I'm arresting him for drink-driving,' the constable replied, pushing Lockhart away and pinning the struggling Mason against the wall. 'He drove into the rear yard and side-swiped three patrol cars, then legged it up here.'

'You can't do that. Leave him alone,' Lockhart shouted, and tried to release his friend.

'Sergeant, stand back and shut up,' Dane snapped.

A uniform inspector appeared, with two more officers following.

'Sorry about this, boss, but I'm afraid Mr Mason is under arrest.'

'Get your hands off me. Do you know who I am?' Fumes of Scotch enveloped everyone as Mason screamed into the face of the constable restraining him. His knees buckled and he had to be supported as they led him away. Dane turned to find all his officers and Jane watching, aghast at the spectacle.

'It seems the DI has had an accident, so we'll have to crack on without him.' He chivvied them all back to the table.

'Before we start, I'd like to introduce Jane Mitchell to you,' he said, indicating her. 'She's a journalist working on a book about the modern police service and will be with us for a few weeks. I'm sure you'll all make her welcome.'

Stunned silence followed.

5

Dane took his time with the briefing; he wanted everyone to focus on the investigation rather than the twin bombshells of Mason's arrest and Jane Mitchell's arrival. After it ended, he returned to his office, chased by an angry Lockhart who barged past Jane, slamming the door in her face.

The sergeant's actions startled him, and he glanced through his office window at her. She held up her hand to show she was fine.

'What are you going to do about Pete?' Lockhart demanded.

'I'm just about to go down and find out what's happening.'

'We can't let those woodentops ruin his career. You've got to do something.'

Dane stared at him for a second. The sergeant's face was working with anger and frustration.

'What would you suggest? Spring him from the cells and spirit him away? The only person threatening his job is Pete himself. This outcome was inevitable.'

'Yeah, he told me what you said yesterday. It's your fault. He's convinced you're out to get him.'

'Aren't you supposed to be his friend? You drink with him every evening after work, you must know how bad he is, but you've done nothing to help him. So, don't lay the blame for this on anyone else. And stop referring to uniform officers as woodentops.'

Lockhart glared at him and then stormed out.

Jane returned with two cups of tea. 'They said you're a teapot, so I made us both one.'

He took a sip. 'Thanks. I'm sorry you had to witness all that within minutes of arriving. It's not a regular occurrence, I assure you.'

'Don't worry, I've seen worse on some of the news desks I've worked at, I can tell you.'

Dane grunted and went down to the custody block where he found the duty inspector.

'What's happening to him?'

'He blew three times over the limit. When he sobers up, we'll charge him.'

'Bloody hell. I'm surprised he could stand, let alone drive.'

'He's in deep trouble. He'll go to prison with that reading,' the inspector said, sadly.

'Can I pop in and see him?'

'Be my guest.'

Mason was sitting on the bench in the cell with his head in his hands, his whole body shaking with sobs. He looked up with tears streaming down his face.

'Are you satisfied?' he snarled when he saw who was standing in the doorway. 'This is what you were after, wasn't it? Getting me thrown out of the job.'

Dane leant against the wall and waited for him to calm down. 'I'll organise someone to drive you home once they've charged you.'

'Let Ian do that, please,' Mason pleaded.

Dane went into the backyard, where two traffic officers were surveying the scene of destruction. One was peering through a theodolite at the other, who was standing at the far end of the yard holding a graduated pole. Three parked patrol cars had been hit and the bumpers and other chunks of bodywork lay scattered across the yard. Mason's car had ploughed through the wall of the property store, and steam was gently wafting around the wreck.

One of the traffic officers turned to Dane and sighed. 'He's lucky he didn't kill someone. Another couple of minutes and this area would've been full of people. He was going at a hell of a speed to do all this.'

'Perhaps he put his foot on the accelerator instead of the brake?' Dane replied.

'Only he can tell us that. I'm amazed he made it here without causing any other damage.'

'That's something, I suppose.'

'Won't help him,' the officer muttered and turned back to his task.

Lockhart appeared and lit a cigarette, puffing furiously as he stamped up and down. Dane joined him and explained the situation and what was to happen to Mason.

'I'm sorry I blew up in there, boss. Pete's a good bloke, but he needs to work to keep his sanity, as well as to eat.'

'Well, he won't be working here again. The best thing he can do is to resign and collect his pension. Look at the mess he made.' He nodded towards the havoc behind him.

'I should've stopped him, but it's difficult with an alcoholic,' Lockhart said sadly.

'We all should have done something sooner. Make sure he gets home when they release him.'

Dane rang Sobers to tell him what had happened and ask for a replacement.

'I've already heard, and I know the perfect candidate for the job. I'll sort that out with Wix,' Sobers said.

Pauline Rose rang him with some good news. 'The lab has found a full DNA profile from the blood on the motel sheet matching a thirteen-year-old girl called Laura Hobbs. She's been on the system for about six months following an arrest and caution for shoplifting in Chelmsford. Her fingerprints are in the motel room as well.'

'Thanks. How're your people getting on at the house?'

'They've finished the rooms and all that's left is the loft. They'll crack on up there once they sort the computer out.'

Dane handed Laura Hobbs's details to Reg Phelan. 'Research this girl and find out everything you can about her as a priority.'

'Will do, boss.'

'I'm going to Parr's house to meet the genius,' he announced, then looked at Jane. 'Would you like to come with me?'

'Yes, please. That would be great,' and she grabbed her bags.

As they drove towards Billericay, Dane asked about her background.

'I read English at Sussex and followed that with a diploma in journalism. Then I did a three-year journalistic apprenticeship slogging around regional newspapers. I must have made the grade because I got a job with a national tabloid, but I wasn't there for long.'

'Why not?'

'I hated the whole set-up. The constant pressure to find a story, any story, by any means. The concept of ethical behaviour didn't exist, and that wasn't how I wanted to work. There was a culture of harassment and bullying and I suffered a lot of that. I wouldn't put up with it though and fought back, which only egged them on. If you complained, they labelled you a troublemaker. The last straw came when two sub-editors cornered me in the lift. They thought the hazing was a rite of passage for any new hack and they dealt out most of it. Anyway, those creeps decided I needed a lesson and tried to strip me.'

'Oh dear, what happened?'

'Well, I've done karate since I was four, played rugby at university and I'm gay. So being groped by those two got my dander up.'

Dane laughed. 'What did you do?'

'I took steps to defend myself and when the doors opened onto the newsroom, they were both out cold on the floor. Someone who beats up editors isn't popular, so they fired me. And before you ask, nothing happened to them. I should have taken the lot of them to an industrial tribunal, but I couldn't be bothered. But it turned out well for me because with my reputation as a thug swilling about, no one would employ me. So, I had to go freelance. I specialised in crime and policing affairs, and I've built up a reputation for writing well-researched articles. How about you?'

Dane was about to tell her she was straying onto dangerous ground but stopped himself. Despite his reservations and only knowing her for a matter of hours, he liked her. She wasn't the usual type of hack he'd come across.

'Grew up, joined the army, served in Ireland, joined the police, and here we are.'

'There you are. It's easy to open up, eh,' she grinned.

'That's all you're getting.'

Inspector Harding greeted them at the front door. 'Morning, sir,' he said, staring at Jane.

Dane introduced her and they followed him up to the attic, where a tall, good-looking man was sitting at the computer. 'This is Julian Wright,' Harding said.

36

He spun round in the chair and smiled. 'Hello. Thank you for calling me in. This is an interesting case. I can tell you the machine has got three high-grade security protocols set up on it. Unless you press the right keys in the correct sequence, everything on the hard drive will fry. This protection is a cut above standard stuff these days and I'd only expect to find it when it's related to organised crime.'

'How long before you can get into it?' Dane asked.

'I'm already in.'

Dane blinked with surprise. 'When did you arrive?'

'About ten minutes ago. There are hundreds of thousands of picture files on it, all kiddie porn. I suggest you bring in my old mates from the Child Exploitation Command at the National Crime Agency. More their line, and I must be back in Sweden in time to give a lecture tomorrow morning.' He turned to Harding. 'Right, Ian, you owe me lunch.'

'My guys will take the computer to our office at headquarters, boss. I've already contacted CEOP and they're sending some people down.'

'Okay, ask them to ring me after they've had a look. And I want to know what's on there.'

'Is that it?' Jane said, as they walked downstairs.

'Yes, we'll wait for the National Crime Agency to determine what this set-up might be linked to. I'm not surprised it's full of indecent pictures of kids. But the examination will take weeks.'

'So where do we go now?'

'We're going to pop over the road for a chat with Mrs Wallace. If she doesn't want you in there, you'll have to stay outside, I'm afraid.'

'Don't tell her who I am, then,' Jane replied, and Dane turned to her with a single eyebrow raised. She held her hands up.

'Yes, I know, you're only joking,' he grinned.

The door was answered by an elderly lady who was almost as wide as she was tall. She squinted at the two strangers on her doorstep.

'Hello, who are you?' she asked, putting her glasses on.

'My name is Detective Superintendent Dane, and this is Jane

Mitchell. Is it convenient to speak with you about what you saw the other night?'

'Of course, come in.' She waved them inside and hobbled painfully into her front room where she showed them each to a seat. She lowered herself gingerly into a comfortable armchair close to the window.

Once they were all settled, Jane said, 'Mrs Wallace, I'm a journalist shadowing Mr Dane. Do you mind if I stay and listen to your conversation?'

'Please do, dear. It's always nice to have visitors.'

Dane asked her to run through what she'd seen and reported to his officers.

'I'm riddled with arthritis,' she explained with a grimace. 'The pain often wakes me in the night. Usually I only need to take a couple of tablets and I get off again. But Thursday was bad and kept me awake. I got up at four to make a hot drink and move about a bit. I was in this chair when I noticed a figure come out through Parr's gate. He wasn't very tall, slim, and wearing a top with a hood pulled up over the head so I couldn't see the face. He jogged away from me and down the street, and through the gap in the hedge at the end of the road.'

'What colour was his clothing?'

'It was all dark.'

'Was he carrying anything?'

'A small backpack.'

'Do you know the Parrs?'

'Oh yes. They lived here for years. Everyone was so pleased when they moved away because we all got some blissful peace and quiet. But then he returned. Alone.'

'Have you seen his wife?'

'No, thank goodness. He used to be in the police, although what they were doing employing him, I don't know. They were both nasty pieces of work.'

'They weren't popular, then?'

Mrs Wallace laughed. 'No one liked them at all. They would throw loud parties and woe betide anyone who had the nerve to complain about the noise. The mouth on her was a disgrace and if you crossed either of them, watch out, because they'd make your life a misery. No, they were both horrible examples of human beings.'

'Who attended their parties?'

'No idea. None of the neighbours were ever invited.'

'Has he had any visitors since he returned?'

'There is one chap who arrived in a battered old black BMW estate. He visited about half a dozen times and was usually in there for around twenty minutes, I suppose.'

'Was he alone?'

'He was when I saw him.'

'Could you describe him?'

'I'd say he was five foot ten, or thereabouts. Slim, and looked Asian or Arab, always scruffy, wearing trainers and jeans.'

'Could he be the person you watched the other morning?'

Mrs Wallace pursed her lips and thought for a few moments. 'The person the other night looked shorter to me. They both had the same build...'

'Do you recall seeing anyone else visiting Parr?'

'There was an expensive-looking silver Mercedes parked outside once or twice but I never saw the driver.'

'How good is your eyesight?'

'Good enough when I wear my glasses, and I had them on.' She hauled herself out of her chair and beckoned Dane over. 'See that red car up there?' He nodded, and she recited the registration number.

'I've got that right, haven't I?' she declared with a grin.

'Yes, you have. Can you read that one?' he said, pointing to his own vehicle.

She read it without hesitation. 'Mind you, I wouldn't be able to see that far without my glasses.'

'Thank you for all your help. If you remember anything else, give me a ring,' Dane said and handed her his card.

They returned to the office, and when they walked in, Reg called Dane over.

'The girl whose DNA was at the scene went missing last Thursday afternoon and reappeared on Friday evening. The manager at the home wouldn't tell me much over the phone. But they reported her missing again this morning.'

'What grading did the local division give her?'

'Low.'

'But she's only thirteen years old!'

'It's not the first time she's done this and everyone's fed up with her.'

'That's no excuse. Okay, you have my authority to increase the risk assessment to high and ring the manager. What's her name?'

'Mrs Bone, Iris Bone.'

'Tell her to expect us in the next hour. I'll want to read the girl's record and speak to the other kids as well.'

'She won't like that.'

'Don't you worry about that, just advise her we're on our way.'

Dane contacted the head of social services for the county, explaining the situation and what he wanted to do. 'Oh, and I've got a journalist in tow. Can I take her with me?'

'Absolutely not. I'm happy to provide you with all the help you need, but that's not possible.'

'I understand.' He put the phone down. 'Listen, Jane, you know I said there'd be a few times I couldn't include you in something? Well, this is one of them. You can't come to the children's home.'

'Why?'

'I'll be talking to the kids and seeing personal information about them all.'

'You'll keep me up to date with what you find, won't you?'

'I promise, so long as it doesn't compromise the investigation or the children. I'm sure you'd not do anything to cause harm, but it's too sensitive an area.'

Lockhart appeared at the door. 'They suspended Pete, and I've just dropped him off. He's a mess and opened another bottle as I was leaving.'

'Okay, keep an eye on him.'

'Will do,' Lockhart replied.

6

It took several minutes of patient negotiation to persuade the person at the other end of the intercom to open the tall wrought-iron gates and admit them. Once the gates creaked open, Reg Phelan drove through, and up a short gravel drive to a large Victorian-era building. It looked rundown and dreary with single-storey twentieth-century brick extensions sprouting from each side of it. Reg parked and Dane rang the doorbell. It took three long rings before someone answered.

'I'm here to see Mrs Bone,' Dane said to the scruffy young man who peered at his warrant card.

'Is she expecting you?'

'Yes, she is, and we're in a hurry.'

'Wait here and I'll check,' he sniffed, and tried to close the door.

Dane was having none of that and barged in, taking the social worker by the elbow before peering at the identification card around his neck.

'Okay, Nick. Take us to the manager now unless you want to find yourself under arrest for obstruction.'

'It's Nicholas, actually,' he replied looking outraged, but led them down a short corridor towards the rear of the building. The floors were covered in worn lino and there was an overwhelming aroma of boiled vegetables and sweat. There was no noise or any sign of children. It reminded Dane of every prison he had visited. They were shown into a gloomy office with a view over an extensive garden beyond.

A middle-aged woman looked up at them from behind her desk. She didn't look happy.

'I'm Iris Bone, the manager of this home.'

Dane identified himself. 'You know why we're here?'

'My boss has ordered me to assist you, and this has something to do with Laura Hobbs.'

'That's right. You reported her missing this morning.'

'Yes, and for the umpteenth time this month. She's getting close to being out of control and causing the staff a lot of problems.'

'Have you any idea where she might be or who she's with?'

'No. As far as we know she wants some time to herself. She hasn't been with us long and had trouble settling in.'

'Have you made any effort to find out for sure?'

'There's not enough staff to do that. If the kids are determined to leave, there's little we can do to stop them or follow them.'

'I'm surprised you don't know who she might be with.'

'We know she isn't with anyone from here, all the others are accounted for. And we can't force them to talk to us.'

Dane drew a deep breath to control his frustration.

'How many children are in your care?'

'Fourteen; eight boys and six girls. Each is on a tailored programme of education and therapy with behavioural psychologists. They all resent authority at the best of times and forcing the police on them could do irreparable harm.'

'I've designated Laura as a high-risk missing person because I believe she's in danger.'

'She always comes home of her own accord, and none of us have seen any injuries on her. And why is a detective superintendent looking for a thirteen-year-old girl?'

'I'm investigating the murder in a motel room at the end of last week.'

'That was the ex-copper, wasn't it?'

'That's right. We found Laura Hobbs's DNA at the crime scene.'

'She couldn't have done that.'

'I'm sure she didn't. But she was in there on the night the victim died. And now she's disappeared again. So, we are extremely concerned for her welfare, and I could do with your help.'

'What is it you want to do?'

'I'd like to read her file and speak to the other children together first, then individually. They might have an idea about her movements or who she's with. I'll need you or one of your staff to act as their appropriate adult while we have those conversations.'

'I'll do that, just to ensure they're not put under any pressure.'

Dane took a moment to quell the angry retort on the tip of his tongue. Bone's comment implied he wasn't to be trusted and it irritated him. She clearly didn't want them there, but angering her

42

even more would only delay his work, so he drew another deep breath.

'I'm only trying to make sure Laura's safe. I won't do anything to harm any of them. You have my assurance on that, but we must do this quickly.'

Bone thought for a moment then checked her watch. 'They're in lessons for the next fifteen minutes. When they're finished, we'll bring them to the dining room.'

They sat in the corridor where Nicholas brought them Laura Hobbs's file. Dane skimmed through and discovered she'd been born in Tower Hamlets, an area of East London the word deprived described perfectly. Her mother was a prostitute and there was no named father. Social services had left her with the mother until a physical examination revealed she was being abused. She was taken into care and her childhood became a never-ending string of children's homes and foster placements. Laura never remained at the same school for more than a year and soon after arriving in Chelmsford she was caught shoplifting, and that's when the police collected her DNA. That was her first brush with the law, and Dane wondered what had prompted it.

There were several passport-size photographs of her, one taken every year and stapled to the inside of the cover. It was a depressing pictorial record of the development of a frightened child into a young girl who'd seen too much. Laura's brown eyes, set amid pinched features framed with lank shoulder-length hair, looked back at the camera in the most recent snap.

She showed no emotion, just a flat deadpan expression. Reading about her miserable life reminded Dane how lucky he was. His upbringing had been so different. A stable home provided by loving parents, never having to worry about where he'd be sleeping that night or which school he'd be at next term. Dane couldn't begin to understand what life was like for Laura. But he wouldn't have been able to handle it without something exploding. Little wonder she's rebellious, he thought, as Mrs Bone led them into the dining room where the children were waiting and introduced them.

Dane assessed the group for a moment, gazing at the assembled young faces. Most of the kids avoided any eye contact.

'I'm looking for Laura Hobbs, and I'd appreciate your help. She's not in any trouble, but it's important we find her because we're worried she might be in danger.'

They fidgeted in their seats, before a boy of about thirteen sitting in the front looked straight at Dane. 'We don't have to help you or even speak to you, so we ain't saying nothing.'

Dane didn't respond and watched the rest of the group. Most appeared disinterested. One girl flicked her thumb incessantly over the screen of her mobile phone. A small boy with a mop of dark unruly hair and heavy, black-rimmed glasses, nodded vigorously when the other lad spoke. He turned to whisper something to the girl nearest him. She threw him a contemptuous look and moved away, miming putting her fingers down her throat. There was a definite gap between this dark-haired boy and the rest of the group. No one else said anything, so they set up in a side room to conduct individual interviews.

'What's the story with the boy who spoke out?' Dane asked Bone.

'Jake Flinders. He's a deeply troubled young man who likes to be the leader of the pack.'

'Let's speak to him first and get him out of the way.'

Flinders swaggered in and Bone pointed to the chair next to her. He slumped into it and stared at Dane. 'I've already told you I ain't talking to you. Are you deaf or something?'

Dane held his gaze and didn't reply, so Flinders shrugged his shoulders and tried to stare him out, only managing a few seconds before he looked away. With an exaggerated sigh he pulled a mobile phone out of his pocket, which Bone took from him.

'You won't need that. You can text your mates once you answer their questions.'

'Well, what do you want?'

'Do you know where Laura is, or who she's with?' Dane asked.

'If I did, I wouldn't tell you. She's got rights and what she does is private.'

'Is she your friend?'

'Course she is. She's me bird.'

'Don't you want to help her?'

'I ain't helping you lock her up.'

'I'm not here to do that, and I can understand why she wants to go off for a while on her own. But I'm afraid she's in danger. The sort that could cost Laura her life. All I want is for her to be safe and well. Don't you?'

Flinders shifted in his chair. 'She doesn't tell me where she goes.'

'Who does she meet?'

'No one. She likes to walk on her own and have a look in the shops, and she helps herself sometimes, that's all.'

'You said she was your bird. Does she think you're her boyfriend?'

'Yeah, course she does.'

'But she won't tell you what she's up to?'

Flinders gave an angry shrug. Dane was sure he knew nothing, so they moved on. It took another hour to interview the rest of the children. The girls all disliked Laura, and most resented the attention she received from John.

'Does Laura have a boyfriend?' Dane asked the last girl to be interviewed.

'You'd better talk to that smelly little creep, Kerr,' she sneered.

Christopher Kerr was the younger boy Dane had spotted earlier. The others had been scathing about him, saying he was horrible and always stank. When Bone led him in, Dane saw another small, frightened child, alone and friendless in the world. His clothes were old, mismatched and shabby. He smelt as if he hadn't washed for days. Bone had already warned them he was a quiet and withdrawn child who needed careful handling.

'What can you tell me about Laura, Christopher?'

'She's nice and sometimes she talks to me.'

'What else?'

'She doesn't bash me up the way the others do,' he whispered.

'Do you like her?'

'Yes.'

'Will you help me find her?'

'I want to. But they'll hurt me if I snitch on her.'

'I won't tell anyone what you say to me, I promise,' Dane said.

Christopher was silent, his head bowed. 'She goes out and meets some people. They pick her up – down the road in their car.'

'Who are they?'

'There's three of them. They ring her up and tell her when to meet them. But they're horrible. One of them hit me.'

'When was that?'

'Last week, on Thursday. I followed her because I wanted to see where she was going. She walked down the road, and they were waiting for her in the car. She saw me and I shouted at her not to get in. One of them come over and hit me.' He sniffed again and wiped his nose on the cuff of his jumper.

'What did he look like?'

'Big bloke with a shaved head. He was about twenty and wearing these white trainers, really expensive Nike ones.'

'What sort of car were they driving?'

'BMW estate. A black one. I know the number. I noticed it when the man got back in, after he hit me.'

'Can you remember what it is?'

Christopher thought for a moment then recited the number. He looked round at the looks of surprise on the adults' faces and shrugged. 'I like cars,' he explained.

'Do you know where they take her?'

'She said they took her to a house. Sometimes she stays there all night. Like last Thursday. When she come home, I saw a big bruise on her arm, and her belly was hurting. I could tell because she was like my mum when my dad hit her. All doubled over and breathing heavy. But they'd given her some money, so she had fags and sweets.'

'Has Laura told you what she has to do to earn the money?'

Christopher shook his head, 'No, she won't talk about it.'

Bone looked shocked. 'Why didn't you speak to one of the staff?'

'I wanted to, but Flinders says we shouldn't talk to you cos you're the enemy. He told me that if I did, I'd be sorry.'

'Did Laura tell Jake what had happened to her?'

'Nah, she hates that boy, thinks he's a prat.'

'Has she called him that?'

'Oh, yeah. He was dead angry, but she punched him, and he cried.' Christopher grinned at the memory. 'The other girls bashed her up in the bogs.'

'Did you see her this morning before she went out?'

'I saw her walk down the drive. I think she must have had another call. She didn't even have any breakfast.'

'Do you have her number?'

'Yes. I can give you that.' He told them the number and Phelan wrote it down with the car registration.

'Thank you, Christopher. I'm sure we'll find her safe now you've helped us.'

'You won't say I said anything, will you?'

'No, I won't. But I'll let Laura know what you did for her if you like,' Dane said.

Christopher's face lit up, and he smiled. 'Yes, please. She's the only one who talks to me in this place, and she stops the others from bullying me as much.'

'What's his story?' Dane asked after Christopher left them.

'Father murdered his mother. They placed him in care because there was no other family to take him. He's recently started to self-harm.'

'I'm not surprised with all that baggage. You'd better keep an eye on him.'

'Don't tell me my job,' Bone snapped.

Dane had had enough. Her job was to protect the children in her care. She had failed miserably in that, and he was fed up with her hostility.

'From what I've seen and heard here, someone needs to remind you what it is. Those men have groomed Laura Hobbs and are probably sexually abusing her. Christopher sounds like he's having a miserable life here being bullied by the others and it's going on under your nose. I hope for your sake we find Laura unharmed.'

As they drove away, Dane rang the office to have the registration number Christopher had given them checked and within seconds Lockhart had a result.

'It's a black BMW 3 series, but we only have the previous keeper's details. I've asked for an intelligence check to be done. I'll ring you when they get back to me.'

'One more thing. Contact the Telephone Unit and ask for a live cell-site check on Laura's mobile phone.' He gave them the number. 'Is anything else happening?'

'No, all quiet here. But your journalist friend has been annoying everyone with her questions.'

'Get used to it. She'll be with us for a month, so give her what she asks for.'

'I don't like it.'

'Find that information and call me,' Dane snapped.

Lockhart was back a few minutes later. 'There are three intelligence reports relating to that vehicle. The owner is Mehmet Uzun, aged twenty, lives in north Chelmsford.' Lockhart recited the address and Phelan turned their car around.

'He's always with two others. Fazil Teke, nineteen, and Guri Hyka, eighteen. They cruise the town centre late at night and there's been allegations they bother girls outside nightclubs. When they were questioned, they said they were trying to chat up the girls and meant no harm. The reporting officers weren't happy with them, though. Uzun is on the voters' register for that address I've given you.'

'Is there anyone around who can join us there?'

'There's a couple of lads doing an enquiry in the town. I'll divert them to meet you and organise a uniform patrol unit to back you up.'

Ten minutes later, Reg Phelan rolled the car to a stop about a hundred yards short of the address. They were in the middle of a council estate of semi-detached houses. Each had a small front garden, most of which had cars parked on them. The BMW was parked on the street. Lockhart rang back to say Laura's phone had been traced to within a hundred yards of the address they were outside.

'I've got a bad feeling about this,' Dane muttered.

The detectives and the patrol car arrived a few minutes later, and Dane set them their tasks.

'I'll go to the front with Reg and one uniform officer. I want you three to nip round the back and make sure no one escapes. Come on, we've been hanging round here long enough.'

When Dane knew the officers were in position, he banged on the door.

A moment later it was answered by a tall, well-built, shaven-headed man. His face dropped when he saw who was standing there, but he quickly recovered and screamed out, 'Mehmet, trouble,' then tried to slam the door. He couldn't prevent Dane from forcing his way in.

They were in a short hallway. Dane saw a sitting room to the left and a flight of stairs to their right. At the end of the hall was the kitchen and the sound of chairs being knocked over. Dane put both hands on the man's chest and pushed, propelling him backwards through the kitchen door, where he lost his balance and fell on his backside. Another young man appeared armed with a knife. Dane drew his extendable baton and lashed it across the man's wrist. He screamed in pain and dropped the weapon, clutching at his injured limb. Beyond him, a third man was holding a long machete. The back door burst open and a uniform officer appeared holding a Taser.

'Taser!' he shouted. There was a click as he pulled the trigger and two tiny leads shot out and embedded themselves in machete man's chest. A crackling sound filled the air as the electric charge pulsed through his body. He went rigid and crashed to the floor.

'Sort this lot out,' Dane said to Phelan and ran up the stairs.

He reached the landing and saw an empty bathroom and two bedrooms. Dane barged into the front bedroom, crashing into a heavyset white man who was hopping on one foot as he frantically tried to get his trousers on. A naked young girl was spreadeagled face down on the bed. Her wrists and ankles were handcuffed to the four posts of the bedstead and livid weals laced her buttocks. A riding crop lay on the floor beside the bed.

The half-dressed man toppled to the floor with a squeal and stared up at Dane, his eyes like saucers. 'What's going on?' he

49

demanded.

Dane placed his foot in the middle of his chest, pinning him down.

'Where are the keys to the handcuffs?'

'I haven't got them.'

'Don't move,' Dane snapped and went to the bedside. 'Laura, are you Laura?' She peered sideways at him, her eyes filled with tears and fear. 'It's all right, I'm a police officer. You're safe.'

She sniffed and nodded. 'Please take these off. They're hurting me.'

'Who put them on you?' Dane said as he pulled a small leather pouch from his inside pocket. He selected a slim lock pick and got to work.

'Mehmet.'

Phelan appeared, and his jaw dropped at the scene in front of him. 'What the…'

'Deal with that one,' Dane said nodding to the man on the floor, 'and call an ambulance.'

'Try to relax your wrists while I get these off,' Dane said to Laura.

As soon as she was free, Laura curled up in a ball. Dane covered her with a blanket and sat beside her. She watched him through wide, fear-filled eyes and shivered until two paramedics arrived and chivvied him out of the room. He leant against the banisters and took a breath, before glancing to his right. Then he put his head round the door to the second bedroom and froze in shock.

Lying on a filthy mattress was another naked woman with one wrist handcuffed to the bedpost. Dane touched her shoulder and gently rolled her over. She was unconscious. Her face was the size of a melon, both lips split, eyes black bloodied slits, and her nose smashed. Deep purple bruises covered the body, testament to a savage beating. A cold fury rose in Dane as he unlocked the handcuff and called one of the paramedics.

Phelan joined him and gaped at the pitiful sight. 'Who is she?'

'I've no idea,' Dane replied, and they left the medic to her work and returned to the kitchen.

'There'll be some transport here in a minute to collect this lot.'

Dane regarded the four prisoners. The three young men stared back with defiance while the man from the bedroom looked petrified. 'Take excellent care of them. I don't want them to have any excuse to wriggle out of what they're going down for.'

Dane rang Bone. 'We've found Laura, and she's on her way to the hospital.'

'What's wrong with her?'

'She has some injuries, but nothing life-threatening.'

'You're not to speak to her or force her to make statements until I've seen her.'

He didn't bother to reply and hung up before ringing the head of social services.

'Leave Ms Bone to me. I'll send a senior case worker and our child psychologist to meet you at the hospital. They'll assess the girl and make sure you get what you need.'

Dane thanked her as a paramedic came down to find him. 'We want to move them both, but Laura is refusing to go anywhere unless you're with her.'

He followed the medic back up to the bedroom and sat on the bed.

'Laura, they must take you to hospital. Would you like me to come with you?'

She nodded. 'Don't let them hurt me again.'

'They won't. I promise you. How long have you been here?'

'They picked me up at ten and brought me here.'

'How many men have you seen?'

'Three, before that fat pig who hit me with the stick. Mehmet tied me to the bed so he could do things to me.'

'There's another girl in the other bedroom. Do you know who she is?'

Laura shook her head.

'Okay. Don't worry, we're going to get some help for you,' Dane said, then went next door and watched as the medics worked to stabilise the mystery woman. 'How is she?'

'In a bad way. As well as the beating, she's probably overdosed on heroin. We need to get her to hospital.'

Apart from the bed, the room was empty. No sign of drug paraphernalia or the woman's clothes. So where did she shoot up? Dane wondered as he glanced out of the front window.

There were now four marked police vehicles and two ambulances parked in the street, all attracting a growing crowd of onlookers. Phelan kept the suspects secure in the kitchen as they carried the girls out. As the medics made Laura comfortable, Dane noticed a silver car parked at the end of the road. A man was standing beside it, watching. Even at that distance, Dane could see the anger working his face.

'Are you coming?' the medic called, and he climbed in.

7

Dane sat in the far seat as the paramedic checked Laura. She watched him through wide, frightened eyes, and he tried to reassure her with a smile. The heavy ambulance lurched around corners, and he had to wedge himself in to stop getting thrown about. When they arrived, he followed as they wheeled Laura through A&E to an examination cubicle. Two young female officers joined him, and he posted one to watch out for Laura and took the other to find the second girl. The outside doors burst open and paramedics hurried through, pushing the stretcher on which lay the mystery woman. A doctor knelt astride the supine body, pumping her chest as another held an oxygen mask in place.

'That doesn't look good,' Dane muttered as the procession turned into a room and the door slammed behind them.

Dane heard his name being called and turned to find a smiling lady in her forties standing in front of him.

'Hi, I'm Sue Page, from Child Protection.'

'Pleased to meet you.'

'Arthur Clarke, our behavioural psychologist, is with me. We just popped in to visit Laura.'

'How did you get on?'

'Not well. She refused to talk to us.'

'What have the doctors said?'

'She's received some painful injuries from the whip, but they're superficial and there's no internal damage. But they'll keep her in overnight for assessment. I'm sorting out a new placement for her.'

'She isn't going back to the home?'

'No, they've relieved Ms Bone of that responsibility. But we have a small problem because Laura told me in no uncertain terms that she'll only speak to you.'

They joined Clarke, and Dane instinctively liked the pair. Their concern for Laura shone through; they wanted the best for her. They agreed how to persuade her, and Dane went into the girl's cubicle and sat next to her bed.

'How're you feeling?'

'I'm sore. It really hurts where that sod hit me.'

'You've been lucky.'

'Yes, and I've been a prat. When will they let me out of here?'

'Tomorrow, but only if the doctors are happy there's nothing wrong with you.'

'What happens to me then?'

'There are two people outside who're trying to sort that out.'

'I don't trust them. They're all the same. They smile and say they understand, but they don't really.'

'They've promised me they'll only do what's best for you. And I need you to speak to my officers and allow them to examine your injuries and take samples from you. We can't do any of that until the social workers and the doctors say you're fit.'

'But I want to help you now.'

'Then do me a favour and trust them.'

Laura looked at him for a second, chewing her lip, and nodded. 'All right, I will, but only if you promise they won't send me back to that dump.'

'You're not going back there.'

She managed a weak smile at that news. 'Okay, I'll see them.'

Dane left Laura with Sue and Clarke and wandered outside to sit on a bench by the main entrance feeling utterly drained by the day's excitement. A small group of patients stood nearby, puffing on their cigarettes. He'd given up years before, but seriously contemplated asking somebody to give him one. He'd always avoided dealing with child abuse cases, knowing he'd have difficulty keeping his objectivity. The scenes at the house had generated a visceral anger in him towards the people responsible. How anyone could treat children in that way was beyond him. Dane's thoughts turned to the other poor woman, so badly beaten he couldn't even hazard a guess as to how old she might be. He had seen his fair share of evil, but this was on another scale, and bolstered his determination to nail the people responsible. With a lungful of secondary cigarette smoke, he went to find the doctor who was looking after her.

Dr Singleton looked as worn out as Dane felt. 'Do you know who she is?'

'No, I don't,' Dane replied, and described how he'd found her.

'How's she doing?'

The doctor sighed and rubbed his hand over his face. 'Not good. She suffered a cardiac arrest in the ambulance. The paramedics only just kept her alive and we're struggling to keep her stable. I'm certain she's overdosed on an opioid. Do you have any information about what she's taken?'

'No, but there are forensic investigators at the scene who'll look out for anything that might help you.'

'Thank you. We'll be moving her to ICU and we'll do scans and whatnot. I usually only see this type of trauma from a high-speed car crash.'

'What's her prognosis?'

'Poor.'

There was nothing more Dane could do at the hospital, so he drove back to headquarters to brief Wix and Sobers.

'Are this lot connected to the Parr murder?' Sobers asked.

'They are through Laura, but it's tentative.'

'When will we charge them?' Wix demanded.

'As soon as we've gathered some evidence. There isn't much connecting Uzun and his cronies to Parr. We have them for the abuse on Laura and the other girl. If they were involved with Parr, we'll have to dig it up. And that'll take time.'

'Well, don't make a meal of it. I've organised a press conference for tomorrow morning, and I want to be able to tell them something positive. I know how you hate them, so I'll deal with that.'

'Please be careful what you release.'

'I'll decide what is, or is not released; not you, Superintendent. I'm in charge of this operation, so you find the evidence you say is lacking.'

Dane bit his tongue and returned to the incident office. Reece Lewin had organised a team to interview the prisoners.

'What do we know about the prisoners?' Dane said.

Lewin checked his notes. 'Paul Foyers is the man you found abusing Laura. He's forty-eight, single and the managing director of an electronics firm in Braintree.'

'Has he any previous convictions?'

'Only an old drink-drive conviction.'

'Good, take his details to Pauline Rose. She can ask for his DNA to be searched against the forensic samples from Laura. How about the other three?'

'Mehmet Uzun is the owner of the BMW estate car and rents the house. He's twenty and a Turkish national. He's been in the country legally for fifteen years. Previous for drugs offences and assault, but has never been to prison. They've taken him to hospital to check his arm. Someone broke it.'

'That'd be me. He came for me with a knife.'

'He shouldn't be there long. Next is Fazil Teke, nineteen years old and also Turkish. We think he's Uzun's cousin, but we'll confirm that later. He has convictions for assault and cautions for possession of cannabis. Then there's Guri Hyka, eighteen, Albanian and a cocky little sod. We're still checking his immigration status.'

'Have they asked for a solicitor?'

'Yes, a firm in London.'

Dane checked his watch. 'You'll not get much done tonight. Bed them all down and be ready to go first thing tomorrow.'

'Will do, boss.'

Dane trudged up the stairs to his office where he found a message from DI Harding. Officers from the Child Exploitation & Online Protection Command (CEOP) had connected Parr's computer to another of their investigations, and to hundreds of other abusers across the world. The sophisticated set-up suggested he was involved in the wholesale of indecent images on behalf of organised crime groups. Parr had not been on CEOP's radar before and they weren't investigating him, nor had they plans to do so. But they promised to inform Harding if that changed. Dane decided that side of the investigation could stay with them. He would concentrate on catching the killer.

Dane was the last to leave the office for home, where he settled in front of the television with an ice-cold beer after a solitary dinner. He thought over his day. It had been frantic and unexpected. The thing he loved about his job was the unpredictability. Some might say finding Laura and the other girl was all in a day's work, but even for him it had been unusual. The image of the battered face and body of the unidentified woman intruded into his thoughts. It saddened him to think she could have a family somewhere worrying about her, never knowing what happened to her.

*

He didn't have time for a run the following morning and drove to the café. As he mopped up the last vestiges of egg yolk and baked beans, Tony joined him.

'Is that better?'

'You bet. My stomach thought my throat had been cut.'

'Happy to be of service. How's it all going?'

'Busy.'

'Listen, I've had a word with a few people. That motel you're interested in...'

'Yeah, what've you heard?'

'It's a brothel.'

'Do you know who runs it?'

'The bloke minding the women is Kenny Johns. I've known him for years. He's a local and eats in here now and again. The story is he collects the girls from a Turk in Southend and sets them up in a room at the Florida. There are usually ten of them working there of an evening.'

'Any idea where Kenny is?'

'No, but give me a few days and I'll see what I can find out.'

'Who's the overall boss?'

'I'm not sure yet. The guy in charge of the Turks is an Albanian. All I've heard about him is that he's dangerous and an animal when it comes to controlling the girls.'

'Where do the women come from?'

'They're all trafficked in from abroad.'

Dane considered this new information. He had suspected something wasn't right at the motel from the start. Now he had two Turks and an Albanian cooling their heels in the cells. He doubted they could run what Tony had described, but they must be connected, so how did they fit in? They'd already identified Kenny Johns as the barman at the Florida, so it became more important to find him.

'Thanks, Tony, it's a great help.'

'No worries. I'll keep me ear to the ground.'

'I'm grateful, but don't put yourself in any danger.'

As Dane arrived at the incident office, he received a call from Sue Page telling him they were bringing Laura to the station for her interview.

He watched from the viewing room as she settled down, fidgeting and rubbing her nose. She listened intently as the specialist police officer explained how the interviews would be recorded and filmed on video. Laura was asked to introduce herself, which she did with a quiet yet confident voice.

'I'd like you to tell us in your own words how you met Mehmet Uzun, Fazil Teke and Guri Hyka and what you've been doing with them,' the officer asked.

Laura hesitated and Dane saw the fear flash through her eyes. 'If I tell you, am I in trouble? I've done some horrible things with them, and they kept saying I'd end up in prison if I told anyone.'

'The only people in trouble are the men who abused you. You're the victim. Whatever you tell us is used as evidence against them. They can't hurt you anymore, and Sue will make certain you're safe in the future.'

Sue Page nodded her agreement. 'None of this is your fault, you have nothing to fear.'

Laura nodded and, reassured, recounted a harrowing but all too familiar tale of being groomed by Mehmet and his two friends. She had met them as she wandered alone around Chelmsford town centre. They bought her food and cigarettes and made her feel wanted. She thought she had some real friends at last and poured her heart out about her background. Mehmet gave her a phone and kept in contact with her by text, slowly winning her trust. One evening he told her he loved her and took her to his bed. After that they had sex whenever they were together. Then Mehmet handed her over to the other two.

She sipped some water, then described how Mehmet told her they liked her, and she should say thank you. She didn't want to and tried to leave the house, but they beat her then repeatedly raped her.

'They filmed themselves doing it, laughing and posing for the camera.' She took another sip, and Dane looked down and noticed his hands were shaking.

'Once they'd finished, Mehmet showed me the films. He told me if I tried to run or report them to the social workers, they'd use them to prove I liked it and wanted them to do it.'

Then Mehmet sold her to other men. With the pictures and her fear of them together, she believed she had no choice but to do what they wanted. In a quiet voice, she told them Mehmet would put her in the front bedroom and she'd be forced to have sex with four or five clients a day. Mehmet and his two friends all lived in the house. Apart from them and the punters, Laura had seen no one else there. The three of them had plenty of cash and Guri kept bragging about his brother and how important he was, but she never met him.

Laura sniffed and stayed silent for nearly a minute before Dane saw the tears coursing down her cheeks.

'Shall we take a break?' Sue suggested.

'I'm all right.' Laura sat up with a determined look on her face and wiped her nose on her sleeve. The officer passed her a box of tissues. 'Thanks.'

'Tell us what happened yesterday.'

'Mehmet brought that pig in and handcuffed me to the bed.' She paused for a moment to compose herself before recounting being raped and beaten with a riding crop by Foyers.

'That really hurt, and the more I screamed, the more he hit me. And then the policeman came and stopped him, thank God.'

People often asked Dane how he handled some of the awful sights he saw and the terrible things he had to deal with. He would always explain that, as a professional investigator, he didn't have the luxury of getting emotional or squeamish. The people he dealt with were victims, sometimes of the most appalling crimes, and it was his job to catch the criminals responsible. He couldn't do that if the sight of blood or a horrible case bothered him. So, he had to keep a professional detachment to do his job. Laura's account confirmed he'd made the right decision to keep away from child abuse investigations. An intense loathing for the creatures who'd done this to Laura was generating an anger inside him. He must control it, or it might damage the investigation.

At that point Sue insisted they take a break. Dane rang Reece Lewin and informed him of what Laura had claimed. 'Find their mobile phones and get them looked at.'

They all trooped back to the interview room half an hour later and Laura told them what happened at the motel.

'Mehmet got a phone call, and he told me he had an important client for me. He seemed nervous and kept saying I'd better do a good job, or I'd be sorry. I was really scared because I'd only ever done stuff in the house. He dragged me up the stairs to the room and left me with him.' She described the abuse she suffered, and that at one point Parr throttled her until she passed out.

Laura stopped and drank some water before continuing. 'I thought they'd given me to him so he could kill me. When Mehmet came back for me, I was so happy I wet myself. They argued when Mehmet saw I couldn't walk. It didn't bother him I'd been hurt. He just had the hump because I wouldn't be able to work for a few days.' Her anger at the memory flared, her fists clenched and her voice shook.

'Did they have a fight?'

'No, they had a row, shouting at each other, like. I think he scared Mehmet. The bloke told him to clear off or there'd be trouble and Mehmet backed down, but he was really angry. We went back to the house, and I stayed the night with them. He made me walk home the next morning.'

'Were the other two with Mehmet when he picked you up?'

'No, they were at the house.'

'Was Parr alive when you left?'

'Yes. When they were arguing, Parr grabbed me by my hair, threw me in the bathroom and told me to get dressed. Then we left together.'

'Could Mehmet or the others have gone out after you returned to the house?'

'No, they all stayed in playing video games.'

'Are you sure? How about when you were asleep?'

'I was awake all night. I couldn't sleep because I was hurting so much. They didn't go out.'

It struck Dane how matter-of-fact Laura was about it all. She had developed a hard shell to cope with her life, something no woman should ever have to do, never mind a thirteen-year-old kid. Her account put Mehmet and his mates in the clear for Parr's death.

They still had many questions to answer, but as murder suspects, they weren't looking good.

The child abuse officers needed to start the laborious process of writing her statement. That would take days to complete, so Dane left them to it. He sat alone in his office for a few minutes and thought about his own daughter, Robyn. She had grown up in Canada with Dane's former wife and they'd had no contact for ten years. They'd recently reunited, but throughout their estrangement he'd never forgotten her or stopped hoping that she was all right. No one cared about Laura, and it was so sad. On an impulse Dane sent a quick message to Robyn, his daughter, to tell her he loved her.

There was a tap on the door, and Reece Lewin and the interview teams came in. They all settled around the conference table and as he briefed them about Laura's account, their faces hardened.

'We'll start with Foyers. I doubt he's involved with Parr's murder, but he is a rapist.' As they pulled their notes together, his phone rang.

Dane answered it and held his hand up as he listened, grinning. 'That was the lab. They've found a full DNA hit on Foyers from the samples we recovered from Laura. So, nail him.'

Foyers refused to answer any questions when interviewed, but was charged with several sexual offences and remanded in custody.

The first round of interviews with the other prisoners began. They each had a solicitor who encouraged the three young men to say nothing at all. Advice they stuck to. Later that evening Dane joined the interview team. They all clustered around a laptop, peering at the screen. 'You need to see this, boss,' Lewin said quietly.

He played a series of short graphic video clips showing the three men taking turns raping Laura. Dane switched the footage off and closed his eyes. His head was pounding and his teeth ground together.

'Well. If they're kind enough to provide us with the evidence to put them away, we should oblige them, don't you think?'

They all nodded. 'No mistakes. Make sure they pay for this. Go get 'em,' Dane said.

'There's something else, boss,' Lewin said and keyed up another clip and then pressed play. Dane recognised the front room of Mehmet's house. Two men were holding a young woman between them. Dane assumed she was the unknown victim, and they were probably Mehmet and Fazil, although their heads were out of the shot. She sagged between them, whimpering piteously. Someone was talking in a language he didn't recognise as a tall, bare-chested man with a full sleeve tattoo covering his left arm appeared in the frame.

Dane winced as he watched the ensuing beating. It reminded him of a boxer working out with a punch bag. The thug started hitting her face, and a blow snapped her head to the right, spraying blood out towards the camera, which jerked to avoid being splashed but in doing so exposed their faces. Dane fiddled with the pause button until he had a clear, still image showing the three men in custody. The callous brutality was sickening. With a final crashing blow, Guri stepped back, panting from the exertion while the voice delivered what sounded like a statement.

Lewin slowly shook his head. 'What sort of man can do that?'

'The type we shouldn't allow to roam free. Get this video to Technical Support. They should be able to give us a clear image of them, and we'll feed this evidence in against them. In the meantime, we need to identify the cameraman, the language and what he was saying.'

The interviews with the suspects continued into the evening. They all replied to every question with a monotonous 'No comment.'

8

Dane drove to the hospital on Wednesday morning to check on the progress of the mystery woman and get a DNA swab from her. The doors to the ICU were unguarded. He looked round and spotted a uniform officer standing by the nurse's station in an adjoining ward enjoying a chat with the staff.

'Aren't you supposed to be guarding a patient?' Dane snapped after tapping him on the shoulder.

'What's it got to do with you?'

Dane held his warrant card up. 'Who're you?'

The young man blanched and stood up straight. 'PC Adams, sir.'

'Well, Constable, get back to your post and stay there.'

'Yes, sir,' he muttered sheepishly, scuttling away.

Turning to the nurses, Dane smiled. 'Where can I find Mr Clarence, please?'

'I'll ring him for you,' one replied. The second said, 'We didn't encourage that policeman to come in here.'

'If he comes back, tell him to clear off and do his job,' Dane replied, then turned to meet the consultant.

'How's the girl doing?'

'We've stabilised her and put her in an induced coma. She'll go into the high dependency unit later today. It'll be several days before we bring her round.'

'I'd like to keep a police guard here. Is that all right?'

'Is she in danger?'

'The men who assaulted her are in custody, but they have friends. I prefer to be cautious.'

Clarence considered that for a moment. 'If it's necessary, then I'll allow it. But make sure they don't spend their time bothering my nurses. They've got enough to do without fending off the advances of randy coppers.'

'Is that what's happening?'

'Only this morning.'

'I'm sorry about that and it won't happen again.'

Dane found Adams lounging at his post and after a few terse words reminding him of his duty, returned to his car. As he did so, his phone rang.

'Dane here.'

'Hello, my name is John Parsons. I'm a senior investigator with Essex Fire and Rescue. I'm at the Florida Motel. I've been told I should talk to you about a fire we've attended here.'

'What's happened?'

'A member of the public spotted flames late last night and contacted us. We arrived to find the place ablaze. We've just finished putting it out, but the place has been razed to the ground.'

'Are there any casualties?'

'Not so far. We're damping down but if anyone died on the premises it'll take some time to detect their remains. I called your control to report the arson and they told me to contact you.'

'I'm dealing with a murder committed there at the end of last week. One of the rooms was a crime scene, but we'd handed it back to the owners.'

Dane promised Parsons an investigator would call him later and sped toward headquarters, his mind racing. Was this a coincidence? Had they missed something at the motel? Pauline Rose and her team had finished their search of the room and he'd authorised the return of the property to Mr Roux. Perhaps the most recent revelations had more relevance to the investigation than he thought. Had there still been some evidence at the site connected to the three in custody? That was possible; Mehmet had been there and, according to Laura, knew Parr. But why destroy everything?

He found Sobers waiting with Wix in her office. They listened as he brought them up to date. Wix was impatient for results and dismissed Dane with a curt reminder that she wanted charges, sooner rather than later. He didn't respond, preferring to avoid another row with her.

The interviews had been progressing while he'd been away, although the suspects had said nothing. The forensic team had discovered a single fingerprint belonging to Mehmet in Parr's kitchen, but he refused to explain how it got there.

Reece Lewin knocked on Dane's door later that afternoon. 'We've received a translation of what the bloke on the video was saying. The language is Albanian, and he says, "This happens when you try to run from Dragon." I've also checked the information about a gang of Turks selling prostitutes in Southend. The Organised Crime Unit has received the same intelligence and is planning to put them under surveillance.'

'Good work. I'll find out what that is from our esteemed Head of Intelligence.'

Dane joined Lewin and the six officers conducting the interviews in the canteen for a cup of tea. They all looked exhausted. It's hard enough to prepare and conduct an effective interrogation of a suspect at the best of times. If the suspect refuses to answer questions, the procedure is doubly difficult. Dane had dealt with many criminals who stuck to their right to silence as a tactic to frustrate the police. But these three were different. The footage of them abusing Laura and beating the other woman was unequivocal and should lead to long prison sentences for them all. Yet they seemed unconcerned, almost indifferent to their predicament. A lot of that would be bravado, and he wondered how long that'd last once they were locked up.

*

Dane met with Tom Hanson – Head of intelligence – and DI Chard from the Organised Crime Unit the following morning. The meeting turned out to be another disappointment. The inspector explained the intelligence from the National Crime Agency about a prostitution ring in Southend had not, so far, been acted on.

'What exactly have they told you?' Dane asked.

'A dozen young women are being touted around town by three Turkish men.'

'Is there anything about an Albanian being the boss?'

'No. We've heard nothing along those lines, although there might be something in it,' Chard replied.

'How so?'

'Prostitution in London is controlled by Turkish and Albanian gangs. They're efficient at trafficking women into the country and notorious for the ruthless methods they use to keep control. These groups are expanding out into the shires in the same way we're seeing with drugs and county lines.'

Dane explained what they'd uncovered at the Chelmsford house and wondered if they were part of the Southend group.

'I doubt it. The three you've got sound too young to be entrusted with their own franchise. They could be family or associates of the characters in Southend and been allowed to set up something of their own, like an apprenticeship,' Chard laughed.

Dane didn't think it was funny. 'Does the name Dragon mean anything to you?'

'No. But given what you've uncovered, we'll start doing some work on it next week. If we come across him, I'll contact you.'

Late that afternoon the prosecutor authorised criminal charges against the three men. Dane watched as they stood in front of the custody sergeant. Mehmet and Fazil both listened to the long litany against them in silence. Guri reacted angrily when he was told he would not be getting bail.

'My brother will take care of this,' Guri snarled.

'Dragon isn't here to help you now,' Dane said.

That caused a reaction and Guri rounded on him. 'Those little sluts won't be around to give evidence.' He snorted with derision. 'Dragon will get me out.' His lawyer grabbed his arm and hissed at him to be quiet.

By this time, Dane knew they hadn't murdered Parr, a point he made to Wix at the gold meeting on Friday afternoon. She'd told the press conference that the individuals responsible for the murder had been arrested and didn't like what she was hearing.

'Why are you so sure they didn't do it?'

'Because there's no evidence against them. Did they know Parr? Probably. We found Mehmet's fingerprint in his home, but there's a witness who puts him there weeks before. That provides him with a reasonable explanation. Why would they murder him? They had a dispute about what he'd done to Laura. But Mehmet regarded her as a piece of meat. Yes, he was angry she'd not be able to work for a while, but kill him for it? No. To cap it all, she confirms the three of them stayed in all night. We have more to do but they're not our killers.'

'What's your focus for next week?' Sobers asked.

'Tracking down Dragon. He's Hyka's brother and probably the man running the prostitutes. I'm not certain we can connect the killing to the prostitution, but it's a line of enquiry to follow. I need to speak to Parr's wife as well.'

'I think you're being too hasty in trying to clear them, so make sure those enquiries are thorough,' Wix snapped.

'Yes, ma'am.'

'By the way, DI Sally Rendell is joining you on Monday.'

'Thanks. She's just the person to get to grips with that team,' Dane said.

Jane Mitchell had followed the week's events with unabashed glee and asked questions incessantly. She'd been in the meeting and travelled back with him. 'I'll be having a sleepless weekend getting everything recorded. What are your plans?'

'My partner's coming home and we're going to finish some decorating and try to relax. I'm on call, though, so things might change.'

'What happens then?'

'If there's a major crime I respond to the scene and start the investigation.'

'But what about the Parr murder?'

'I'll assess who can pick up any fresh case and on Monday pass it over to them. We all lead several investigations at the same time. Five murders each is the average. Do you want to come if I get called out?'

'Yes, please, that would be great. I'd love to see how you deal with the discovery of the body, so give me a buzz.'

'Even if it's in the middle of the night?'

'Of course.'

Dane admired her infectious enthusiasm, and she hadn't caused too much disruption. Lockhart had taken every opportunity to moan about her, but no one else seemed bothered by her presence.

Dane told everyone who the new detective inspector was to be and noticed Lockhart's lip curl at the news. He visited Laura, who'd finished making her statement and was about to leave to meet her foster parents.

'Can I rely on you to keep out of trouble?' Dane said.

'Yeah. I've been a stupid prat, and I don't want to get into that sort of trouble again. But at least I ain't got to go back to that dump. I hated it there, no one liked me and the people in charge were horrible.'

'What did they do to you?'

'None of them ever hurt us. But they wouldn't listen to me. I know I can be a bit of a pain, but they treated me like a stupid little girl. I didn't get on with the other kids, either.'

'You had one friend there.'

'Who?'

'Christopher.'

Laura smiled. 'I felt sorry for him. He's a creepy git but all the others ganged up on him, especially Flinders. I know how horrible it is to be the one everyone hates.'

'Christopher put me onto Mehmet, so you'd better tell him how much that means to you.'

'I'll text him,' she announced, but then her face fell. 'No, I can't do that, they took my mobile away.'

'How about writing him a letter?' Dane suggested, but her look of utter shock made him smile. 'It's not that old-fashioned, is it?'

'You're having a laugh. I'll get another one and message him.'

Dane pulled her phone out of his pocket. 'We've finished with it, and I suspect your need is greater than ours. There's some credit on there for you.'

He watched as her fingers dashed over the keyboard to check if she had any messages. Then she looked up at him. 'You've put twenty quid on it.'

'Don't use it all at once.' He handed her his card. 'That's got my mobile number on it, put it on your phone or keep the card with you. It's up to you but if you find yourself in danger again, or you need an ear, call me.'

She turned the card slowly in her fingers. 'Do you mean that?'

'Of course I do.'

'Thank you.' She sniffed and wiped her nose. 'No one's ever

done that for me before. I promise I'll only ring if it's a proper emergency.'

It was late afternoon when Dane left her, so he headed straight home where Vicky was waiting for him. They cooked together before getting on with some decorating. As they worked, he told her that Jane Mitchell was not as bad as he'd expected.

'I'm glad it's working out. I'd like to meet her.'

'Perhaps we can invite her out for a meal?'

'Good idea.'

They finished the last bedroom on Saturday afternoon, marking the end of the renovations and a cause for celebration. As Dane cleared up the tools, Vicky got to work in the kitchen preparing for their guests that evening.

John Lord and his wife Olivia arrived bearing a case of very expensive wine as a housewarming present.

Lord was an exceptionally tall, good-looking man in his late forties. Their paths had first crossed in Cambridge at the same time as Dane met Vicky and they were now firm friends. Lord was a veteran of the Coldstream Guards and Special Air Service. After resigning his commission, he'd started a security company called Simple Solutions. Dane couldn't think of a more misleading name because what Lord did was anything but simple. They specialised in, among many other things, intelligence gathering, surveillance, kidnapping resolution and hostage negotiations. Lord recruited his staff from the military and intelligence communities, and they had an international reputation for achieving results. A reputation recently enhanced when it became known that Lord helped Dane with a daring rescue. The story had horrified Dane's commanders, fascinated the national press and provided excellent publicity for Simple Solutions. Olivia was the second daughter of a duke and almost as tall as her husband. She had rowed for Great Britain in the Olympics and now proudly proclaimed herself a full-time mum bringing up their two young sons.

After the meal, Dane and Lord took their drinks onto the patio while Olivia and Vicky made the coffee.

'I see you're busy again,' Lord said.

Dane explained about the events of the previous week, with the murder of Parr and what had happened to Laura.

Lord shook his head in disgust. 'I don't know how you keep your hands off them. People who do that sort of thing to children disgust me. I'd put a bullet in their skull if I had half a chance.'

'I frequently feel the same urge. What have you been up to?'

'Just returned from Columbia. We negotiated the release of a twelve-year-old girl, the daughter of a judge. She'd been snatched by a drug lord.'

'Was she all right?'

'She's alive, though minus half her left ear. How she recovers from that is anyone's guess.'

'Was she held for long?'

'Eight months. It was a complex case and not helped by the behaviour of the judge, but we got there in the end.'

They were joined by the ladies and chatted into the night enjoying each other's company and the excellent wine.

Dane struggled on his Sunday morning run as the hangover refused to go away. None of the others had accepted his invitation to join him so didn't see his reaction when he called into the local newsagents to buy the papers.

The banner headline on one tabloid screamed out at him: *Shame of perverted ex-cop murdered in sex game.* His headache got worse as he trudged home.

The smell of frying bacon lifted his spirits slightly when he walked into the kitchen. He dropped the papers on the table and the other three gathered round and read the offending article.

It described the circumstances of Parr's murder and details of his computer room in explicit detail.

'This has all come from within the police,' Dane said.

'See who the author is?' Vicky replied.

He glanced at the byline and swore under his breath. 'Angus Boyd. I suppose it had to be him.'

Boyd was a freelance journalist who specialised in police and national security stories. He'd been writing negative articles about Dane for more than a year and seemed obsessed with him. It came as no surprise to see his name above this story. But Dane was angrier about someone leaking such sensitive information.

'He's been pestering me for an interview for months. But after reading what he'd written about you I declined. I don't like the sound of him,' Lord said.

'He seems to have a very good source,' Olivia added.

Their breakfast was interrupted as Dane's phone rang. 'Have you seen the papers?' Wix barked.

'I've just read it. Someone's been talking out of turn.'

'We've got to respond.'

'I wouldn't do that just yet. We should refuse to comment about the specifics and try to discover who the leak is.'

'Who would do this? Could it be that journalist?'

'It might be, but I doubt it. Anyway, you vetted her and vouched for her discretion,' Dane said.

'Yes, and she came very well recommended. But you never know if you can really trust them, do you?'

Dane shook his head at her breathtaking hypocrisy.

Lord and Olivia prepared to leave after breakfast.

'Good luck with catching your traitor,' Lord said as he shook hands with Dane.

'I hope I can get my hands on them before they do any more damage,' Dane replied.

'If I can be of any help, you only have to call.'

'Thanks, that's very good of you.'

As Lord's car disappeared round the corner Dane put his arm round Vicky's shoulders and gave her a squeeze.

'Right, what have you got planned for me for the rest of the day?'

'I'd like to go to IKEA. I've seen some cushions I think would go nicely in the lounge and a couple of other bits and pieces.'

Dane was as keen as Vicky to finish the refurbishment of their new home, so they set out straight away.

'What's on the cards for you this week?' Vicky asked.

'The Parr investigation. It was always going to be a challenge, but it'll be even more complicated now I know someone is leaking to the press.'

'Any idea who it could be?'

'No. I barely know most of the people on the team so there are no obvious suspects.'

'You don't think it could be the journalist?'

'I doubt it. She's been given unprecedented access to us and an exclusive. I can't see how it could do her any good to betray our confidence like this.'

'I agree. I am looking forward to meeting her, though.'

'And what's in store for you?' Dane asked.

'More of the usual. We're all working on the central team project. I'll be pleased when it's all over.'

'I know what you mean. I could do with seeing more of you.'

Vicky smiled and squeezed his arm. 'Same here.'

They held hands as they searched the massive furniture store. Vicky loved a bit of retail therapy and Dane hoped this short interlude would help her relax. He smiled at her obvious pleasure at finding the occasional bargain and soon they had a full trolley. They returned home with cushions, picture frames and some impulse purchases and put the finishing touches to their new home. As Vicky packed, Dane stood on the patio with a mug of tea. He was beginning to dread this time of the weekend. It felt cruel that Vicky had to spend so long away from him. He knew she felt the same, but he would never stand in the way of her career. They held each other tight before she left, and Dane felt her tears on his cheek.

*

He was jolted awake by the shrill ringing of his phone. As he groped for the handset, he saw it was two o'clock and groaned.

9

Geraldine Binks drove onto the driveway outside her detached bungalow in the seaside town of Clacton in Essex. She turned the engine off and sat for a minute, nervously looking at the front door. There were no lights showing, but she knew Graham wouldn't have gone to bed until she got back. It was nearly half past midnight, and she should have been home hours ago. That had been the deal, and she had broken the rules. Geraldine rocked gently in the seat, wringing her hands and rehearsing her excuse. When she had it straight, she collected her weekend bag from the boot and, with a deep breath, went in.

'Hello, it's only me,' she called out cheerfully. 'Sorry I'm so late but the traffic has been awful…'

A heavy silence greeted Geraldine, and an unpleasant musty smell made her nose crinkle. She peered into the empty sitting room, and then walked down the passage to the kitchen. At the far end, a ladder gave access into the loft, and she could see the lights were on up there.

She stood under the open hatch and called out, 'Graham, are you up there? I'm going to make a cup of tea – do you want one?'

There was no reply. 'Suit yourself,' she muttered and went to the fridge. There was a single milk bottle which only had a dribble in the bottom of it and there was no bread. Exactly as she'd left it the previous Wednesday. 'What have you been doing, you lazy…' She looked back at the open loft hatch. She knew that once ensconced, he could be there for hours. It didn't occur to her to go up. That was against the rules.

Geraldine picked up her bag and opened the bedroom door. The smell was stronger now as she walked across the room towards her wardrobe in the darkness. At the bed, she tripped and fell headlong, landing on top of something soft and cold. She put her hand out and felt a foot, then a rope, as the stench of rotten meat enveloped her, making her gag. With a yell of fear she scrambled to her feet and turned the light on, revealing the horror in front of her. She stifled a moan of terror and staggered backwards into the hall, where she slumped to the floor.

'Oh, Graham. What have you done?' she whispered, staring at the macabre spectacle. She shivered and clasped her hands together. Tears welled as she looked around and, spying her handbag, crawled over to it and retrieved her mobile phone.

Geraldine listened to the ringing tone with increasing frustration. 'Pick it up, please…' she muttered, then heard the call connect.

'It's me. I've just got home and found Graham dead. I don't know what to do.'

The soothing voice calmed her and Geraldine listened, nodding at the instructions she received. When she hung up, she edged her way fearfully past the stinking corpse and pulled Graham's bedside cabinet away from the wall. She lifted the carpet below it revealing a loose floorboard. Hidden under that was a plastic box containing a thick wad of cash, her passport and a mobile phone. She put it all in a bumbag and secured it round her waist. After rearranging everything, she dialled 999.

*

Dane took a moment to rub his eyes and make sure he was awake before he answered the call.

'Sorry to wake you, sir. It's Inspector Marr at Clacton. We've got a body here who's been trussed up the same as Colin Parr. The victim's wife found him when she returned from a weekend away.'

'I'm on my way,' Dane replied, now wide awake.

Dane was halfway to Clacton when he remembered he'd promised to ring Jane Mitchell. He thought it unlikely she was Boyd's source but decided there'd be plenty more opportunities for her to attend a call-out. It took him nearly an hour to reach the address on a narrow residential street already bustling with police officers. Neighbours lined the road or stood in their doorways watching the commotion.

Dane found Inspector Marr who looked relieved to see him. 'Morning. What've you got for me, then?'

'The lady who lives here let herself in and discovered her husband, then rang the ambulance. They took one look at the body and called us. She made a right fuss when they did that.'

'Where is she?'

'Over there in my car.'

Geraldine Binks looked tiny, and Dane estimated she was in her early forties as he crouched down next to her.

He introduced himself. 'I'm sorry for your loss, but as your husband's death is suspicious there are certain things I must do. Can you tell me about his movements over the weekend?'

'No, I can't. I've been in Scotland since last Wednesday.'

'Was he expecting anyone to visit him while you were away?'

'Not that I'm aware of. He preferred to stay around the house. He might take the occasional walk down to the beach for some fresh air.'

'How about the neighbours? Did you socialise with them?'

'Not really, we keep ourselves to ourselves.'

Dane nodded. 'Is there someone who can put you up for a few days?'

Geraldine hesitated, and he saw fear bloom in her eyes. 'I want to stay here. This is my home. Why should I go somewhere else?'

'We'll need to examine the property for a couple of days, at least.'

'Graham wouldn't like that at all. We never let strangers in. That was the rule,' she whispered, almost to herself.

'I'm sorry, but we must do our job. We'll arrange a hotel for you to stay in and be as quick as we can, I promise.'

'But what will I do for clothes and things?'

'We'll take care of all that for you. Now, please go with these officers. I'll come and see you later.'

Pauline Rose arrived, and once dressed in a forensic suit, Dane led them through the metal gate outside the bungalow. There were two double-glazed bay windows each side of the entrance. In the hall they passed the bedroom to the left, the living room to the right, and checked the kitchen first. All the usual white goods were in place and a ladder led up to the loft. The lounge contained a threadbare settee and armchair, an old TV and a sideboard, but no photographs or ornaments.

The body lay at the foot of the king-size bed in the bedroom. The scene was virtually identical to the Parr murder, except the injuries caused by the handcuffs were relatively light and this victim was fully clothed.

Dane crouched beside the corpse. The pungent odour of decay permeated the room as body fluids soaked the man's trousers at the groin. Flies' eggs were evident in the eyes, nose and mouth of the victim, but there were no obvious signs of a struggle. So, he either knew his killer and willingly let them in, or they quickly subdued him. He must have been dead for several days, given the level of decomposition.

When Dane had finished, he climbed up through the hatch and into the loft, which was bathed in harsh neon light.

It took a lot to surprise Dane, but the scene that met his eyes certainly did. He was standing in a carbon copy of the attic in Billericay. Bookcases loaded with albums, and at the far end a computer on a desk with an expensive leather chair next to it. He picked his way past a small pile of photo albums in the middle of the floor.

Dane knew they would contain the same awful images they'd found at Parr's. How were the two men connected? Were they business partners? Had they both upset the same person? From what he'd seen so far, that sounded the most likely explanation, but why had it happened now?

With a sigh, he rejoined Pauline and together they planned the forensic examination.

As the sun came up, Dane rang Sobers. 'I suggest we link the two murders and I take the investigation.'

'I agree,' Sobers replied.

'I've called a team to Clacton for a briefing. Pauline's team has started work, and the post-mortem will be later this afternoon. I'll have to get Justin over again. I'm also concerned about the wife.' He described her demeanour and attitude earlier.

'She's probably in shock.'

'Perhaps, but she mentioned something weird about rules and not letting strangers in. I'll get Hayley Cross in to act as her family liaison officer. She'll find out what's going on.'

'Okay. I'll brief the chief.'

*

By seven, he had everything set up at the scene and drove over to Clacton police station to meet the arriving officers. He spent an hour briefing them and had just finished when Sally Rendell rang.

'Good morning. Sorry, but I'm tied up with a new job. Where are you?' Dane said.

'I'm at the incident office,' Sally replied.

'Hang on there and get the sergeants to brief you on the Parr case. I'll meet you later.'

Dane made it to headquarters by ten thirty and bumped into Sobers.

'Wix lost it when I told her we'd agreed to link the offences and actually ripped a strip off of me,' Sobers said.

'What's her problem?'

'She's adamant it should be her decision, not yours. I can't hold your hand. I've got to go to Hertfordshire HQ for a conference.'

'Don't worry about me. I can handle her. So long as you're backing me on linking them.'

'I am, and the chief's onside as well.'

Wix kept him waiting before her secretary ushered him in. 'Right, what's the story with this new murder?' she snapped.

He sat down without being asked and told her what he'd found in Clacton.

'What connects these two cases?'

Dane quelled his immediate impulse to be sarcastic and gave her a reasoned argument.

'It's up to me to decide if we link crimes and who investigates them. I might have wanted someone else to take this case.'

'Who did you have in mind?' Dane replied evenly.

'It doesn't matter now, does it? You took it upon yourself to make that decision.'

'I did that because it's my job to manage all the investigation teams and deploy the SIOs. When did that change?'

'I'm in charge of crime investigations for this force, so I am responsible for who does what.'

'But my role is to keep that mundane stuff off your desk. Sobers is happy with the way I run the section and so is the chief constable. So, what have I done wrong? Why are you so hostile towards me?'

Wix glared at him, a muscle working along the line of her jaw. Her face was pale, and he could see she was furious. 'You're a throwback to another, long-departed era.'

Dane hadn't expected that and took a moment to consider his response. 'Perhaps you should explain that bizarre statement.'

'You shouldn't be leading a sensitive and important part of the force. You're a Neanderthal. And you've killed people.'

Wix was obviously referring to the previous November when Dane shot three terrorists. But he couldn't see any relevance to what was happening now.

'Your view of me as a police officer, and a person, flies in the face of every assessment ever made of me. I'm not a bully, and nor do I bend or break the rules. I won't tolerate unacceptable behaviour as you saw when I confronted the situation with DI Mason. I work hard and to the best of my ability. And yes, I have had to kill people. But only in self-defence, and I gave them all the opportunity to surrender, at some considerable risk to myself. You clearly dislike me, and I suspect would rather I wasn't here. So, if you don't want me working with you, get rid of me. But if you try, make sure you've got the evidence to justify your actions because I won't go quietly. And if we're being honest with each other, you should know that I'm not impressed with you, either.'

Wix's face turned puce with anger. 'Who do you think you are, talking to me like that?'

'What makes you think I'll stand here and take your insults without a reply? Your interesting management style and bullying belong to that long-departed era you profess to hate. And you have the nerve to call me a Neanderthal.' A simmering silence lasted for a few seconds before he said. 'Well? Am I sacked?'

'No. But you're on thin ice. Get on with your job and make certain I'm kept informed of all developments regarding this case.'

'Yes, ma'am, and with that in mind I'll tell you I've asked the IT specialist from Sweden to come again.'

Wix looked like she would explode, but Dane could justify everything he'd done, and she knew it. 'Get out of here.'

Dane sat in his car and decompressed. He'd never been shy in speaking truth to power, but he'd gone too far with Wix. She would never admit to any faults, so his criticism would be meaningless to her, but he felt better for saying what he had. The row had been brewing for a while, and he'd had enough of her hostility. Whatever he thought of her, though, she remained his boss. He would be careful in his future dealings with her and not allow her any opportunity to be vindictive, although he doubted she'd need an excuse. He sighed with frustration; all he ever wanted to do was catch the real bad guys. He drove back to the incident room where an angry Jane Mitchell confronted him.

'Didn't we agree I could come with you when you got called out?' she snapped, following him into his office.

'We did, but I forgot until I arrived there. And I needed to talk to you to clear the air.'

'You mean about the article?'

'Yes.'

'I suppose you assumed I'm the source.'

'No. Well, to be honest it crossed my mind.' He held his hand up to placate her. 'Look, the information can only have come from within this organisation. What did you expect me to think?'

She sighed. 'Boyd has the scoop, which'll give him serious kudos. You might not like it, but that's how my world works. You're only as good as your last story. We cover the same field as competitors. Why would I gift him the byline and let him increase his profile with this? I am not his source.'

'Thank you. That was all I wanted to hear, and you make an excellent point. But a crime scene in the early hours of the morning wasn't the place for this sort of discussion. I had to see your face when you told me. I trust you and I won't exclude you from anything else around here.'

'Good, and another thing, Angus Boyd is one of the two I left in the lift. I'm hardly likely to pass him an exclusive, am I? Now let's move on. Tell me about this fresh case.'

'I must say hello to my new inspector first, then we can talk.'

Jane grinned. 'I've already met her. She's going to liven this place up.'

'You could be right there.'

The inspector's office door was closed, with the blinds down. He knocked and looked in. All three sergeants sat there, facing Sally, who was behind her desk. 'Hi, sir, I'll be with you shortly.'

A few minutes later, she joined him.

'Come in.' He pointed towards a chair as he got up and shook hands with her.

'Nice to have you on board. Are you up to speed with the current investigation?'

'Yes, and I've had an interesting chat with the sergeants.'

Dane raised an eyebrow. 'Interesting?'

'Let's just say they weren't expecting someone like me.'

Probably not, he thought, as he regarded the short black woman sitting opposite him. The close-cropped hair and the line of gold studs along her ear lobe were striking enough, but it was the masculine style of her clothes that sometimes drew comment. But the important thing was she had an impressive record as a detective.

'Let's get down to business.' He spent the next hour explaining what he wanted her to do.

10

Hayley Cross strode into the office at midday. Dane watched as she bumped into Sally Rendell with exclamations of surprise and a hug. They were obviously old friends but couldn't have looked more different if they'd tried. Hayley was six feet tall and dressed in her habitual smart black trouser suit and white blouse, Sally nearly a foot shorter and looking like a banker. Jane Mitchell joined them and within seconds, the three were laughing out loud at something.

Dane poked his head out. 'If it's not too much trouble, could I borrow her for some work?'

Hayley turned and gave him a beaming smile. 'Hi, boss, what you got for me this time?'

They'd worked together for many years. She was a friend, and the best detective Dane knew, and he was pleased to have an excuse to bring her into the investigation. He told her about the Parr case, what had happened that morning, and described Geraldine Binks.

'I want you to find out everything about their background and life together. Graham Binks was sixty-six, so there's an obvious age gap. I've arranged for us to visit her this afternoon. I'll get her to tell us the basics, then you can get to know her better and gain her trust. We also need to discover what she knows about the set-up in the attic.'

Geraldine Binks opened the door to her hotel room and looked nervously up and down the corridor before leading them inside. Seeing her in daylight, Dane realised she was much younger than he'd thought. About five feet four tall, with a pale oval face, she was painfully thin. Her clothes were modern but designed for teenagers. She looked more like a nervous and frightened adolescent girl than a mature woman.

'Thank you for seeing us,' Dane said, then introduced Hayley, explaining what her role would be. 'If you're up to it, could you give me some background about you both, please?'

'Graham was the manager of my children's home. My birth mother abandoned me as a baby, and I spent my childhood in care. He took me under his wing and when I turned sixteen we ran away together.'

Dane shot a glance at Hayley who pursed her lips. 'How did that go down with his employers?' Hayley asked.

'Not well.'

'How old was he then, fifty-one?'

'That's right, he took early retirement.'

'Did he do that before you eloped?'

Geraldine nodded. 'We had to do it that way, otherwise he'd have lost his pension. He was accused of all sorts of horrible things. No one would believe that I loved him, and it was my choice to be with him.'

'Where did you live?'

'We had to keep moving while social services were looking for us. We married when I turned eighteen and bought the house five years ago.'

'Do you work?' Dane said.

She shook her head. 'I've never had a job. Graham didn't like me going out without him. We live – lived – on his pension and savings.'

'They must be considerable to afford to live on them for all this time.'

'He had an inheritance from his parents, and he's quite good on the stocks and shares. He was in charge of the money. I don't know anything about that sort of thing.'

Geraldine spoke in a soft voice and avoided eye contact with either of them.

'How about friends? Do you have any round here?' Hayley asked.

'No one local. I've got a friend who I visited over the weekend.'

'Could we have her name?'

'Why would you want that?'

'We need to confirm where you were for the last few days,' Dane said.

'You don't think I did that to him, do you?' she replied, looking up.

'No, and I'm sure your friend will confirm she was with you. But we must speak to her as a matter of routine.'

'Well, I'll ask if she doesn't mind you talking to her. She lives near Inverness.'

'That's a long way to travel for a weekend.'

'It takes a while to get there, but it's worth it.'

'Why didn't Graham go with you?'

'He never came with me to Scotland. The journey was too much for him, to be honest.'

'Did anyone visit you at your home?'

'Some of his friends from his photo club would come round and disappear up into the attic.'

Dane waited a beat, hoping she'd expand on her answer, but she stared down into her lap and stayed silent. He glanced at Hayley and could see she was as perplexed as him.

Why won't she open up? Surely she wants to help us catch her husband's killer?

'How long has he been interested in photography?'

'Ever since I've known him. He liked wildlife and landscape pictures the most,' she replied vaguely.

'I saw none on the walls or anywhere in the house.'

'They're all in his albums. I don't like clutter around the house.'

'Is the car yours?'

'No, it belongs to Graham. We both use it, but me more than him for the shopping.'

'What's in the loft?'

'All his camera stuff and his pictures. He had a computer up there as well, I think.'

'Have you been up there?'

'Never. I wasn't allowed up in the loft, so I stayed out. It was his space. That was the rule.'

'Do you have a picture of him?'

'No,' she said, and tears sprang into her eyes. 'We weren't into family pictures.'

'We're doing a press release later today with an appeal for any witnesses to come forward. Graham will be identified as the victim, and it should be on the TV and in the local papers. Your husband was murdered in an unusual way. Another man died recently in almost identical circumstances. His name was Colin Parr. Did you know him?'

She hesitated for a second and looked down. 'That's not a name I've heard before. It means nothing to me.'

That didn't ring true to Dane, and he wondered why she was being so evasive. He glanced at Hayley, who shook her head.

'Thank you again for seeing us. Hayley will arrange a time to write all this down in a statement. Is that okay?'

'How long must I stay in the hotel?'

'I hope we'll finish our work soon. You should be able to go home in a couple of days.'

'Oh, I'm not planning on returning there. I'm going to sell up and go to Scotland.'

'What do you think?' Dane asked when they got back to the car.

'I bet you anything she was abused throughout her childhood and that saint Graham was the prime offender. She's the one he couldn't put down, which is why they had to decamp when she turned sixteen. At that age, she'd leave the care system to go into the community and fend for herself. He couldn't control her then, and it wouldn't surprise me if they were on to him. She's been under his thumb ever since, and still is. He's drummed the need to say as little as possible into her and she's petrified of breaking his rules and giving up his secrets, whatever they are.'

'That's interesting. She seemed scared of breaking the rules last night. And I wonder what his connection is to Parr. I'm sure she recognised his name. Did you know him?'

'Yes, I did. He was an unpleasant, sneering bully who didn't like female officers at the best of times and this gobby black one got right up his nose. Everyone hated him. You must remember him?'

'I do. He tried to discipline me when I was a probationer at Basildon.'

'What did you do?'

'I dealt with a missing girl from a children's home. I submitted a report criticising the managers of the place. They had no interest in what she was getting up to. A bit like Laura Hobbs last week. She was a persistent missing person, and no one ever bothered to find out why. Anyway, the manager complained to Parr that I'd been rude and unprofessional by questioning him in front of his staff. But my chief inspector backed me up, and they had a huge row. Parr was promoted soon after that, and I never crossed his path again. Will you get on with finding background on the Binks family and work your famous contacts to discover what was happening at that home? I've got to do the press conference with Wix.'

'What's she like?' Hayley said.

'She's charming,' he replied, deadpan.

'That bad, huh?'

'I'll catch up with you after the post-mortem.'

*

They started twenty minutes late because Wix couldn't be found. Polly from the press office was panicking because most of the camera crews had other assignments and were threatening to pack up and leave.

Jane joined them as they waited. 'Boyd is out there with a photographer,' she said.

'Which one is he?'

She pointed him out through the window. 'Third row, second seat in from the left.'

Dane marked his position, then stared at his face for a few seconds, fixing the man's features in his memory.

Wix bustled up to them with no explanation of apology. 'Are we ready?'

'Yes, but we're behind schedule. I'm due at the mortuary in half an hour, so I won't hang round for questions,' Dane said.

'I'll handle them,' she replied, and led them in. Wix opened with a lengthy statement describing the circumstances of the discovery of the body before handing over to Dane. He made the standard appeal for anyone with any knowledge of recent movements, or friends of the couple to contact the incident room. He also confirmed the two murders were linked and, when he finished, stood to leave. Boyd shouted out that he had a question for him.

'I'm late, sorry, I have to go,' Dane announced and left, followed by Jane.

'How often does a conference like that result in any useful information?' Jane asked.

'It's not unknown, otherwise I wouldn't subject myself to them. People might see something, but then convince themselves it isn't important. An appeal often jolts them into action and they ring in, so it is worth the effort.'

'Boyd seemed keen to put a question to you.'

'I noticed.'

Jane stood in a corner of the mortuary and watched as Dr Hume started his work.

After half an hour Dane noticed she was very quiet and looked queasy. He moved beside her. 'Is this what you were expecting?'

'I suppose so, although nothing you read prepares you for the real thing. Do they all smell as bad as this?'

'Not really, but it's the middle of summer, so a body will start decomposing soon after death. That's what causes the stink. You get used to it after a while.'

'How many have you been to?'

'Hundreds. They're an important part of the investigation. If this one proves the link between the two killings, we're looking for a potential serial killer.'

'What's next?'

'Find the connection between the victims and see if that led to their deaths. Once I have that, we'll be on the right track.'

The post-mortem took three hours and produced the expected result. The killer restrained Binks with handcuffs, then the ropes. Damage to the muscles in his back and shoulders testified to his being in the stress position for at least an hour before he died, and his testicles were injured. There was no evidence of an electrical stun gun being used.

*

They arrived back at the office in time for the evening briefing, and Dane was flicking through his notebook, when he received a call from Polly.

I think you need to know what happened after you left.'

'Go on.'

'Angus Boyd made a fuss about you walking out, saying he had a legitimate question to ask and you ignored him. Then he complained about Jane Mitchell being given preferential treatment and demanded the same access. Wix explained what Jane was doing, but Boyd kept insisting it wasn't fair. Then she announced she'd think about his request and get back to him tomorrow. The rest joined in, demanding they be let in as well. It turned into a circus and our message got lost in it.'

'Okay, Polly, thanks for the heads up.'

Dane returned to his office where he took a moment to bring his anger under control, then rang Wix. Her secretary said she'd gone home. He tried her mobile which diverted to answerphone. It was obvious she wasn't going to pick up a call from him so he called from a landline, and this time she picked up straight away.

'It's Dane. We need to speak about what developed after I left the presser earlier.'

'Why?'

'What are you intending to do regarding Boyd's request for access to the investigation?'

'I'm considering it.'

'What's to consider? The answer has to be no.'

'You do not tell me what to do. It's my decision and I'll make it in my own time,' Wix snapped.

'If you don't assure me now that you'll say no, my next call will be to the chief constable. I cannot believe you're even contemplating this sort of request, especially from Boyd. This is a murder investigation, not a bloody circus.'

'This is all to do with Boyd, isn't it? I saw how you avoided him at the conference.'

'I didn't avoid anyone. I had to leave, and you knew why I was going and agreed to deal with questions.'

'You can't ignore him.'

'I can, and I'll not let him divert attention from a message we want to get across. Apart from anything else, someone is already leaking information to him. He'll print whatever he gets regardless of the damage it might cause. Are you really so naïve as to believe he'd honour an agreement not to publish stuff he sees until after a court case? It'll be in the papers the next morning.'

'You don't know that.'

'Yes, I do. You're obviously not going to give me that assurance, so I'll appeal to the chief.'

'Wait, just wait. I must think about this.'

'If you let him in, you create a precedent. All the others will be on at you constantly for access. It's bad enough having Jane Mitchell in there. That's like a red rag to them.'

'How are things working with her?'

'She's a talented journalist and not getting in the way. And I'm certain she's not the source of the leak. Despite my reservations, I agree with you now that this'll be good for us. But you can't let the rest of them in.'

'All right. I'll say no to them all.'

'Thank you,' he said and hung up.

11

Dane settled himself down at the head of the table and surveyed the forty officers and staff in front of him. They were all watching him intently, and he realised he was scowling. With an effort he smiled, not wanting them to think something was wrong. The extra detectives were from the other major investigation teams, drafted in for the duration of the enquiry. He'd noticed a spring in their step as they arrived for this meeting. It was an interesting case, and one any detective would be desperate to be part of. But he could still feel the acid bubbling in his stomach caused by his latest exchange with Wix.

What is the matter with her? It's almost as if she wants me to fail.

Whatever her motivation, he wouldn't let her damage the morale of his team. Taking a deep breath, he briefed them on what they'd learnt at the post-mortem.

Sally and the sergeants had prepared for the extra workload, and everyone soon knew what their jobs would be. Ian Lockhart informed them that the house-to-house enquiries around Parr's home were complete, and they were moving on to Clacton.

'What do we know about Colin Parr?'

DC Tom Jones raised his hand. 'I've been doing that, sir. He retired seventeen years ago. His file covers his postings and promotions throughout his police career. There were a few complaints about him, all minor issues like being rude to people, but none were criminal or proved. He finished his service at headquarters, where he oversaw the CID. I can't find anyone who will admit to being his friend and no one who remembers him has a good word to say about him or his wife.'

'What about her?'

'Her name is Joyce Eileen Parr, and she remains his next of kin. He had a bank account in Southend with a couple of thousand pounds in it and another one which his police pension gets paid into. This pays a monthly direct debit to a French bank. I found an address and number for a Mrs J Parr in a small village about twenty miles from Bergerac.'

Dane looked at his watch. 'Give her a ring now. If it's our Mrs Parr, tell her the bad news and inform her you and I will get out to see her as soon as possible.'

Detective Sergeant Cooper from the High-tech Crime Unit informed everyone that the CEOP investigators had established Parr's computer was involved in the supply of indecent images of children. They believed he was acting as a middleman and selling them on. So far, they'd found no links to other bank accounts or individuals. The set-up in the Binks house appeared identical.

'Are you sure neither of the victims are of interest to the National Crime Agency?' Dane asked Cooper.

'They've assured me they aren't, sir. I have three emails in which they confirm that.'

Pauline Rose confirmed her team had completed their examination of Parr's home and started in Clacton. 'We recovered a lot of prints from the motel room. Several are from the victim and Laura Hobbs. The rest are from the cleaner, Roux, and a couple on a bottle of Scotch from the barman. That leaves a dozen unmatched. These could be from so-called guests or punters who've not been in trouble with the police before.'

Tom Jones returned. 'I've just spoken to her. She had heard about his death and told me she couldn't care less. We're welcome to visit anytime we like because she's always in, and she sounded like she was drunk.'

'Book us on the morning flight for the day after tomorrow. Now: Binks. Hayley, what did you find out about him?'

'He was a social worker for thirty years and an administrator of children's homes in the county. Social services have a record of three full-blooded investigations and several other complaints. All bar one, which was made by a co-worker, came from kids in care and he was cleared of any wrongdoing in all of them. He took early retirement and Geraldine immediately ran off with him. They reappeared in Essex a couple of years later after getting married. While the authorities were looking for them, they uncovered some unsavoury goings-on at the last home he'd worked in. They believe he was having a sexual relationship with Geraldine while she was there. They could never prove it, though, and when they eventually caught up with them she refused to co-operate, and they dropped the whole thing.'

'We'll examine that side of his life when you interview her. But if we're right and she is a victim of abuse, we must treat her carefully. When are you meeting her?'

'Tomorrow morning,' Hayley replied.

'Reece, do an ANPR check on her registration number. She told us she'd just returned from Inverness, so she should have passed some cameras on the way. See if we can plot her movements and do the same with her mobile phone. I want to know where she's been and the name and address of the friend she was staying with. Now, there is something else I need to mention. You'll all be aware of the article in the newspaper over the weekend about the Parr investigation.' There was a rising murmur, and some cast accusing glances at Jane.

'To say I'm unhappy is an understatement. Most of the information quoted is accurate and must originate from within the police. I hope the leaker is not a member of this team, but if they are, I will find them. It's important that what we've now discovered about Binks and his wife stays in these four walls. No one is to talk to any journalist except Jane, of course. I'm certain she's not the source of the story, and she has my complete confidence.'

Dane had detected an undercurrent of hostility towards Jane, with some officers ignoring her, and she followed him into his office as the meeting broke up. 'Thanks for that. I appreciate it. Boyd rang me earlier.'

'Oh really? What did he want?'

'He suggested it would be a good idea if we did lunch. He claimed we'd got off on the wrong foot all those years ago and he'd been meaning to apologise for his behaviour.'

'That's nice.'

'Aren't you going to ask me if I'll be meeting him?'

'What you do is not my business. I'd certainly not presume to tell you who you can meet.'

'Well, I declined his kind offer. He then suggested I was making a terrible mistake, and that he could be good for my career. And if I didn't talk to him, I would regret it.'

'It took him that long to change his tune, did it? What did you say to that threat?'

'I told him where to go. I reminded him he's a rubbish journalist who gives the rest of us a bad name. Then I hung up on him.'

'I guess that means you trust me, eh?'

'Well, yes, I suppose I do. I've watched you work for the last week and you're nothing like the monster that idiot keeps trying to portray. He's livid you granted me this access and he won't stop agitating until he gets the same.'

'That won't happen. He'll never get through the door of any office I'm working in.'

Sally poked her head in. 'We've received several anonymous calls about Binks. The general line is that he was a dirty paedophile and deserves everything he got. And Polly's been on to say that she's also heard from a couple of journalists who have received similar calls and want a comment from us.'

Dane rang Polly straight away. 'Is Boyd one of the journalists who's asking?'

'No. They're all from local news desks.'

'Okay, you can tell them we're investigating several lines of enquiry, and we don't comment about anonymous allegations. If any of the people who've rung would like to contact us, we'll be interested in speaking to them.'

'They won't be happy with that,' Polly replied.

'That's all we're saying now. I haven't explored this with Geraldine yet, so I'm not talking to them before we know what she has to say.'

Dane looked up and waved to Hayley. 'Get hold of Geraldine and tell her we're on our way,' he said and explained what had been happening.

A few minutes later, she was back. 'A reporter's already found her, and she's barricaded herself in her room. She's not a happy bunny.'

'Okay, Sally, contact Witness Protection. We need somewhere

safe to stash her for a few days. We can't leave her in there now.'

'I'm on it,' she replied.

As Dane parked outside the hotel, half a dozen reporters surrounded them, shouting questions. He ignored them and strode into reception to be met by the harassed manager.

'I've asked you all to leave. You're upsetting my guests,' he shouted, then gestured to Dane. 'Can't you do something?'

'There'll be some uniform officers here soon, they'll keep them out.' He turned to the journalists. 'You heard the man. He doesn't want you on the premises, and I won't be making any comment, so do me a favour and leave.'

They all reluctantly wandered out as the manager grabbed Dane's arm. 'She has got to go. I'm sorry, but this is too much.'

'We're moving her. Make up the bill and I'll settle it.'

'Thank you,' he replied, looking relieved.

It took Hayley a minute to persuade Geraldine to open the door. As they waited in the corridor, a local reporter came out of a room and walked towards them, smiling. 'I'm a guest,' he announced, pulling out his notebook.

Geraldine peered out, and seeing who it was, released the security chain to let them in.

Dane confronted the journalist. 'If you're still here when I come out of that room, you'll find yourself arrested for witness intimidation,' he warned and followed Hayley.

'What did you tell them? They've been banging on the door, saying the most horrible things and offering me money,' Geraldine sobbed and fell onto the bed.

'All we did was ask for help to discover the killer. But there've been calls alleging Graham was a paedophile.'

'That's not true, any of it. He was a good man and always looked after me. He never laid a hand on me,' she wailed.

'We're going to take you out of here. Get your things together and we'll go out the back.'

Hayley stayed with her as Dane went to settle the bill. The reporter was still lurking at the end of the corridor but kept his distance. Down in reception, Dane poked his head outside and saw there were now three uniform officers keeping the press pack at bay. Dane called one in and had a quick word with him before driving round the rear of the building as Hayley brought Geraldine down. They bundled her into the back seat as several journalists appeared. Seeing they were leaving, they all sprinted for their vehicles. After Hayley sped through the only exit, two patrol cars blocked it, stopping anyone from following.

Geraldine sat quietly throughout the journey to a large country house. It was secluded, in its own extensive grounds, and frequently used for the temporary housing of a protected witness. The couple who owned the property were retired police officers and used to these emergency visits.

Once in her room, Dane asked her to hand over her mobile phone.

'Why do I have to do that?' Geraldine asked.

'We must maintain the security of this place. Not only for your safety but also that of the couple who're looking after you,' Dane replied.

'What do I do if I want to call someone?'

'You use the landline. This isn't an option, Geraldine. We'll store your phone, and no one will have access to it or download what's on it.'

'You're certain those people from the papers won't find me here?'

'As long as you follow the rules here you'll be safe.' Dane deliberately used the word rules to watch her reaction. There was something wrong with her and he couldn't put his finger on it. He was sure she wasn't being entirely truthful with him and wondered why.

Hayley promised to return the next morning to start with the statement. By the time they left, Geraldine had calmed down and even managed a smile.

12

Early the following morning, Dane received a text from Tony and, armed with a legitimate excuse for a cooked breakfast, called in at the café. He was later than usual and took a spare seat on a table with two truck drivers and enjoyed their company as he ate. When they left, Tony joined him.

'I've picked up a couple of snippets you might be interested in.'

'What's that?'

'Kenny Johns is dossing with his little brother, Baz. I'm told he got himself hurt bad and is keeping his head down.'

'Thanks for that. Any news on the Albanian?'

'He's called Dragon, but I don't know if that's his real name. I haven't been able to find out where he lives, either. He drives a silver Merc, and everyone's scared of him.'

'Why?'

'Word is if you cross him, he'll kill you without batting an eyelid. There are stories circulating about what he does to girls who try to run, and they ain't nice. He films what he does to them, then shows them to the others to scare them out of trying to escape.'

'Sounds like a charmer. If you hear anything on where I can find him, I'd appreciate a call.'

'No worries.'

'I'd better get to work. Food was great as usual.'

'We always try to please.'

An hour later, Dane was with Reg Phelan and another two officers outside a first-floor flat on the outskirts of Basildon. A woman in her early twenties with bleached blonde hair and an anxious expression answered the door. She looked relieved to find four police officers on her doorstep and nodded over her shoulder.

'You'll be after Kenny. He's in here bleeding all over my settee.'

'Who're you?' Dane asked as she led them along the short hallway to a sitting room. The flat stank of burnt meat.

'Tracey. I'm Baz's wife.'

There were two men in there, both well over six foot tall and heavily muscled. One, in his twenties, was sitting in an armchair playing a video game on a gigantic television. He looked startled when they followed Tracey in and glanced at the second man who was lying on the settee before turning to Dane.

'Are you the doctor?'

'No, he isn't, you idiot. It's the police,' Tracey shouted, then turned to Dane. 'This is my dimwit of a husband, Baz. That's Kenny.'

She pointed to the comatose man whose condition was shocking. Vicious, deep burns covered his body with huge weeping blisters on his swollen face and chest. Open suppurating wounds dripped blood and pus from his charred arms and hands.

'What happened to him?' Dane said.

'The pair of them turned up here like this late Wednesday night. I thought they'd gone out to the pub. But it turns out they set fire to a hotel.' Tracey bent down in front of her husband. 'Didn't you?' she screamed as Baz cowered in the chair. Dane noticed he had burns on his arms and face, although he was nowhere near as bad as his brother.

'Have they seen a doctor?'

'No.'

'Why not?'

'Because the bastard who dropped them here told them to sit tight and he'd send one for them. And they believed him, like a pair of idiots.' She was clearly at the end of her tether and looked as if she were about to launch herself at Jimmy. Dane took her by the arm.

'Come on, let's get this sorted, shall we? You sit down, and we'll call an ambulance.' He nodded to Phelan, who pulled his phone out and left the room.

She slumped down in the second armchair next to her husband and he reached out to take her hand. 'I'm sorry, Trace…'

Dane got a chair from the dining table and sat beside Baz. 'I've got to caution you, Baz, because I believe you've committed a crime. Do you understand?'

Baz nodded and Dane recited the legal phrase. 'Do you want to tell me how you got in this state?'

He hesitated, and Tracey said quietly, 'Tell him everything, or I will, and then you'll be out on your stupid ear. I've had enough, I swear to God.'

Baz, for all his bulk, flinched as if she'd slapped him, then looked down at his hands and shuddered. 'Me and Kenny burnt the motel. That one up on the A12.'

'Why?'

'Because he wanted it done.'

'Who did?'

'Dragon. But it all blew up in our faces. Then he dumped us here. I told him Kenny needed help, and he promised he'd get a doctor. We've been waiting…'

'I've been telling them to go to the hospital, but he wouldn't have it. Baz won't do anything unless Kenny says he can,' Tracey said bitterly.

Phelan returned. 'They're rolling. Should be here in a few minutes.'

Dane turned to Tracey. 'Okay. Why don't you put some clothes and stuff together for these two? They'll be in there for a while, I think.'

'You gonna nick them after that?'

'Yes. They're both in trouble. But the most important thing now is they get treatment for their injuries. We'll worry about the rest of it later.'

As Tracey went to pack a bag, Dane turned to Baz and inspected his arms. 'That looks painful.'

'Stings a bit,' he muttered, then looked at his brother as tears filled his eyes. 'He's gonna be all right, ain't he?'

'He should be once he's treated and cleaned up.'

Dane had to restrain the urge to ask more questions. He'd established the crime and, given Baz's condition, if he continued the interview it would be deemed inadmissible as evidence. There would be plenty of time to talk to them once they'd left the hospital, and he didn't think they'd remain silent. The paramedics arrived and, after administering emergency treatment to Kenny, transported them both to the specialist burns unit.

Back at the office Dane rang Hayley Cross. 'How're you getting on with Geraldine?'

'She's a strange one. I'll lay money Binks was abusing her from an early age. But she won't admit it and still insists they didn't start having sex until long after they ran away. She says they were inseparable, but from what little I've gleaned I think he kept her a virtual prisoner. He wouldn't let her have her own bank account and gave her a set amount every week for housekeeping. She reluctantly admitted their sex life had stopped and blames herself for putting on weight and not being as attractive as she used to be.'

'There's more fat on a chip.'

'I agree with you.'

'If he was that controlling, how come she could visit her friends on her own?'

'That started recently, and it surprised her when he suggested it. I think he had an ulterior motive and wanted her out of the house. He was only interested in children and when she matured, he probably moved on to others. You've seen the way she dresses and looks. She's desperately trying to stay young, and it's sad. I asked her about Parr again, but she's adamant she doesn't know him.'

'Has she given you the name of her friend in Inverness yet?'

'No, she says there was no reply when she called.'

'Tell her to do it today. Put your foot down.'

'Will do.'

Tom Jones poked his head in and informed him they were booked on the early flight to Bergerac the following morning. After he'd gone, Dane asked Sally how she was settling in and noticed her hesitation.

'What's up?'

'Nothing I can't handle, just a few people being silly.'

'If it persists, we talk about it.'

'Don't worry, I can manage. In the meantime, Reece Lewin might have some news on the ANPR front.'

The sergeant revealed the movements of the Binkses' car. 'It never went to Scotland. She drove to Weston-super-Mare via the

M25, M4 and M5 last Thursday and came back the same way on Sunday. The timings coincide with Geraldine getting home and finding the body. I'm searching for any CCTV cameras on the route that could give us an image of the driver.'

'Good, well done. Is there anything new from the Child Exploitation Command?'

'No, nothing more from them.'

Dane thanked Reece, who left to be replaced by Lockhart, who reported the house-to-house enquiries around the Binks home were complete but produced no useful information.

'Can I have a word in private?' Lockhart said, glancing at Sally.

'I've got some things to do,' she murmured and closed the door behind her.

Lockhart watched her go with barely disguised dislike. 'You need to know there are rumblings about what she's doing, and the boys don't like some of her decisions. Especially regarding the makeup of teams and who does what.'

'That's her role. She's in charge of the efficient running of this team.'

'Up to now, it's been me and the other sergeants who sort that out.'

'Not anymore. Things are changing. You, and your boys, will follow her instructions to the letter and give her your complete support. Anything else?'

Lockhart had clearly not expected this response, so changed the subject. 'I saw Pete last night. He's not in a good way. They've served him with discipline notices and it looks like they're going to sack him.'

'What did he expect? He drove into work three times over the legal drink-drive limit and wrecked the backyard.'

'But he's ill, and can't afford to lose his job. Can't you speak to someone?'

'And say what, exactly? The best thing he can do is resign and take his pension.'

'You don't care about him, do you?'

'It's a shame to see anyone's career end like this, but he brought it on himself. The days of the old boys' network getting someone off have long gone.'

After Lockhart had left looking thunderous, Dane rang Hayley. 'Are you still with her?'

'Yes.'

'I'm on my way. Wait with her until I get there.'

*

Geraldine gave him a beaming smile when he arrived at the safe house.

'To what do we owe this unexpected pleasure?'

'I've received some interesting information I thought I should share with you. Have you contacted your friend yet?'

'No. I tried earlier, but I think she might have gone away for a few days.'

'If you give us her name and address, we could track her down.'

'No, I don't want to involve her until I know she's happy to meet you.'

'We've got to talk to her, Geraldine.'

'I understand, and I will co-operate, but I can't just give you her number. She's my oldest friend and isn't that keen on the police, to be honest.'

'Why's that?'

'She had a few unpleasant experiences with coppers when we were in care together.'

Dane nodded, as if he understood her position. 'You remember I told you that you must be truthful, don't you?'

'Oh yes.'

'Without that trust, we might not catch the people responsible for murdering your husband.'

'I've said I'll do everything I can to help you.'

'Good, so start again and tell us where you really were last weekend. Because you weren't in Inverness, or Scotland.'

'I was up there…'

'Have you heard of automatic number plate recognition?'

'No.'

'It's a system that uses roadside cameras to record the registration numbers of vehicles that pass them. I fed your car's details into it,' he said, and watched as she went pale. 'So perhaps you could explain why you were on the motorway to and from the West Country?'

There was silence for a few seconds. Dane glanced at Hayley, but her face registered nothing. She'd obviously guessed something was afoot.

'How dare you check up on me? I'm a victim, not the suspect,' Geraldine shouted.

'Who says you're not? It's always very difficult for me to decide the status of someone when they lie to me. Now, where did you go and who were you with? I know you've been travelling down there regularly. It won't take long to find some CCTV footage that'll show who was driving the car, and I doubt it was your late husband.'

Geraldine slumped in her chair before going to stare out of the window. 'We made a pact and promised each other never to give our addresses away to anyone. That's why I said I was in Scotland. I'll ring her in the morning and once she's given me her permission, I'll tell you, but not before.'

Dane watched her for a moment. 'You have until lunchtime tomorrow. Then I'll have to insist you tell Hayley who she is.'

'I'm not trying to hide anything, but that's the way it is.'

Dane left them and walked down to the living room, where the owner of the property was watching television. 'Has our guest used your phone to make any telephone calls?'

The man nodded confirmation and got up to hand Dane a printed list of the numbers, showing seven calls to three different numbers.

'Keep an eye on her tonight. I don't trust her. She's up to something.'

'No worries,' the man said as he showed Dane out.

Dane returned to the incident room instead of going straight home. Someone would be working a late shift and he wanted the telephone numbers checked out immediately. As he reached the door, he heard a raised voice from within the office.

13

'I'm telling you. They dumped her on us because she's no good. We must stick together and fight her.' Lockhart's voice carried through the door.

'You don't like her because she won't let you skive off down the bookies or the pub,' Lewin replied. 'She hasn't done me any harm, and it's nice to have some direction around here for a change.'

'She's useless. Dane's no better, either.'

'You want to be careful. He likes her and most of the office is on her side,' Phelan put in.

'Dane engineered her coming here. Pete's going to get the sack because he refuses to lift a finger to help. She'll ruin everything, and she's a dyke. It's bad enough having that journalist in here looking over our shoulders all the time. They'll be at it in the stationery cupboard before long.'

'What do you mean?' Phelan asked.

'Oh, come on, you haven't twigged that Mitchell's one as well? Dane's here to split us all up. He gets rid of Pete, brings in the hack so he can look good, and Rendell to do his dirty work. All that feeds his own agenda, he's checked all the boxes to show how multi-ethnic he is. That black bitch will ruin everything if we don't stand up to her.'

Dane clenched his fists to control his rising anger. He'd heard enough and stepped round the corner. There were two detective constables sitting beside the three sergeants and they all looked up in surprise. Lockhart's face blanched when he saw him.

'Pack your personal possessions and get out of here. Someone'll contact you to tell you where you'll be working in the future,' Dane said.

'But—'

'You four.' Dane turned to the others. 'Wait in my office.'

'I wasn't being serous,' Lockhart whispered.

'Leave.'

Dane watched in silence as Lockhart emptied his drawers and, with a parting venomous glare, walked out.

Dane joined the remaining men. 'I want you to sit down separately and write your statements regarding what's gone on here. Include everything he said about Inspector Rendell, Jane Mitchell and me.'

'I ain't happy doing that,' Detective Constable Harris replied quietly.

'You either make a statement or leave with Lockhart. It's entirely up to you. If you decide not to, you'll face the same disciplinary charges as him, for doing nothing to stop racist, sexist and homophobic language. You all know what happens to those who ignore such behaviour. So, what's it to be, Harris?'

'Okay, I'll do it.'

'Wise choice. Sit separately and get on with it. When you've finished, bring them to me.'

Dane slumped in his chair and watched as the nearest officers started scribbling their statements. He rang Sobers and told him what had happened.

Sobers was silent for a moment, and then sighed. 'I'll contact Professional Standards and they can take it from here. I'll come over to see you all now.'

The force was, rightly, unforgiving of officers who behaved like Lockhart, and those who didn't challenge such language. That Lockhart was confident enough to speak so openly revealed much about what had been going on in the office before Dane's arrival. It was pure luck he'd been there and he knew if he hadn't, the others wouldn't have reported it.

*

Dane cooked a lonely supper before ringing Vicky, and they spoke for an hour. He didn't tell her about Lockhart at first, but described the ongoing problem with Wix.

'You're obviously not her favourite person,' Vicky said.

'You can say that again. I don't understand what I've done for her to dislike me so much.'

'She has responsibility for your area of policing and needs to be seen to be in control. I bet she thinks you make her look weak when you take decisive action. Or when you make decisions she wouldn't have considered. It's all to do with power, and she won't brook anything or anyone who stands in her way.'

'Christ, is that what they're teaching you? I hope you don't turn into one of those clones.'

'Not a chance. I've got you to keep my feet firmly on the ground.'

'But why would she choose to work like that?' Dane moaned, and then told her what had happened earlier.

'Is Lockhart mad? That'll cost him his job,' Vicky said.

'I doubt he even thought about that.'

'It doesn't say much about the other people in the room either.'

'Sobers has already read them the riot act and I'll be reinforcing that with the rest of the team. It wouldn't surprise me to hear some complaints about Lockhart now he's gone. But I'm off to France in the morning, so it'll have to wait until I get back.'

*

Dane slept badly, the sound of Lockhart's voice churning in his head all night, and he felt tired and grumpy when Tom Jones picked him up. As they waited in Departures, he had lengthy telephone conversations with Wix, the chief, and the head of Professional Standards. Sobers caught him just as they boarded and told him a new detective sergeant had been found to replace Lockhart and would arrive on Friday.

'That's great. Who is it?'

'Yvonne Clyde.'

'Never heard of her. Where's she from?'

'Recently transferred to us from the Met. Wix was very keen to send her to you. There might be a history with those two.'

'They probably know each other. It doesn't matter to me as long as she's good at the job. Got to go, we're about to take off and the flight attendant is going to beat me up if I don't switch this off.'

They collected their hire car at Bergerac airport and Tom drove north through the stifling midsummer heat. No one was about in the tiny villages they passed through where the roads narrowed and the sunlight rebounded off the walls. Dane stared out of the window as he contemplated the events of the previous evening. Now he saw he'd made a dreadful mistake by putting Debbie

Evans in charge of that team. The baleful influence of Mason and Lockhart had overwhelmed her and the other sergeants in their thrall. It would have taken a powerful personality to break their grip, and she didn't possess the gravitas or experience.

So, he'd sent her into a situation she couldn't control. It didn't matter that she hadn't asked for help when she needed it. He'd let her down. That could only provide Wix with ammunition to use against him, and he knew he mustn't make the same error again. The comment by Lewin that everyone else in the office supported the changes gave him a small crumb of comfort.

'This is it,' Tom announced and turned onto a short gravel driveway that squeezed through an ancient stone archway to a paved courtyard. Dane admired the picturesque farmhouse and then gazed over the countryside. It was a beautiful sight. The land fell away across a wide valley, and the nearest property sat on top of a hill half a mile away. He turned as heels clattered over a tiled surface towards them. The door opened to reveal a woman in her mid-sixties with a shock of bleached blonde hair waxed into a fixed position over her left shoulder. She was wearing a sheer silk housecoat with a tiny bikini underneath and high-heeled sandals. Dark eyeliner ringed her eyes and bright red lipstick her mouth.

'Hello, you must be the fuzz. I'm Joyce Parr,' she declared and stood back, waving them in, a heavy glass tumbler half full of a clear liquid in her hand. 'Come on outside, we mustn't waste this lovely weather.'

She slurred her words and was unsteady on her feet as she led the way through the living room and onto the patio. Dane paused at the sight of the stunning view before Joyce waved them towards a couple of chairs. She swept the housecoat off, exposing her tanned, skinny body, and stretched herself out like a cat on a sunlounger next to the pool. The chair was hot in the sun and Dane wished he hadn't worn a suit and tie.

'Do you mind if we sit over here in the shade?' he asked.

'Squat where you want, dear. What can I do for you?'

Dane explained about the discovery of her husband and offered his condolences on her loss.

'Don't worry about me, darling. He's gone, so I get everything,' she smiled and gave a mock salute with the tumbler. 'Do you want something to drink? Wine, or a Scotch?'

'No, thank you, although a glass of water would be welcome.'

'Water! My God, what's happened to the modern police force? In my day, no one would turn down a Scotch. Are you all going soft?'

'We've got work to do, and a bellyful of booze wouldn't help.'

'Oh well, please yourself, there's water in the kitchen through there.' Tom headed off. 'In the meantime, I'll just freshen this up.'

She heaved herself up and tottered over to a table laden with bottles and poured a generous slug of vodka and added ice but no mixer as Tom returned with two glasses.

'Well now, how can I help you?' Joyce asked once she'd settled back onto the lounger.

'Could you give us some background to your life with your husband?'

'I certainly can, darling. I joined the police in the seventies when us girls had to work in the women's and children's department. I met Colin at a party. We soon discovered we had lots in common and married about a year later.'

'What were those interests?'

'Sex. As much as possible with each other and as many others as we could find,' she replied, and roared with laughter at their reaction. 'What a pair of prigs. I make no excuses. I love sex and I'll get it wherever I can. If you fancy a bit, I'm up for a threesome right now. No? Oh well, don't worry, you're on duty and shouldn't do that sort of thing. But that's what we liked.'

Her bluntness nonplussed Dane, and for a moment he was unsure how to react.

'So, is that what you did throughout your marriage?'

'Most of the time, yes. I left the job, and he climbed up through the ranks. I suppose these days you'd call our relationship swinging. We travelled all over the country to meet other couples who liked to do what we did and had fun with them. Colin was just as at home with a bloke or a woman. I prefer two blokes, one at each end.' She hooted with laughter again, enjoying the opportunity to shock them.

This is an act, what's she up to?

106

'Did any of his colleagues share your lifestyle?'

'Of course. There are dozens of us, including several very senior officers.'

'Who are they?'

She arched an eyebrow. 'That's my secret.'

'When did you buy this place?'

'About twenty years ago, and it took ages to do it up the way we liked. His salary financed everything.'

'Did you work?'

'No, I'm always too shagged out to do anything as boring as that. Although I did project-manage the renovations here.'

'You've done a terrific job. It's lovely,' Tom said.

'Thank you, sweetie, that's the nicest thing anyone's said to me for donkey's years. He retired, and we did some travelling until we came over here full time. We rented out our house in Billericay as an insurance policy.'

'Why not sell it?'

'We both loved it here, but we don't speak the lingo and you can't trust the water or the medical services. So, we kept the other place on in case it didn't work out.'

'Why did Colin go home?'

'Our relationship had been going stale for a few years. Ever since I passed fifty, really. He lost interest in me and found what he wanted elsewhere. It's easier to hook up with others back there, so he cleared off and left me here.'

'Did that bother you?'

'Yes, it did, strangely. I've had sex with more people than I can remember. But always with Colin's blessing, and more often than not, he'd be watching.'

'What made him lose interest in you?'

'I grew old.' She was quiet for a moment, looking forlornly over the glorious landscape in front of her. 'I don't go without. It might surprise you to learn what these Frenchies like to get up to. Mind you, the pool boy refuses to come here on his own anymore.' She giggled, and gulped her vodka, spilling some of it down her chin.

Out of the corner of his eye Dane caught the look of distaste on Tom's face.

107

'When did Colin leave?'

'End of last year, and I hadn't seen him since.'

'I understand he received a visit here from the local police?' Dane asked, and saw the sharp, calculating glance she shot him as for a moment her mask slipped.

'A couple of their detectives turned up here and accused him of some sort of internet thing with pictures. It put the wind up him.'

'Did they arrest him?'

'No. They were here for an hour and asked a load of questions. They didn't come back.'

'Did he have a computer here?'

'Oh yes, he used it to download porn. His tastes varied, everything except animals – even he drew the line at that. But he liked kids the most, male and female, young brats between eleven and thirteen.'

'How about you? What do you prefer?'

'I like big blokes with monster muscles banging away, and I've occasionally indulged in a bit of lesbian. But I'm not into the kiddy stuff, that's not my style.'

Dane heard a sharp intake of breath from Tom but pressed on.

'Did he make money from the internet?'

She shook her head. 'We're well off with his pension and investments. He didn't need to work, and the pictures were just a hobby.'

'It must have cost a pretty penny to renovate this place.'

'It did, and it took ages to complete. We paid for it out of his wages. The lump sum from the pension gave us enough to finish it all.'

'Did he bring other people here for sex?'

'Oh yes, we hosted regular weekend parties here for years. When we grew apart, we did our own thing.'

'We found a sophisticated computer set up in the attic of your home in Billericay.'

'That'll be the one he used to keep here. He took it all with him when he left.'

'And the photograph albums?'

'Yes, he wouldn't leave them behind. He valued them more than me.'

'Did you see what was in them?'

'Of course. You'll find some saucy snaps of me in my youth in some of them.'

'But they're full of the most disgusting pictures of children being abused,' Tom interjected, looking shocked.

Joyce shrugged. 'He loved his collection and was always adding to it.'

'You don't consider there's anything wrong with the images he collected?' Dane replied.

'No, it wasn't to my taste but who am I to police what he liked?' She saw the looks on their faces and snapped. 'Don't give me that moral "I should have done something" tosh. I'm just as much the deviant as him, but I didn't hide it.'

'Who else knew about his hobby?' Dane asked.

'I don't know.'

Dane sighed. 'And who might want to murder him?'

'I've no idea unless it's something connected to his hobby. His need for sex was constant. He'd happily pay for it. Perhaps he had someone round who took things too far.'

'That's an excellent point and shows how important it is we find out who you were swinging with. Who would stand to lose by being exposed by Colin? Could he have been blackmailing someone?'

'I doubt that. He was as susceptible to blackmail as any of them. The people we socialised with are a small tight club. We don't snitch because once the hypocrites with morals are involved, everyone would go down, and no one wants that.' She punctuated the speech with another swig of vodka.

'Did he leave any albums here?'

'No, he took all of that with him.'

'May we look around?'

'Not unless you've come armed with a warrant,' she slurred.

'Do you know Graham Binks?'

'No, why?'

'Someone murdered him, and in the same way your husband died.'

'Sorry I've never heard of … what was his name?'

'Binks.'

'No, means nothing to me,' she replied without even pretending to hesitate and think.

Tom asked if he could use the toilet. 'Of course, sweetie, in there to the right.' She climbed up from the lounger.

'It's okay. I can find my way.'

'I'm sure you will, dear, but I need a top-up,' she leered as he disappeared through the French windows. 'He's a nice boy. They didn't make them like that in my day.' She chuckled and poured the last of the vodka into her tumbler. As she turned, her heel slipped on the tiles and she stumbled. Dane leapt up and caught her before she hit the patio and helped her steady herself. She shrugged him off and staggered back to the lounger.

Dane watched as she lowered herself back down, now certain she was playing a game with him. *What do you hope to achieve by this?*

'Didn't spill a drop. Now, what else do you want to talk about, Mr Policeman?'

'Would you be willing to give us a statement about all this?'

Joyce screamed with laughter. 'You are joking. Put everything on paper? No way. I've no intention of going back to dear old Blighty so there's nothing you can do to me.' She giggled, emptied her glass, then her head slumped to her chest and she passed out.

Tom reappeared through the French doors. 'What happened?'

'The bottle has taken its toll. Did you have a look about?'

'Yes, and the whole place is a tip. The kitchen stinks, the bedroom is even worse, and I'd avoid the bog if I were you.'

'Any sign of computers?'

'Only a laptop with a hole through the screen.'

They lifted the comatose Mrs Parr and laid her in the recovery position on the settee inside and made sure she couldn't roll over. Dane picked up her glass and sniffed. Then, with a smile, he put it next to the bottles of booze.

The house was furnished to a high standard with expensive fixtures and fittings. Dane doubted Parr's pension, as good as it was, could have stretched to all this luxury. On the other side of the courtyard, they'd converted the old barn into a garage with space for six vehicles. It had two toilets which struck him as odd; why two? Joyce Parr was still in her alcoholic stupor when they left.

'What a vile woman. We should do something about her,' Tom said, as they drove away.

'What did you think of her vodka-induced haze?'

'I doubt she'll even remember our visit when she wakes up, much less what she said. It's a shame that none of it would be admissible in evidence.'

'She wasn't as drunk as she wanted us to believe. It was all an act. And a very good one at that.'

Tom turned to Dane with an astonished look, nearly driving them off the road. 'How…?'

'I smelt her glass. There was more tonic in there than vodka. She gave herself away when I asked about the police visit.'

'How did you know about that?'

'I didn't. Something scared Parr enough for him to return to Billericay. Given what the National Crime Agency people found on his computer, it had to be criminal. My question caught her on the hop, so she had to adjust her story and confirm the gendarmes were interested in him. Now I'd like to find out what they wanted from him.'

'You're a sneaky bugger, boss.'

'Comes with the training, but don't mention this to anyone else. She was deflecting us, to make us think of them as nothing more than a pair of sexual deviants. There's much more to this. I'll ask the NCA to find out why Parr was interviewed.' As Tom dropped their hire car off at the airport, Dane got a call from Pauline Rose.

'We've had a result with some fingerprints,' she declared. 'Two prints belonging to a known sex offender. One on the kitchen worktop in Parr's place and the other on the ladder at Binks's house.'

'Who is it?'

'His name is James Patey, current address Chelmsford.'

That cheered Dane up. Then Hayley rang with bad news. 'Geraldine's legged it and taken all her stuff. I checked the local taxi company. One of their drivers picked her up at three this morning and dropped her at Ipswich railway station.'

'She had little cash and no cards, so how did she pay for that?' he asked.

'She ordered the cab and told them to collect her at the gates of the safe house. She found enough cash. The driver mentioned she was talking on her mobile and arranging to meet someone later today.'

'How did she get that out of the safe?'

'She didn't. It was a different phone. The taxi company have given me the number she used, and I'll get it checked but that'll take days. Sorry, boss, I didn't see this coming at all.'

'Don't worry, nor did I, and it's not your fault. She's made us both look like fools. Find her.'

14

Sally Rendell greeted him the following morning and Dane regaled her with Joyce Parr's salacious description of her degenerate lifestyle. Sally passed him the briefing package they'd prepared.

James Patey was thirty-two and five foot six inches tall with a slim build. He could certainly fit the general description of the person Mrs Wallace spotted leaving Parr's house. A police mugshot showed the head and shoulders of a surly, dark-haired man with severe acne. Patey had a long criminal record for shoplifting, burglary, and drug offences, besides three convictions for indecent assault and one for rape when he was fifteen.

Sally sat quietly, watching Dane reading. It had seemed to come as no surprise to her when he'd told her about Lockhart's behaviour. She'd announced it to everyone the day before and nobody on the team had appeared bothered about his sacking. They were all more interested in the imminent arrest, and there was a buzz in the office.

There was a knock on the door and Jane walked in. 'May I join you?'

'Yes, of course,' he replied, and told her all about his visit to France.

'She sounds charming,' Jane said as he finished.

'Her life revolved around Parr and their hobby. She'd like us to think she's a sad widow drowning her sorrows in vodka alone in a foreign country.'

'You don't believe her, do you?'

'Let's just say there's more to her than meets the eye, but she has lost her husband.'

'You're too nice. She should rot behind bars for what she's condoned all these years,' Sally said.

'We'll return to her, but we have more pressing things to worry about. Now, where's Patey?' Dane said.

'There are two detectives outside his block of flats, but he isn't there. They'll arrest him for both murders if he appears. Failing that, he's due to sign on at the job centre in Chelmsford tomorrow, so we'll catch him there.'

'Sounds like a plan to me. How are the Johns brothers?'

'Kenny's burns have become infected, and he'll be in there for a few weeks. Baz isn't so bad, and they'll release him soon.'

'Is there a guard on them?'

'Yes, but the doctor isn't happy with the intrusion.'

'I'll nip up there and try to placate them and check up on the mystery woman we found with Laura while I'm at it.'

Dane found the amiable sister in the specialist burns unit who explained their reservations about having officers on their ward.

'There's a real risk of infection if we let too many people in here.'

'I understand. We'll do whatever you want, but they're both under arrest, so we can't leave them unguarded. How is Kenny doing?'

'Not good.'

Dane went for a quick word with Baz and found Tracey sitting beside the bed.

'I wanted to check how you're getting on. Is there anything you need?'

'We're okay, thanks,' Tracey replied.

Baz's face was still red and swollen. His hands and arms were smeared with ointment and a drip was rehydrating him. But he looked better than when Dane had last seen him.

'Kenny is lucky to be alive, but he's not doing good,' Baz's voice cracked. 'They won't let me see him. Listen, I'll tell you everything you want to know. Dragon left us to die, and I won't let him get away with that.'

'We can talk about that once you're out of here. Have you any other family?' Dane asked.

'No, it's just me and him. Our parents are dead, so we take care of each other.'

'He didn't do that last week, did he?' Tracey said bitterly.

'Don't be like that, love. I'm as much to blame.'

Dane left them and walked up two flights of stairs to the high dependency unit where he was perturbed to find no sign of a police guard. As he got to the nurse's station, he noticed a figure appear from a room halfway along the corridor and head away from Dane. A nurse was coming the other way and as she passed the stranger, she turned with a puzzled expression. The man was slim, with a shaven head and wearing a doctor's white coat. She watched him, and then turned into the room he'd emerged from. Moments later there was a scream followed by the piercing screech of an alarm. The nurse reappeared at the door and yelled at the top of her voice, 'Help, help me!'

Dane sprinted to the door to be confronted by an appalling scene. The mystery woman lay on the bed, her head thrown back as blood poured from the dreadful gash across her throat, drenching the nurse as she tried in vain to stem the torrent. A second nurse arrived, barging Dane aside and bringing him to his senses. He looked along the corridor in time to see the killer disappear through a fire escape. Dane reached it seconds later and pushed, but the door only moved a few inches before slamming against an obstruction. He peered through the window in time to see his quarry pause, half a flight of stairs below him, then glance up and smile before darting out of sight. Dragon. Dane put his shoulder to the door, but it wouldn't budge.

He gave up and ran back to the room. Mr Clarence was standing in the corridor outside, anger darkening his face. 'Where's your so-called guard?'

'That's what I'd like to know. Where do the stairs beyond the fire escape lead to?'

'What? Why are you—'

'The man responsible ran through there and blocked the door. Where do they go?' Dane said, his voice rising in urgency.

'Down to the basement level, there's an exit to the service road.' Dane looked through the window and saw the road three floors below, snaking past the building. He'd never get down there in time. He didn't have a radio and there was no signal on his mobile. By the time he got through to the control room to raise the alarm, he knew the killer was long gone.

Twenty minutes later, PC Adams ambled in, carrying a cup of coffee and a paper bag containing something greasy. He stopped at the sight of the commotion before being confronted by an angry Dane. 'Where have you been?'

'I needed the loo, and I bought some scoff. What's happened?'

'Someone murdered the woman you were supposed to be guarding. Sit over there. And don't move until I tell you to.' Dane pointed to a row of chairs.

The next few hours were a blur as Pauline and her team arrived and got down to work. Detectives gently interviewed the traumatised nurses. One provided an excellent description of the man she'd seen, and it matched Dane's recollection of him. Three armed sentries whose presence was no longer an irritation replaced the lone officer guarding the Johns brothers.

Dane asked a nurse if anyone had visited the dead girl when PC Adams tapped him on the shoulder.

'I was on duty yesterday afternoon and a woman asked about her.'

'Did she give you a name?'

'Ivanka. She said she was Eastern European and that she and the girl were friends.'

'What else did she tell you?'

'Nothing really, we chatted for a minute or two, then she left.'

'Well, what did you chat about?' Dane demanded, his frustration rising.

'We sort of passed the time of day.'

'Did she say what her connection was to the girl?'

'No, she didn't.'

'Did you ask her?'

'No, I didn't think to.'

'Did you get her number?'

Adams looked down, his face colouring, and shuffled nervously.

'Let me guess. You met her today for a coffee?' Dane snapped.

'Yes,' Adams whispered. 'In the canteen, I wasn't there for long…'

'Time enough for someone to slip in and slice that poor woman's throat open. Did you bother to learn her surname when you were having your chat?'

'She told me it was Putin.'

'You didn't think that odd?'

'Why would I?'

There was a stunned silence as Dane closed his eyes and drew a deep breath. The ward manager, a middle-aged Irish lady with a shock of red hair, turned to him.

'Holy Mother of God. Where did you find this fool?'

It was several hours before Dane got away, and as he did, Wix rang him.

'Where are you?'

'Just leaving the hospital.'

'Come straight to my office,' she snapped and hung up. Her brusque manner didn't surprise him but forewarned him something was amiss.

As he crawled along in the early evening traffic, it occurred to him that Laura Hobbs would now need protection, so he contacted Sue Page.

'How many people know where she is?'

'It's not a secret. Anyone with access to her file can find that out. Why?'

Dane explained what had happened. 'We've got to assume she's in danger. Can you seal her file and check if anyone's been making enquiries about her? I'll also need the details of the foster parents.'

'I'll get on it and ring you later.'

Dane did not doubt that Dragon would go after Laura, and a frisson of fear surged through him as he thought of the woman in that hospital room. He ran up the stairs to Wix's office and bumped into Sobers.

'What are you doing here?'

'I've been summonsed and she doesn't sound happy. Do you know what's wrong now?' Dane replied.

'No, let's find out.'

Wix looked up when they entered, surprised to see Sobers. 'Do you need something?'

'I came to discuss staffing for the investigation and bumped into Mr Dane.'

Wix had another visitor: a heavily built squat man with an angry expression. He regarded the two newcomers with the hint of a sneer.

'This is John Friend from the National Crime Agency,' Wix said. 'He's had to come to see me because Dane has compromised one of their operations. We'd both like to know why you travelled to France without first checking with his office.'

'Why would I talk to them before visiting the bereaved wife of a murder victim?' Dane replied.

'Because if you had you'd have been told not to go there,' Friend snapped.

'So, you are investigating the Parrs?'

'I'm not at liberty to disclose that information…'

Dane faced Wix. 'I've been in contact with the National Crime Agency from day one of this investigation. I have asked them repeatedly if they were looking at Parr or Binks, and I have their assurances, in writing, they were not. There are no "interest flags" on any national intelligence database. So, either there was a breakdown in communications or, more likely, someone there has lied to me. Now this guy strolls in here and has the gall to accuse me of compromising their operation. And you believe him without question.'

Before Wix could say anything, Sobers said to Friend, 'Who's your boss?'

'I work in Organised Immigration Crime.'

Sobers clicked his fingers and held his hand out. 'ID.'

Friend handed his wallet over. 'Says here you're a G3?' Sobers said.

'That's correct.'

'The equivalent to a detective inspector,' he announced to Wix.

'You, wait outside,' Sobers ordered Friend, then rounded on Wix. 'You might be happy for a junior officer to waltz in here and throw accusations around, but I'm not.' He pulled his mobile phone out and dialled a number. Soon after, they were taking a secure conference call from Aly Sims, Director of Operations from the NCA, an old friend of Sobers'.

'First, let me apologise for the breakdown in communications,' Sims said. 'I'm not sure why you haven't received the information, but I'll find out tomorrow. We are working with the French and

118

Italian authorities investigating a people-smuggling ring that's trafficking women and children across Europe. Most originate from Albania and are being transported through Italy and France, with many of them coming to Britain.'

'I assume this is for the sex trade,' Dane replied.

'Yes, but some kids are being used in the organ-transplant business. The French police were watching Parr when he was living in France because they suspected he was involved with the smugglers.'

'Do they know what his role was?'

'Not for certain, but they suspected he was facilitating the movements through France and into the UK. The prime movers are the Italian mafia.'

Dane's head snapped up at that. *Is that what Joyce was trying to hide?* 'Was his death linked to this activity?'

'They've nothing to suggest that. But I'll ask our Italian counterparts if they have anything. We have no record of Binks featuring in any of this, but I'll ensure that's double-checked.'

'Could you find out if there's any intelligence about a man called Dragon? He's an Albanian and the leader of a group of Turkish pimps in Southend. He's the suspect for a murder earlier today.'

'I'll sort that out, and the senior investigator in charge of this operation will contact Mr Dane. Would you be kind enough to tell Friend to be in my office first thing tomorrow morning?'

After Friend left, Dane considered what they'd just been told. This could change the whole focus of the investigation and, if there was now an international element, cause him a few problems. Wix made no apology for what had happened and dismissed them with a curt nod. Dane returned to the empty incident room, where he made up his notes.

It was typical of Wix to automatically assume he'd done something wrong. Dane hoped she felt some personal embarrassment that might allow her to ease up on him for a bit, but he wouldn't hold his breath. As he arrived home, he realised he'd left his notebook on his desk. He considered going back for it, but decided it was too late. It was safe there. As he lay in bed, the image of the unknown girl's lifeblood pouring away wouldn't leave his consciousness and was the last thing he thought about as he dropped off.

*

Sally conducted the morning briefing, and the teams were leaving when a woman entered the room and walked over to Dane.

'Hello, sir, I'm Detective Sergeant Yvonne Clyde reporting for duty.'

'Nice to meet you. Take a pew while I sort a few bits out, then we'll get to know each other. Would you like a cuppa?'

'No, thanks, I don't drink the stuff, but I can brew you one while I wait.'

'Lovely, a sergeant who knows how to make tea.'

Her face clouded, and Dane realised his misstep. 'I'm sorry, that was my weak attempt at an ice-breaker.'

'It's okay, boss. You might not want it after you've tasted it,' she countered and smiled before heading for the kitchen.

Dane sipped the excellent brew and regarded Detective Sergeant Clyde. She was in her thirties and slight, with light brown hair cut in a bob that framed her face. Her glasses seemed to enlarge her piercing blue eyes.

'I'm happy to have you here. As you've probably noticed, we're busy, so I need you to get straight to work. I've never heard of you, so why don't you give me a potted history of Yvonne?'

'I prefer to be called Vonn. I originate from the West Country and joined the Met six years ago.'

'Why did you move out to Essex?'

'I was on a CID team in central London where I had a real problem with persistent sexual harassment. I refused to put up with that and complained about the worst offenders. That didn't make me very popular, and it became impossible for me to work with them. Ms Wix was extremely supportive and suggested I transfer to Essex, and I'm pleased I took her advice. This is a great opportunity for me, and I'll do the best I can for you.'

'It's good to have you here. Have a natter with the DI and she'll put you to work.'

Vonn smiled and got up to go, and then turned back to him. 'Do you mind people going out for a run at lunchtimes?'

120

'Not at all, provided it doesn't interfere with your work.'

'Great. I get twitchy if I can't run at least four times a week.'

'I know the feeling. Good luck.'

*

The cops lurking outside the job centre spotted Patey as he arrived and called more officers into position. When their target came out, they closed in. Dane listened on the police radio and heard frantic calls for assistance as Patey ran for it and led them all a merry chase through Chelmsford. After twenty minutes a breathless, triumphant voice declared they'd arrested him.

Dane reached the cell block in time to watch four burly officers carry the wriggling Patey into the custody office. Blood streamed from a cut over his eye as he screamed obscenities. Once he stopped struggling, they removed the handcuffs and stood him in front of the custody officer, who told him the reason for his arrest.

'Murder? What're you trying to fit me up with this time? I want my brief and I ain't talking to no one until he gets here.'

Dane found the dishevelled group of officers involved in the chase in the canteen. 'What happened?'

A young sergeant sitting in the corner said, 'I tried to arrest him, and he was off like a greyhound. We eventually cornered him in a building site where he was hiding among a load of concrete pipes and we had to threaten to send a dog in after him.'

'How did he damage his eye?'

'He deliberately head-butted the cage in the van as we were getting him out.'

'I've got that recorded on my bodycam,' another officer put in.

'Okay. Well done, everyone, that's a good nicking. Have we found the keys to his flat?'

'I retrieved them. I was going to take them over there to the search team,' Vonn said.

'I'll come with you.'

Dane and Pauline looked around as Vonn waited at the door. The small bedsit just outside the centre of Chelmsford was filthy. A sofa bed was against the wall, and grubby clothes scattered across the floor. The kitchenette had a sink, a small fridge and a grease-encrusted hob.

'It's a wonder he hasn't died of botulism,' Pauline gasped, holding her nose.

A large flat-screen TV, satellite box, games console and a pile of DVDs stood in the corner.

'He isn't so poor he can't afford the electronics,' Dane commented.

Pinned to the wall were four pictures of primary-school-age children, a boy and three girls. They were all wearing identical red pullovers, their faces creased with a false smile for the camera. The photos were in discoloured white cardboard frames. Dane pulled them off the wall. Scribbled on the rear of the boy's picture was, 'Me, school 1996'.

So, this was Patey as a child and Dane wondered why he would keep an old snap of himself on show. The other three pictures had nothing written on them, and there was no family resemblance between any of the children. On impulse, he pulled them out of the frames and found a small piece of paper with a telephone number on it behind Patey's picture. As he replaced them all on the wall, he noted the flat expressions of the girls. Those kids were not happy.

They could find nothing relating to either of the murders, so returned to the station. With Vonn beside him Dane watched the monitor as the interviewing officers led Patey into the small interview room. His solicitor, a sour-faced woman, sat beside him.

Patey answered every question about Parr with a 'no comment' delivered in a flat monotone. After forty minutes, they concentrated on Binks. Once again, Patey refused to answer and appeared bored by the proceedings.

He was chewing his nails when they asked him to explain how his fingerprints came to be in Parr's house. He looked startled and faltered for a moment before giving his stock reply.

'Were you in there during the early hours of the day we discovered the victim's body?'

Patey paused for a few seconds, and then gestured to his solicitor. 'We need to talk.'

'You heard him. Stop the interview now.'

An hour later, they returned, and the lawyer handed over several sheets of paper.

'My client has made a prepared statement. He will not answer any further questions.'

Dane joined the officers to read what Patey had written. He stated he'd known Colin Parr for years and was a frequent visitor to the house in Billericay until the Parrs moved away. They'd bumped into each other about a month before Colin's death. Parr invited him round for a drink and he'd been there twice since, but not on the night in question. Patey then addressed the possibility of his fingerprints being found in Binks's home, stating they were friends and he'd visited the house in Clacton several times. Patey reiterated that he knew nothing at all about the murder of either victim.

In the custody room the solicitor was trying to browbeat the custody officer into releasing her client as Dane joined them. 'Good evening. I'm the officer in charge of this investigation.'

'You have no justification for detaining my client.'

'There are more questions we need to put to him before we consult with the CPS over whether we charge or bail. We'll do that in the morning.'

Dane looked at Patey, who returned his stare. Then his eyes flicked over Dane's shoulder with a momentary look of surprise, which he masked, turning away. This reaction puzzled Dane and he glanced behind him. But no one was there.

Dane rang Wix and informed her they'd probably have to release Patey on bail.

'Aren't you going to charge him?'

'There isn't enough evidence to do that yet.'

'Why not, for God's sake? You've got his prints at both scenes. What more do you need?'

'He has a plausible explanation for being in each house which, at the moment, I can't disprove.'

'I want this sorted out and soon.'

'I'm working on it,' Dane replied, and hung up. *It's like dealing with a spoilt child*, he thought as he locked his desk and drove home.

15

Dane felt relaxed as he set out for headquarters the following morning. They would release Patey later, and he had an idea for dealing with him. That meant he'd have to see Wix, something he'd rather not have to do at that time of the day, but it would be worth the effort. No sooner had he pulled away from the house than he received a call from Polly in the press office.

'Have you seen the papers this morning?'

'No, why?' he replied with a sinking feeling in the pit of his stomach.

'Boyd. He's been at it again.'

'I'm on my way in. I'll check it when I get there.'

He found the offending article online. A colour picture of Joyce Parr, reclining on the sunlounger beside her swimming pool, glass in hand, filled the page. The banner headline read 'The French Connection' alongside the author's byline.

'Angus Boyd,' Dane grumbled as he scanned the piece. It covered his trip to France with lurid stories about the wild sex parties held by the Parrs in France and Billericay. A statement attributed to *sources* revealed Dane was working with the French police investigating links between Parr and a people-smuggling ring operating from Albania. Dane found Sobers unlocking his office door and told him the bad news.

'It confirms someone is leaking and it must be from my team.'

Sobers read the article and sighed. 'You're probably right. You have enough to deal with. Leave this with me. I'll sort something out and we'll trap whoever it is.'

'I'd better ring her. If they've staked her out, we should ask the locals to help, if that's what she wants,' Dane said and checked his watch. He wondered if she'd be up but rang anyway. To his surprise, she answered straight away.

'Mrs Parr, it's Superintendent Dane here.'

'Who are you?'

'We met the other day when I visited you about your ex-husband.'

'Oh, yes, sorry. It's a bit early for me. What can I do for you?'

'I'm ringing about the visit you've had from the British press.'

'That was fun. This journalist turned up on the doorstep yesterday morning, asking about Colin and what our life was like together. I invited him in, and we had a pleasant chat over a few drinks.'

'Have you seen what he's written?'

'No.'

'It doesn't show you in a good light. Was the journalist's name Boyd?'

'That's right.'

'Did he tell you how he found you?'

'He said he'd been following the investigation into my ex-husband's death and understood we liked to swing. So, we chatted about that.'

'I'm sorry to have brought this on you. Would you like me to arrange for some police protection?'

'No,' she yelped. 'Christ no, that's the last thing I need. Don't worry about it. I never read the papers and I'm really not bothered. There's nothing they can do to me here, and the French don't care about other people's sex lives.'

'Do you know a man called James or Jim Patey?'

'Jimmy? He's been hanging around for ages. Colin met him years ago, and they stayed in contact.'

'Was he one of Colin's friends?'

She laughed. 'More like one of his young bits of meat. But yes he was.'

'When did you last see or speak to him?'

'He rang me after he read about the murder to give me his condolences. He wanted to come over, but I told him no thanks. Lovely talking to you, but I've got to go,' she said and hung up.

Dane thought about their conversation and her reaction to his offer of police protection stuck in his mind. He could understand her not wanting any, but it was her choice of words that he found odd. Why, he wondered, should it be the last thing she needed? Then it hit him. *She's taken over from her husband. That's why she doesn't want any police about.*

He flicked through the pages of his notebook until he came to the entry covering his visit to France and the subsequent discussion with Aly Sims. The passages in Boyd's article, accredited to unnamed 'sources', could only have come from this book. No one else had been told the full details of his conversation with the NCA chief, so someone must have looked at his notes to find that information. Dane felt betrayed. Most journalists cultivated police officers; indeed, quite a few cops had their own media contacts. The mutual need for that cross-pollination was important and usually stayed within accepted boundaries. But this was a calculated betrayal of trust by a corrupt employee selling out the investigation to Boyd. The call to Joyce Parr reminded him of the telephone number he'd found on the back of the photo in Patey's flat and, on impulse, he dialled it. After three rings, she answered, and he hung up. *So, she has two phones.*

Dane wandered through to Tom Hanson's office. 'You are not a popular man,' Tom greeted him.

'Who hates me now?'

'Someone called Friend has been on complaining. They're livid that all this about the Parrs has leaked to the press.'

'I'm just as fed up as they are. But I'm going to find whoever's responsible. In the meantime, I need a surveillance team to follow Patey to gather lifestyle information on him.'

'They're available, but we'll have to clear the deployment with Wix.'

Dane's request elicited the expected response. 'Have you any idea how much this will cost?' Wix exploded.

'Of course I do, and I'm not asking for a laugh. If we watch where he goes and who he meets, we might take the case forward.'

'I don't like it. Twenty-four-hour coverage will use up all our surveillance resources.'

'I'm aware of that, but it's my considered opinion that we must do this, otherwise we'll miss vital evidence.'

For all her bluster, Dane knew he was in a sound position. This was a reasonable and proportionate operational request, and difficult for her to deny.

She gave a deep sigh and nodded. 'Okay. I'll sanction this deployment, but I want a daily update on what we're achieving.'

As Hanson organised the surveillance, Dane returned to the incident room. The final interview with Patey finished as they booked Baz Johns into a cell.

Half an hour later, the team was in position, and they released Patey.

Baz's lawyer met Dane with a handshake. 'He's instructed me to tell you he intends to make a full confession about the fire and give you information about someone called Dragon. His sole condition is that he'll only talk to you.'

Dane agreed to that stipulation and took Hayley to sit in with him.

Baz waited quietly as they prepared to start the interview. He'd been discharged from the hospital the previous morning, but Dane had decided not to arrest him straight away. Kenny Johns had died, and his brother was inconsolable. With no immediate need to lock him up, Dane allowed Baz to take some time to grieve and make arrangements for the funeral. Dane hadn't been expecting him to turn up for another day or so.

'Thanks for yesterday. You didn't have to do that, and I appreciate it,' Baz said.

'Are you sure you've had enough time to sort things out?'

'Yeah. Tracey's getting it all organised. I want this done and dusted.'

'Why don't you start at the beginning? Give us some background on you and your brother, and how you both came to work for Dragon.'

Baz explained that his late mother had been a prostitute in Southend who brought up he and Kenny, who was twelve years older, on her own. When she'd died, Kenny took him under his wing and they'd been together ever since. They worked on building sites and at other manual jobs during the day and were bouncers at Southend's nightclubs at night. Their hard-man reputation preceded them, and Dragon offered them both a job.

'Tell me about that.'

'He needed a couple of handy blokes to mind the stock.'

'And his stock is?'

'Girls.'

'Who are they?'

'They're all from where he comes from, Albania. They live in two houses in the town, and we ended up looking after the motel.'

'How many are there?'

'There's twenty-eight of them.'

How come we didn't know his already?

'Do they entertain clients in the houses in Southend?'

'No. They used the Florida for that, ten of them working there every night. It was me and Kenny's job to get them there, and make sure none of the punters took any liberties. When they finished their shift, we took them back.'

'When did Dragon first arrive in Southend?'

'Only a few months before we started with him. He's got two Turks working for him as well.'

'What does he look like?'

Baz considered that for a moment. 'About five eight tall and slim, but he works out in a gym. Dark complexion with a shaven head and he always has about five days of stubble on his chin. Likes to wear casual clothes, jeans, T-shirt and expensive trainers. He doesn't say much, but he's hard as nails, and vicious. He rules them with a rod of iron.'

'How do you mean?'

'If any of the girls gets out of line, he'll give them a savage beating. As a message to the others. He nearly killed one girl after she tried to run away. It was frightening, I can tell you.'

'What happened to her?'

'No idea, and I didn't ask, but she was never around after that.'

'Where does he live?'

'Not a clue. He drives out to Southend for the day every morning, just like he's going to the factory.'

'What does he drive?'

'A brand-new Mercedes. He loves that car. The Turks use a minivan. They hire that and change it twice a week. We used it to move the girls about.'

'Did you live there?'

'Me and Tracey are in the flat.'

'Was she aware of what you were doing?'

Baz looked down, shamefaced, and shook his head. 'She thought we were doing a bit of minding and working nightclub doors and stuff like that. Dragon pays us a decent whack, so she didn't ask too many questions. Until we come home all burnt up, then she went mental.'

'Was it always you and Kenny at the motel?'

'We worked together, but when we had some time off Dragon's Turks took over.'

'Where did Kenny live?'

'He had a room at the Florida.'

'How does Mr Roux fit into this set-up?'

'Dragon is the local boss, but there are people over him. We reckon Roux worked for them and kept an eye on their investment.'

'How did a customer go about booking themselves a girl?'

'They'd ring the motel and we'd set it up. It's a popular place, always busy. They made serious money. Roux pretended to be the manager.'

'Who was working there the night Parr died?'

'Kenny, I was off. Him and Roux found the body. He came round mine that afternoon, bricking himself.'

'Did you know Colin Parr?'

'Oh yeah.'

'As a punter?'

Baz laughed. 'You could say that. He had free use of the stock whenever he wanted.'

'Was he the boss, then?'

'No, he took care of the money. He would be there two or three times a month for a meeting with Dragon. Once he'd finished that side of the business, he'd choose a girl. They all hated it when he came.'

'Why?'

'Because after being with him, the girl would be off the road for a few days.'

'You mean he beat them up?'

'Yeah.'

'What did Kenny tell you about that evening?'

'He got a call from Dragon to take a bottle up to the room, which he did. Parr was in there with a load of cash all laid out in piles on the table.'

'There wasn't any there when we searched it,' Dane interjected.

'It was in a bag Parr always carried about. Roux hid it before your lot arrived.'

'Go on.'

'Kenny heard Dragon and Parr arguing. They stopped when he knocked on the door, but it was tense in there when he gave them the bottle. Dragon came to the office later, and they talked about the girls and how much business they were all doing. Then he left.'

'Did he mention the young girl taken to Parr's room?'

'He said there'd been one, but she wasn't one of Dragon's stock.'

'We found her. A Turk called Mehmet supplied her.'

Baz nodded. 'I know him, he's looking after Dragon's brother, Guri.'

'What's their set-up in Chelmsford?'

'Mehmet's the younger brother of Arif, one of the Southend Turks. Dragon gave him and Guri the chance to prove themselves by recruiting their own stock and setting up their own business.'

'So, Kenny comes round yours the day they find the body. What does he tell you?'

'He told me about Parr and how the place was crawling with cops.'

'Who called the police?'

'Roux did. Kenny thought he was mad, but Roux was sure they could talk their way out of it because Parr had obviously made a mistake and killed himself.'

'That didn't work too well, did it?'

'That's why Kenny wanted to keep out of sight.'

'And he knew we'd want to talk to him.'

'Yes.'

'What happened next?'

'Dragon rang Kenny. Told him he'd done the right thing and to stay low. Couple of nights later we were down the pub when he called about a job he wanted doing.'

'The motel?'

'Yep. He picks us up in the van with Arif and Hakki. He's the other Turk, and we go out to the Florida. They had four jerry cans and Dragon told us to burn it down.'

'Did he say why?'

'Because you lot had nicked his brother, and because of that and the murder the Florida was blown as a brothel. Dragon wanted it gone to destroy any evidence. He thought that would force you to release Guri.'

That didn't sound logical to Dane, given the video evidence Dragon must have known they had. It sounded more likely Dragon was lashing out over the loss of the motel and denying others the opportunity to use it.

'So, what did you do?'

Jimmy paused for a few moments, and tears filled his eyes. 'We sloshed the petrol round one side and the Turks did the other. The problem was we were full of beer and splashed some over ourselves. Then Dragon flicked a fag end to set it off, and everything blew up with an almighty bang. And next thing, Kenny's burning. By the time I put the flames out, we're both burnt.'

'Did Dragon do it deliberately?'

'Nah. It caught us in the flashback. If he'd been trying to kill us, he wouldn't have taken us home, would he?'

'Why didn't you take yourselves to hospital? You must have been in agony.'

'Because Kenny was certain Dragon would bring us a doctor. How stupid can you be? We should have done what Tracey said.'

'How is Dragon connected to Parr?'

'Parr was involved with getting the women into the country. He was close to the people bankrolling the whole thing, which was why Dragon had to deal with him. But they hated each other. You could see their hackles up when they were together. Dragon always had a right old moan when Parr damaged his stock.'

'Did they fight? Is that what Kenny heard?'

Jimmy shrugged his shoulders. 'No, they were just having a shouting match.'

'Could Dragon have killed Parr?'

'From what I've seen of him, he's capable of it. But I can't say he did it. Kenny never thought he did either.'

'Who did he think did it?'

'He really had no idea. We couldn't figure how they got in there, either.'

'We found a girl beaten half to death at the house used by Guri and his pals. Do you know anything about her?'

'Dragon mentioned someone had run, but not that they'd caught her. She the one at the hospital?'

Dane nodded. 'Did you talk to the girls?'

'No. Dragon didn't want us doing that. And none of them spoke a word of English, anyway.'

'Does the name James or Jimmy Patey mean anything to you?'

'No.'

'How about Graham Binks?'

'Those names mean nothing to me.'

That was the extent of Jimmy's knowledge, so they took him back to his cell to wait to be charged. Dane rang Inspector Chard from the Organised Crime Unit and gave him the addresses in Southend.

'The first place is where we've been watching. There's been no movement in or out all week and we're sure it's empty. I'll get my people to check the other one.'

Dane guessed they'd find another empty house. Dragon knew his operation in the town was blown and those poor women would now be a long way away from Southend. Parr's involvement with the prostitution was an interesting revelation and might provide a motive for his murder. Dragon was a killer and the man Dane chased from the hospital. But did he kill Parr? Possibly, but why, and if he did, when did he do it? Laura left Parr alive hours after Kenny had seen Dragon. And if the Albanian killed him, even in a fit of unplanned anger, why would he leave the body lying around in his own brothel? Surely, he'd have disposed of it to avoid having the place crawling with police. Roux reporting the death had ruined a very lucrative business. And that would hurt profits, which the people they worked for wouldn't like.

Dane now had the connection between Mehmet, Guri and Dragon. That explained a few things, and a sudden memory popped into his head. As they'd loaded Laura into the ambulance, he recalled the man standing next to a Mercedes watching them. That must have been Dragon, furious at the arrest of his brother and even more angry because of the disruption to his business.

All of which meant he had to ensure the safety of Baz, his wife Tracey and Laura Hobbs. Another battle for resources with Wix. Meanwhile, the Albanian remained a suspect for Parr's killing and of that poor girl in the hospital, so he had to be his priority, but how to track him down? He pondered the problem and had an idea; a smile creased his face as he reached for a street map of Southend and called Hayley in.

'I want you to go to the CCTV control room in Southend.' Dane showed her the locations of the houses Baz had mentioned. 'Both these streets are just outside the camera coverage, but the roads at the ends are in it. View the footage from the area. Go back two weeks. See if you can pick out a nice new silver Merc and a minivan.'

Once she'd gone, Dane gazed through the glass walls of his office and watched the officers working at their computers in the incident room. He wondered who the traitor was. Jane Mitchell bustled in through the door, laden down with her usual bags and a sheaf of newspapers under her arm. She looked round till she spotted him.

'I promise you I didn't say a word to that louse,' she declared breathlessly as she dumped her cargo on a chair.

'Have you any idea who his source might be?'

'None, but it's a doozy.'

'Not how I'd describe them.'

'No. I suppose you wouldn't. But that's how my world works. We all live or die by how good our sources are. He's tried to ring me again, by the way. I'm ignoring him.'

'Would you mind giving me his number?'

'Why do you want it?'

'It might help me find out who's talking to him.'

'I'll have to think about it. We all swap numbers, but there's an unwritten rule that you don't pass them on without the owner's permission. And while I hate Boyd with a passion, I can't just hand his over.'

'I understand,' Dane said, but couldn't hide his frustration.

'Look, I'm not saying no, but it's difficult. Now, what are you doing today?'

'We've got a team following Patey. I'm off to visit their control room to check how they're getting on. Would you like to join me?'

'Yes, please.'

They found Detective Inspector Crane in the darkened surveillance control centre surrounded by computer screens and TV monitors. The occasional burst of radio chatter came from a loudspeaker. A large map on a screen showed half a dozen blue dots, each representing the position of an officer as they kept their prey under observation.

'We've got him in our net,' the inspector explained after Dane introduced Jane.

'What's happened since he left the nick?'

'We watched him go back to the building site where he was arrested and recover a mobile phone. Then he settled into the nearest pub and made some calls. We had a car outside with the IMSI grabber. It took us an hour, but we've snagged his number,' Crane announced with a grin, handing a piece of paper to Dane.

'Brilliant. What's he up to now?'

'He's having a beer.'

'What's that thing you used to get his phone number?' Jane asked.

'It's an electronic device that mimics a mobile phone mast and snares an outgoing phone signal. So, when Patey made a call, one of our surveillance operators pointed it at his phone and diverted his signal through it, which gives us the number.'

Her mouth dropped with surprise. 'Is that legal?'

'Yes, it is.'

'Sounds like something a civil liberties activist would hit the streets about.'

'We have to justify its use and get high-level authorisation to deploy it. Once we have what we need, the device is switched off.

And the surveillance commissioners audit our use to make sure we minimise the intrusion.'

'Even so. Can I write about it?'

'Of course, it's not a secret.'

They took the number up to the Telephone Unit, where Dane gave the details of Paley's phone to the clerk. She assured him they'd get the information he needed ASAP. But as it was only a Level 2 investigation, it might take a few days. Dane blew his cheeks out in frustration but thanked her.

'I thought they'd give you that at once,' Jane said.

'Welcome to my world. She receives hundreds of requests a week. There are only so many people employed to search for the information in the mobile phone companies. So, they have to stick to the priorities. My request is urgent to me, but it isn't life-threatening, so I wait my turn.'

'That's crazy. I bet I'd be able to get it immediately.'

'I believe you. But I'd rather not know how you'd do that.'

She smiled, then handed him a slip of paper. 'Boyd's number. Don't tell anyone I gave it to you.'

He nodded, touched by her trust in him.

16

Hayley returned with a result the following afternoon. 'This Mercedes was a regular visitor turning into both roads until last week,' she said, and showed him a picture of the vehicle and its registration number.

'Who's the owner?' Dane asked.

'It's a clone. The number belongs to an identical car owned by a city councillor in Glasgow. I spoke to him, and he's seriously angry. The poor guy's been getting congestion charge demands and fixed penalty parking notices from London for more than a year.'

'Is there any way we can use those charges to work out where Dragon lives?'

'I'm working on that. Give me a day or two. In the meantime, I thought you'd appreciate these.' She dropped half a dozen black and white photos on the desk.

Dane scooped them up and smiled. Four clear head-and-shoulder shots of the Albanian and his Turkish associates. 'Well done, mate, you've surpassed yourself this time.'

'You're too kind, boss. Can I have a raise?'

'If only it was down to me. Get these circulated. With a bit of luck, someone might know where they are.'

After Hayley left, Dane rang Friend in London.

'I'm sending over several pictures of a suspect with his details. Could you pass them to your intelligence department to see if they can help identify him?'

'I'll see what we can do,' Friend drawled.

'You don't want to irritate me any more than you already have. Ms Sims has assured me of complete co-operation from your office. This guy is the suspect for two murders, so I'll look forward to hearing from you soon.'

*

Vicky came home on the Friday evening exhausted; she was in the middle of a set project with three other students, so would spend much of her weekend writing up their week's work. But she had the following few days off and planned to recharge her batteries. Dane kept busy around the house, shopping, mowing the lawn, tidying the flowerbeds and taking regular calls from Chard, who updated him with Patey's activities.

The young man led an erratic lifestyle after rising late in the day. The surveillance team soon established his principal employment was selling drugs in pubs and clubs where he worked until closing time. They had no useful information regarding the murder investigation to report to Wix on Monday.

'We've only been looking at him for a few days. We can't hope to get a result this soon. These things take time, but he'll lead us to something interesting,' Dane suggested.

'Two more days, then we review this again. But I'm warning you, you'll have a tough job persuading me to keep it going.'

'Have you seen my request for some protection for Baz and Laura?'

'Yes. I've authorised a panic alarm to be installed at Baz Johns's home and I talked to Sue Page about the girl. They're confident she's safe and agree with me it's very unlikely Dragon will find her. The foster parents are aware of the situation.'

Dane knew Wix and the social services were probably right, but it didn't stop him from worrying. Later that morning, he sat down with Sally and the sergeants, reviewing the work they'd completed so far. They had outstanding enquiries with the telephones and the finances, but they always took time. The forensic exhibits had produced nothing startling, so they had little to go on in relation to either murder. Dragon was now the main line of enquiry, with officers out trying to track him down.

After the meeting broke up, Dane sat back, closed his eyes and considered the case.

Parr had been a sexual predator of the worst kind and had got away with it. That offended Dane, but there was nothing he could do about it now. Parr's recent activities had led the French police to his door, which caused him to lose his nerve and decamp for the relative safety of England. Laura's and Baz's situations had revealed a network of offenders, trafficking and abusing young women, who operated across Europe. Was this connected to the murders? Joyce Parr had to know far more than she was letting on, but she wouldn't volunteer any useful information to assist them. Dane considered having her arrested and extradited to face charges, but given the complete lack of any hard evidence, he dismissed the idea. It would distract the investigation, and he didn't think she knew who killed her husband, anyway. The person seen leaving Parr's house had still not been located. Could it be Patey? Or Dragon? The physical description of both fitted, and while he knew Dragon killed the girl in the hospital, he wasn't so sure about Patey as a murderer.

Binks and Parr had to be connected. The method used to murder them, the Patey link and the similarities in the computer set-up suggested that. But no fingerprints, except Patey's, were at both scenes.

Geraldine's disappearance needed looking into. She had given her statement and been patient while the police finished searching her house. But the minute she had the opportunity, she disappeared. She was a witness and so not obliged to hang around or inform him if she wanted to leave, but they had to find her. Hayley still hadn't identified the friend she'd been visiting. So neither wife had been completely truthful, and he wondered why. What did they know about their husbands' activities and how could he persuade them to tell him?

*

On Wednesday morning, Wix cancelled the surveillance on Patey. Dane had to admit they'd learnt nothing to assist the investigation, but still thought her decision was a mistake. He found Jane, and they picked up Vicky for a planned lunch.

They enjoyed a pleasant meal, relaxing in a lovely country pub that boasted a TV chef and an excellent menu. The two women got on like a house on fire. Vicky invited Jane to Cambridge and agreed to be interviewed for her book. She had caught up with all her work, so planned a shopping trip that afternoon and Dane was going to drop her off in Chelmsford. As they reached the outskirts of city, Dane's mobile rang.

'Is it you?' a tremulous voice asked.

'This is Dane. Who's that?'

'It's Laura – Hobbs.'

Dane was instantly alert. 'Are you okay?'

'Hang on… Sorry, I'm in trouble. I can talk now.'

'What's happening?'

'Christopher rang me earlier. Flinders nicked his mobile,' she replied breathlessly.

'Start at the beginning.'

'Me and Christopher, we've been texting. I thought he sent one this morning asking me to meet him in Chelmsford. It said he's got a big problem and needs my help. My foster mum said it would be all right, so I caught the train. As we were coming into the station, he called from the telephone at the home and told me Flinders bashed him up yesterday and nicked his phone. Christopher followed him when he went out and watched Flinders give it to three blokes in a big silver Mercèdes who looked like the ones who hurt me. He thought they were after me. Then I spotted Mehmet's brother waiting down by the ticket place at Chelmsford station with another bloke.'

'Where are you?'

'I'm hiding by the cathedral. I ducked out the rear entrance of the station, but they must have had someone over there because when I come round the corner, they chased me, but I lost them.'

'Can you get to the police station?'

'No, I tried that first, but there's a bloke standing out the front. He looks like one of them, so I doubled back. What should I do? They're looking for me.' She sounded tense and frightened, and he squeezed the steering wheel as he put his foot down.

'Are you out of sight?'

'Yeah, I think so. If they find me, there're a couple of ways I can go.'

'Have you got enough credit to stay on the line?'

'I don't know.'

'Hang up, and I'll call you back.' Dane glanced at Vicky. 'Contact the control room and organise some support while I ring her.'

Laura's phone rang out twice before she answered in a breathless voice. 'They spotted me. I'm heading for the market, where it's crowded.'

'Good idea. Keep the line open. We're five minutes away,' he urged.

Vicky was talking to an operator in the police control room. 'This is not a joke or a hoax. There's a young girl being chased by at least three men in Chelmsford town centre.' She paused and listened to the reply. 'I've told you who I am, and I'm sitting next to him – what? No, he can't come to the phone, he's driving.' She gestured to Dane and rolled her eyes.

'Ring Sobers,' he suggested, as they sped past Bromfield Hospital.

She nodded and redialled. The heavy afternoon traffic was obstructing their progress and he didn't have blue lights or siren. Jane squealed as he swerved around long queues of vehicles and roared through junctions against red lights and across roundabouts, tyres screeching in protest. Angry blasts on horns followed his manoeuvres with flashing headlights and obscene gestures from other drivers. Laura was silent for a while, and he called out to her.

'I'm here,' she replied, panting. 'One of the stallholders has let me squat down behind their counter.'

'I'll be there soon.'

Vicky had reached Sobers. Dane saw her smile at something his boss said, then swerved to avoid a bus pulling out into the lane he was barrelling down at sixty miles an hour. Vicky cried out and dropped her phone.

'Sorry about that,' Dane said, as she bent down to retrieve it.

'He's sending a response unit.'

'Good.' A cry came from the speaker, and he shouted, 'Laura?'

A scuffle and loud angry voices, then someone running. 'They found me.'

Dane blasted through another red light, lights flashing and his own horn blaring. He passed under a tall railway viaduct and saw the multi-storey car park over the market two hundred yards ahead. He checked the mirror and glimpsed Jane hanging on for grim death, her eyes shining with excitement. A long line of vehicles waiting at the roundabout and an uninterrupted stream of traffic coming in the opposite direction blocked the road. Dane swung the wheel, bouncing over the pavement, and skidded to a halt on the grass outside an office block. He abandoned the car and sprinted across the road, narrowly avoiding being flattened, and hurdled the crash barriers in the central reservation.

Chelmsford market is a compact maze of walkways comprising dozens of stalls, all cheek-by-jowl and selling a wide range of bric-a-brac, fabric, clothes, books and many of life's necessities. He stopped just inside the entrance, holding his phone to his ear, Vicky and Jane now behind him.

There was a commotion to his right, close to some stairs leading into the car park. He ran round two stalls to find Dragon had Laura by the hair as the two Turks threatened an angry crowd of stallholders, slashing at them with knives. Dane didn't break stride as he passed a stall selling jars of health food. Scooping one up, he hurled it at the nearest Turk. It shattered on impact with the side of his head and he dropped like a stone. His friend turned to confront Dane as Jane skipped past and kicked him hard between the legs. The force of the blow lifted him off his feet, and he collapsed in a heap with a gurgling wail of pain. Dragon dragged Laura back through the doorway.

'We've got them,' Vicky shouted as Dane followed. He could hear Laura squealing in pain on the stairs above him and sprinted up two flights to a door leading to the parking floor, where he peered through the glass. Dragon was struggling with Laura, dragging her towards the parapet twenty yards away. He flung open the door and walked towards them; Dragon put the knife to Laura's throat.

'If you come any closer, I'll cut her head off.'

Dane stopped and held his hands up. 'Okay. Take it easy.' The growing clamour of sirens echoed through the city centre as patrol cars converged around the market. 'You'll not escape from here. Just let her go.'

The door opened behind him and Dane glanced over his shoulder, seeing armed officers come through and fan out to cover Dragon. 'You won't stop any court case against you or Guri by killing her. It'll only make things worse for the pair of you.'

Three more officers appeared and Dragon hissed, then half turned, dragging Laura in front of him. As he did so, she sank her teeth into his exposed wrist. He howled in pain and dropped the knife as he tried to prise her mouth open, then he punched her head, causing her legs to buckle, and shook her off, sending her staggering. Dane leapt forward and hauled her out of his reach as the officers raised their rifles and took aim. Without hesitation, Dragon vaulted over the parapet. Dane peered over, expecting to see him lying broken on the pavement. Instead, he watched the Albanian nimbly drop off the canopy he'd landed on twenty feet below. A crowd of startled onlookers stared in astonishment as he ran off and disappeared into the crowds.

'How did he do that?' he muttered and turned to Laura, who was shaking. 'Are you all right?'

'I think so.' Blood stained her teeth and mouth, which he gently wiped off with his handkerchief.

Vicky appeared. 'Those two downstairs are in custody,' she said and looked around. 'Where is he?'

'He jumped.'

'What!'

'Straight over, he didn't hesitate, then bounced up and ran off.'

She peered over and shrugged. 'If any normal person did that, they'd be in bits. Do we need to take Laura to the hospital?'

'Yes,' Dane replied.

'No. I'm okay. I ain't going there,' Laura replied.

Jane joined them. 'That was the most fun I've ever had standing up. I am absolutely stoked,' she announced, a huge grin on her face. And they all laughed, releasing some of the tension.

'That was some kick, but why didn't you use the karate?' Dane asked.

'I always find a good old boot in the bollocks very effective in ending a punch-up,' Jane replied to more amusement.

They spent hours making their statements. The authorities removed Christopher from the children's home, and brought him to headquarters where he was reunited with Laura. They'd be taken to a place of safety by Witness Protection. Christopher was able to give an excellent description of the men he saw with

Flinders and had noted the Mercedes' registration number. Dane went to see them before they left, and Laura threw her arms round him, taking him by surprise.

'Thanks for getting me out of that mess,' she said.

'That's all right. All part of the service. You'll both be safe now.'

The Turkish pimps refused to say anything during their interviews, but nevertheless the prosecutors charged them with a variety of offences. John Flinders admitted being paid a hundred pounds to steal Christopher's phone and hand it over to Dragon. He'd been willing to help the Albanian track Laura down, partly for the money, and partly to get back at her because she'd disrespected him. Meanwhile, Dragon made good his escape.

17

As Dane arrived at the incident office the following morning, he passed a slight figure sprinting along the road, her arms and legs pounding. It was Vonn Clyde. She jogged up to him as he parked, her face flushed and glistening with sweat.

'Hello, boss,' she panted, leaning over and holding her knees. She was wearing a tight vest and shorts with gaudy, bright purple running shoes. Her body was firm and muscular without an ounce of spare fat, but behind the glow of exercise, he thought she looked pale and unwell.

'I'm not sure about those shoes, Vonn. They could put you off your breakfast.' It was all top-of-the-range gear which, he knew, cost a fortune; she was obviously a serious runner.

'Always use the best, I say.'

'How far did you run?'

'Just the five miles. I'm busy this morning, so I'll go out again when I get off this evening.'

'Are you training for anything in particular?'

'No, but I like to keep my mileage up,' she replied, and jogged off to warm down.

Sally had some news from the checks they'd run on Geraldine's phone since her unexpected departure. 'Hayley's got a number Geraldine rang five minutes before she contacted 999 to report finding her husband dead. She's following up on that this morning.'

'Is there anything new from the forensics?'

'The examination of the rope threw up nothing useful. It's all the same type and available in every good DIY store for a few quid a yard.'

'Any more fingerprints identified?'

'Yes. They've matched some prints from Parr's house with a couple in the motel room and the fire escape door at the hospital.'

'They must be Dragon's,' Dane suggested.

'I agree, but there's no match on our national database. I've asked Reg to put a search request through Interpol.'

'How long will that take?'

'They didn't say,' Sally replied.

Vonn Clyde had taken over responsibility for intelligence on the investigation and confirmed that Patey had lived in his flat for six years, could not work and received incapacity benefits.

'What's his disability? Because he looked pretty lively when we were trying to arrest him,' Dane replied

'Social services say he suffered trauma when he was a child. Resulting in physiological damage, rendering him incapable of holding down any kind of employment. He's never had a proper job. One of the few things we learnt from the surveillance is his involvement in the supply of drugs. This corroborates other intelligence and explains how he can afford the luxury items.'

'What about his previous convictions? Do they tell us anything?'

'Not really. When he was fourteen, a girl under thirteen from the care home he was in accused him of rape. She ran away and reported it to the police. He received a caution because there was a suspicion the victim was a willing partner. As if that should be a factor,' Vonn snapped with a sudden flash of anger.

'Where was that?'

'Outside Maldon. He spent his youth in council-run homes and left school with no qualifications. His other convictions were for shoplifting and indecent assaults when he was a juvenile. He's been arrested twice as an adult for soliciting around public toilets, and there were unconfirmed reports he was working as a rent boy. Social services won't release his care record or allow us to read it.'

'Why not?'

'The official reason is he hasn't given his consent.'

'We'll work round that for the time being. Mrs Parr suggested her husband abused Patey, she referred to him as "one of his young bits of meat". Could that have driven him into prostitution and is he still selling himself?' Dane considered that for a moment. 'We'll have to try and persuade social services otherwise. Good work, Vonn.'

18

Dane arrived at the fortified gates protecting the National Crime Agency headquarters in Spring Gardens. The security guards inspected his credentials, and then escorted him to the office of Brian White, a heavyset man in his late forties who greeted him with a firm handshake.

'First, let me apologise again for Friend. He's a direct entry investigator with a background in law and doesn't enjoy talking to anyone, never mind the police. He took it on himself to go out to Essex and I'm sorry if he caused you any trouble,' White said.

'He got a bit of a shock when he ran into my boss.'

'Sobers.'

'You know him?'

'I was a Detective Chief Superintendent in the major crime command in the Met before I came here. We were on a few courses together. Now, what do you need?'

'I take it you're aware of the two murders I'm investigating, with the child abuse pictures and the computers we've recovered?'

'Yes, we're very interested in them. They're going to be a gold mine of intelligence for us.'

'That's great, but not much use to me in trying to find who murdered their owners. I passed the details of our suspect to your investigation team. I hope you've got something for me.'

White handed him a buff folder. 'Have a look at this.'

Dane opened the file and saw a mugshot and résumé. Dragon Hyka, thirty-five, and a native of Tirana, Albania. Although the picture was a few years old, it was the man Dane had seen in the hospital and with Laura. The report explained that Dragon was a blood relation to a powerful mafia chieftain in the capital who oversaw his lengthy criminal apprenticeship. In his early twenties he was sent to Naples to work with a Camorra clan and complete his training. Before long he came to the attention of the Italian police who tracked his movement across Europe until he entered the UK illegally. They considered him a significant player within the Albanian mafia and the Naples gang regarded him as family. He was known to be a major facilitator of people smuggling over the Adriatic and believed to have murdered at least a dozen victims in Italy and France.

'He was in Chelmsford on Wednesday attempting to murder a young girl,' Dane said. The image of Laura in the hands of Dragon flashed through his mind and he shuddered at the thought of how close they'd come to disaster.

'I saw the report and we've been watching out for him, but he appears to have disappeared from his known haunts. We'll keep an eye out and if we get any information about his whereabouts, we'll let you know.'

'Thanks, that'd be a great help.'

'Now, the computers you've recovered are both classic set-ups for collecting and distributing these awful images. We're part of the Virtual Global Taskforce fighting this filthy business, a taskforce that includes police and private sector agencies from all over the world.'

'I've heard of it.'

'We hoover up as many pictures of children being sexually abused as we can find. Then we use facial mapping and other gizmos to trace their movements through other collections we've seized.'

'It sounds a bit like collecting cigarette cards,' Dane said.

'That's a good analogy. The creeps who collect this sort of stuff swap and sell them. They all communicate through cyberspace using very sophisticated technology and well-protected websites. No one can get access to them without the right introductions and passwords.

'There are chat rooms and blogs circulating that'd make you puke. We're working to infiltrate them. We conduct undercover operations from this building, with some success. Your two collections appear almost identical, and both your victims accessed their images from the same sources. We think they were involved in distributing them, like a clearing house. But we've not established a direct connection between the two computers yet. We're still looking, though.'

'Where do the photos come from?'

'Clandestine websites behind complex firewalls and security screens, many of which are in Eastern Europe or the Far East. To cut a long story short, the computer belonging to Parr has connections with the mafia clan in Naples that Dragon worked with. This group runs the ring we're looking at, which is where he comes in. An excellent source put us onto Parr, and we made the French police aware because he was living there.'

'What was his involvement?'

'Parr and his wife established a network of safe houses and staging points in France and southern England. What we don't yet have is the route and method used to bring the cargo into the UK.'

'A witness has told us Parr worked with Dragon and was, apparently, senior to him.'

'That's interesting and confirms a couple of things we knew. Parr was deeply involved in the organisation. He had a large stake in what they were doing and earned a great deal of money from it. And he had free use of the women and children being trafficked through his safe houses.'

Dane felt sick. 'Is that what they're smuggling? Kids, for the sex trade?'

'Yes, predominantly, but some kids go for organ harvesting and other abominations. It's disgusting and your man was in the middle of it.'

'How about Joyce Parr? Is she involved?'

'The French think so. They've had her under surveillance for a while and they noted your visit.'

'Parr worked with dangerous people. Is there any intelligence about who murdered him, or wanted him dead?'

'None whatsoever. Parr returned to this country because he thought the French were about to arrest him. Joyce Parr is made of sterner stuff and refused to leave. There's a steady stream of visitors to the house, most of whom we know are mafiosi. It's likely she still operates on their behalf, and the gendarmerie are maintaining surveillance.'

'You can tell them she's an accomplished actor.' Dane described his visit. 'She invited a reporter in and told him about their parties. I'm sure she's done that to distract us from what's really going on. I don't think she knows who killed her husband, or why.'

'The French believe she's a crucial link in the chain. They'd prefer you didn't visit there again. If you need to see her, contact

148

me and I'll make the arrangements.'

Dane stood and looked out of the office window. All he could see were the arches under a railway embankment on the other side of the road. He wasn't happy to have to refer to White whenever he needed to see his witness, but there was no point arguing against it. A thought occurred to him, and he turned back to his host.

'Could Parr have been in trouble with his masters?'

'It's possible. You don't want to cross those guys because if you do, they'll execute you. I'm not sure that's the case here, though. If he'd been skimming money off or otherwise upsetting them, they'd kill his wife as well.'

'I agree, and why would they murder Binks?'

'You've linked the two?'

'Oh yes, they were both murdered in the same way.' Dane described the scenes.

White looked thoughtful. 'Listen, this could be a coincidence, but that is a classic Italian mafia execution method. It's called *incaprettato* and roughly translates to mean "goat tying". It has connotations with sodomy, which the mafia abhor. If they're going to murder an enemy who's offended against their code and they hold that person in complete contempt, they'll use that as a message to show the victim was the lowest form of life.'

'How do you know that?'

'I spent three years at the British Embassy in Rome, and I studied organised crime there. I'm an authority on the mafia, as we all insist on calling it. In fact, that's the wrong description to use because it isn't one organisation. In Naples, for example, there are more than a hundred clans or families all working to their own ends and independent of each other. They're collectively called Camorra, and they're all vicious. It's the same with the Albanians. They boast about fifteen clans nationwide, all based on family ties operating across the country. They are all powerful and utterly ruthless. The Camorra and the Albanians are close. There's even a history of them over here.'

'That's new to me.'

'There was a strong Camorra connection in Scotland and once they settle, they stay.'

'Are you aware of anything similar in Essex?'

'Well, Albanian gangs are well established in London now and control the prostitution and drugs in Southend.'

This intrigued Dane. The Italian connection with the murder modus operandi was interesting given Parr's apparent mafia involvement, but where did Binks fit in?

'Would Dragon kill that way?'

White considered the question for a few moments. 'To be honest, I'd expect him to use a knife.'

'I've seen him do just that.' Dane recounted the incident at the hospital.

'Dragon comes from a culture that lives by a code that's beyond our comprehension as law-abiding folk. In his eyes, that poor woman or those kids in care pose a threat to him and his clan, and, as you saw, he's ruthless. When you catch him, he won't say a word, and will accept whatever sentence they give him as an occupational hazard.'

'How do they smuggle the people into Britain?'

'They arrive in bulk, which suggests a boat, or more probably containers. We're working on a couple of leads about who's facilitating that.'

There was nothing more to discuss so they agreed to stay in regular contact and Dane set out for Essex. He'd only reached Westminster when his mobile rang.

'Boss, it's Sally. Detective Sergeant Poole from the Sex Offender Unit is at a flat in Shoeburyness where they've discovered one of their clients dead. The scene's identical to that of Parr and Binks.'

Dane glanced at his watch. 'I'm just about to get on the underground. I'll go straight there, so send someone to meet me at the station. Who's the victim?'

'His name is George Wilson, and he used to be an Anglican vicar.'

'Why isn't he still in the clergy?'

'He's a convicted sex offender, and they defrocked him.'

The journey took a frustrating two hours, but when Dane made it to the flat he found a hive of activity. He spoke to a subdued Sergeant Poole.

'What can you tell me about this bloke?'

'He pleaded guilty to indecency with children and his offending stretched back decades. They placed him here on his release from prison. We call on him once a month and until the last time we came, he'd always been here.'

'But he wasn't here then?'

'Well, we didn't get a reply, but as it was an unannounced visit, we left it. He's never been a problem and consistently stuck to the rules. We noticed the smell when we arrived earlier, which is why we broke in. He was a tidy old boy, but someone's ransacked the place. There's stuff thrown everywhere. He's on the floor in the sitting room and he's been dead for a while.'

Dane and Pauline Rose entered the scene. As the sergeant had described, the former vicar's possessions were strewn about, clothes ripped apart, the threadbare carpet pulled up and the bath panel torn off.

'They took their time searching for something,' Dane muttered.

The body lay face down, naked and tied the same as the other two. Thousands of trapped bluebottles and house flies buzzed around, threatening to fly up a nose or into an unsuspecting open mouth, and the stench stuck in his throat. He studied the pile of skin and bones. The rope had almost severed the head. It was a grisly and smelly scene. How was this old man connected to the Italian mafia, he wondered.

'How did his offending originally come to light?' Dane asked Poole once they got out of the flat.

'He groped a choirboy whose dad reported him to the police. Their investigation led to dozens of families coming forward. Wilson had been abusing kids for ages. When they searched his vicarage, they discovered photo albums containing thousands of indecent images of children. He eventually admitted collecting them since his youth.'

'Did he own a computer?'

'No. And he didn't have one here, nor was there any suggestion he was up to his old tricks. We're always on the lookout for that sort of thing. We prearranged most of our visits, but we'd occasionally drop in out of the blue and we never caught him out. If we'd found anything like that, we would've revoked his licence and sent him back to jail.'

Sally Rendell joined them. 'Boss, you'd better come and meet Mrs Blyth. She lives next door and has some interesting information for us.'

He followed her and met the lady, who was sitting at her table with a strong cup of tea. She had a kind face, but her strained expression showed her distress.

'Hello. I would say it's nice to see you, but given the circumstances...'

Dane sat beside her. 'I'm afraid this is always horrible and must be a shock to you. I understand you've something to tell us about your neighbour?'

'Poor Mr Wilson. We'd become friendly since he moved in. He mentioned he was a vicar and had come here to retire. I'm a Catholic, so we didn't attend church together, but he often helped by going to the shops for me and making sure I always had what I needed.'

'When did you last see him?'

'It must be the best part of a month. We were chatting when he told me he was expecting a visitor. Someone he hadn't seen for a long while, a dear friend from his past, he said. He was so excited about it.'

'Did he tell you who that person was?'

'No, he didn't mention a name, but I saw a young man arrive the next day. I was just tottering back from the church, and they were at his door, and I heard Mr Wilson say, "Hello, Jimmy, how lovely to see you," and then he invited him in.'

'Can you describe the visitor?'

'Early thirties, quite slim, and he had black hair. He had a backpack thing with him, you know, oh, what do they call them?'

'A rucksack?'

'Yes, and it looked heavy. Anyway, I haven't seen Mr Wilson since.'

'Thank you very much, Mrs Blyth. Someone will come and take your statement.'

'I'm happy to help. What should I do about his mail? I've got letters here for him from a storage company. I helped him out last year when he wanted to hire a unit, but he didn't have a bank account. So, I did it for him and set up a direct debit to pay the rent for it. He gives me the cash to cover it.'

She showed Dane the letters and he couldn't contain the smile as he read the address of the storage company. *What's the old boy hiding there?*

Dane, Sally and Sergeant Poole drove to the large warehouse on the outskirts of Southend. The manager took them to Wilson's unit which was one of the larger ones available. Inside, they found it lined with shelving, holding hundreds of photo albums. A quick look confirmed they contained indecent photographs of children.

'Didn't you say the original investigators discovered a collection like this?' Dane asked Poole.

The sergeant nodded, looking around the unit in horror. 'I'm sorry. We had no idea he'd started collecting again.'

'These characters are clever and devious. He wouldn't make it easy for you or leave them lying about for you to see. But I doubt he's amassed this lot in the relatively short time since he left prison.'

It must belong to someone else. Is he looking after it for a friend or did he inherit it? They viewed the CCTV and watched a slight figure wearing dark clothing with a hoody up and sunglasses arrive on foot and go to the unit a month before. The person was carrying a rucksack and when he emerged an hour later, it looked bulkier. The date coincided with Jimmy's visit as reported by Mrs Blyth.

Dane turned to Sally. 'Is the observation point on Patey's flat up and running?'

'We set it up this morning, but there's been no sign of him all day.'

'We'd better pay him a visit. I think he's a much better candidate for our killer than the Camorra.'

19

All his available detectives were spreading out to work on this latest murder, so Dane and Sally drove to Chelmsford together to arrest Patey. He banged on the door but there was no answer. He dropped to his knees and peered through the letterbox.

'There's a strong whiff coming from in there.'

Sally raised her eyebrows. 'You don't think he's done himself in, do you?'

'The place stank when I came here with Vonn, so it's hard to tell. But we'll soon find out.' He examined the lock, pulled a slim leather pouch from his pocket and a few seconds later, the door swung open.

'When did that skill become part of the SIO course?' Sally asked.

'You'd be amazed at the stuff you pick up over the years in this job.'

The putrid stench of decomposition was overwhelming. The door to the sitting room was closed, and Dane paused for a moment before pushing it open. A swarm of flies engulfed them. Patey lay on the floor, head drawn grotesquely towards his heels by the rope connecting his neck to his ankles. His face was bloated and purple, and maggots were pouring from every orifice and crawling away to find somewhere cool and dry to pupate.

Dane took in the scene before him. 'Looks like we're a few days too late and he wasn't our killer after all.'

It was many hours before they recovered both bodies to the mortuary in Chelmsford. Dr Hume arrived at half past seven the following morning, full of his usual bonhomie.

The examinations confirmed the expected cause of death for both victims. The killer had broken Wilson's jaw and four ribs in the attack on him.

Patey had bled from the existing cut over his eye but had no other injuries. It didn't appear that the killer had searched his home, in contrast to the other scenes. But it was difficult to be certain, given the chaos already in the flat.

A forensic entomologist spent hours poring over each scene, gleefully collecting samples of maggots as he did so. As he finished at Patey's, Dane asked him if he could determine the time of death.

He considered the question, checked his notes and a couple of test tubes containing his specimens. 'He died last Wednesday, no earlier than late afternoon. That's the best I can do at the moment.'

At first, Dane thought the scientist was joking. 'You're serious?'

'Of course I am. These little beauties,' he shook one of his specimen holders, 'live a very precise life cycle. I'll calculate a more accurate timescale once I've had time to examine them in greater detail. But that's the day he died.'

Wednesday afternoon. Within hours of Wix cancelling the surveillance operation. Was that a coincidence? No one outside a tiny circle of people was aware Patey was being watched in the first place, much less when the team stood down. Had they seen the officers and noticed when they'd gone and taken the opportunity? It didn't seem likely, so perhaps Patey's murder was simple bad luck. But why did he die? What was it that drew him in to suffer the same fate as the other three? Dane couldn't answer that yet. It was mid-morning before he could brief Wix and he sat opposite her, watching as she read his report. A muscle twitched over her left eye, and she touched the skin with her finger as if to stop it moving.

'This appears to be getting out of hand.'

'Not completely, but we must up our game and catch him, and quick.'

'What do you need?'

'Another half a dozen investigators. That should cover it.'

'That's a lot to find one man. It's got to be Dragon.'

'He could be responsible for Parr at a push, but I'm not sure about Binks or Wilson, and he didn't kill Patey.'

'The scientist can only suggest an approximate time frame for his death.'

'The entomologist can give you the date of birth of any maggot at a glance from twenty feet away. When Patey was being trussed up, Dragon was busy trying to murder Laura. Do you really think he escaped from us then popped round to kill him before running for it?' Dane shook his head. 'That didn't happen. He's still a potential suspect for Parr, and a definite for the girl in the hospital. So, I need what I've asked for now. Otherwise I'll struggle to identify this killer.'

Wix drew a sharp breath. 'You're enjoying this, aren't you?'

'What do you mean?'

'You can't wait to shove the fact that I broke off the surveillance on Patey down my throat. To say I told you so, can you?'

'You shouldn't judge everyone by your own standards. You made that decision, and you'll have to account for it. I fancied him as a possible suspect, or at least someone with information about what happened. But I never considered he was at risk of becoming a victim. We didn't agree when you closed it down. But I was protecting my patch for selfish investigative reasons. You assessed the operation wasn't achieving its goals or justifying the expense and took decisive action. That's your job, you did it, and I won't criticise you for it. And I don't waste my time with recriminations or point-scoring because there are more important things to worry about.'

Wix looked surprised by his response, and then considered his request. 'Yes, all right, I'll authorise the extra staff. Now, what's next?'

'I'm going back to basics. As it stands, the method links all four killings. They were all sex offenders, and they were probably associates and shared a secret. I must find that connection which could tell us what it is about them that drove someone to murder them.'

'You'd better get on, and please keep me informed. I suppose we should do a press conference.'

'I've set that up for later this afternoon. We're on at five.' Wix nodded her agreement and Dane left her and walked to his car, where he spent a few minutes deep in thought.

There had to be far more to all of this than was obvious, but he couldn't put his finger on what it was. He did what he usually did when he wanted inspiration and returned to the crime scene. The specialists were finishing up their work in Patey's flat as Pauline watched and she greeted Dane as he stood quietly in the room, looking around. There was something missing. What was it? Then he remembered.

'Who moved the pictures?'

'Which ones?'

'The four snaps of the children. They were pinned up on the wall over the TV.' Dane pointed to the now empty spot.

Pauline looked around, puzzled, 'I've not touched them, and I doubt any of the others have either, but I'll check.'

Dane had a mental image of them, three young girls and Patey. Pauline returned, leafing through the forensic search register.

'Nope, we didn't seize or remove them.'

'Were they photographed?'

'Not specifically, but they might show up in the general shots we took in here.'

'Check when you get time, please. If they appear, do me some blow-ups.' Dane wondered where they could be. They'd had pride of place. Why would Patey put them away, or why would the killer take them?

'Is there anything else of interest?'

Pauline shook her head. 'Nothing to help us immediately.'

Dane returned to the incident office, where he found Hayley. 'How are you getting on with finding Geraldine?'

'I'm sure she's in Weston-super-Mare. The telephone number she called when she found Graham is a mobile phone belonging to a pub landlord. The local police made the usual enquiries, but he couldn't, or wouldn't, help.'

'Does the landlord know her?'

'He says not, but the licensing officer doesn't believe him. He has a reputation for not cooperating and nearly lost his licence because of it.'

'We haven't got time to go ourselves, so ask your contact down there to keep trying, please. I'm meeting the bishop later. With a bit of luck, he might shed some light on the vicar's activities.'

*

Dane arrived at the lovely old Georgian building opposite Chelmsford Cathedral a few minutes early. The efficient secretary showed him into a surprisingly small office and asked him to take a seat. The room was elegantly furnished, with old bookshelves lining the walls. An antique desk stood in front of open French windows that looked over a beautiful garden and a manicured lawn with croquet hoops set in it. A majestic oak tree finished off the idyllic scene.

The secretary returned pushing a tea trolley laden with a big pot and two dainty cups and saucers. She was followed by Bishop Leonard Simpson who greeted Dane and then sat behind his desk. As the tea was dispensed, Dane watched the clergyman, who looked as though he should smell of mothballs. He didn't, but his thin, pinched face wore a pained expression.

'How may I help you, Mr Dane?'

'I'd like some information about George Wilson,' Dane replied.

'Ah, there's not much I can tell you. They sent him to prison long before I came to Essex.'

'I understand that, but I'm interested in where he served and when. From that I hope to find a connection with the other murder victims.'

'Why do you think they're all connected?'

'They all died in the same way, and they were all paedophiles. I've discovered one confirmed link between them all, a young man called Patey.'

'Well, surely…' Simpson interrupted.

'He's dead. I need to dissect the victims' lives to establish the link between them all. There might be something in Wilson's background to help catch whoever has done this. And prevent them from killing again.'

'Is any of this going to be made public?'

'That depends on what I discover. I might need to ask for people who suffered at Wilson's hands to come forward, but what's in your records will remain confidential.'

Simpson didn't look happy but passed over a slim buff folder. 'This is the complete history of George Wilson's time as a member of the clergy. I must insist you read it in here.'

Simpson sipped his tea as Dane started reading.

Wilson had been born in 1940 and brought up in South London. Details of his formative years were sketchy and confined to a single page pro-forma he had filled out. He was ordained as a deacon in 1970, and held several ministries over the following thirty years, each one further out into rural Essex. Wilson's last post had been at a small parish church about eight miles from Maldon. On a separate list was a record of the various schools, children's homes and playgroups he visited.

'Was it usual for a vicar to spend so much time with children?'

'The primary function of the priest is to bring the word of God to his parishioners, and that means everyone. To see him on the Board of Visitors at a children's or old people's home is not suspicious. In fact, I would expect it.'

'Are there any records of complaints made against him?'

'There are, but what relevance have they now? He's dead.'

'I'll look for a pattern of behaviour, what victims complained of and the locations. I'm doing the same with them all.'

'I don't want this material to go outside this office.'

'Some of it might have to, especially if it shows the link. They were unpleasant men who should have paid for their crimes through the courts, not by being murdered. You should understand that.'

'I do understand, but I must protect the church from further reputational damage.'

'What happens if I take you to court to get access to your records? People will say, here they go again; they're closing ranks and protecting paedophiles. I give you my word that no criticism will come from my office regarding the way Wilson might have been investigated.'

Simpson drummed his fingers on the desk as he considered what Dane had said before opening a drawer and handing over another slim folder. 'I would ask that you only make notes from this. I cannot let you take it away.'

'And I have to warn you to keep it safe and available for the court if it becomes necessary.'

'I suppose I've no choice.' Simpson sighed as Dane opened the cover.

There was a list of twenty complaints received by several bishops and parish pastoral councils. Each was an allegation of inappropriate behaviour with a child, and it was obvious to Dane that there'd been a pattern to his offending. In every case Wilson was accused of enticing the child to his rectory for Bible classes or some other pastoral reason and while they were there he assaulted them. There was little information about any of the investigations or who conducted them, but the outcome was always the same. Wilson's assertions that the children were lying were accepted and he was exonerated.

The last six pages were different. They related to an investigation into Wilson after he'd been convicted and imprisoned. This report was more detailed, but someone had redacted all the text on the last page with a felt-tip pen.

Dane showed it to Simpson. 'A professional investigator has written this. Do you know who it was?'

'He's a retired police officer, John Morgan. I suspect you might recognise his name,' Simpson replied.

'You mean the former Deputy Chief Constable of Essex?'

'Yes, he lives in Colchester. I'll get his address and phone number for you.'

Dane read through the file again as he waited. Morgan had spoken to many of the complainants after Wilson had pleaded guilty.

'This is Mr Morgan's original report. Who redacted the last page?' Dane said when Simpson returned.

The bishop glanced at it and shrugged. 'I'm afraid I can't help you. This was all years before my time.'

'You should prepare your office for the likelihood of dozens more victims of Wilson's coming forward.'

'These allegations rocked us all, in every faith. We all failed to protect the most vulnerable in our society and we must make sure it doesn't happen again. I will pray for your success in finding the person responsible for these awful crimes.'

'Thank you for your help. I'll do my best to keep these matters as confidential as possible.'

20

Dane remembered John Morgan, the deputy chief constable when he'd joined the police, as being exceptionally tall. Morgan was renowned for his polite manner, steely determination and devout Christian faith. Dane recalled attending a briefing held in a small chapel on the Essex coast many years before. Dozens of uniform officers and detectives were crowded into the building and a hush descended as Morgan entered the room. His voice boomed out.

'Get those hats off – this is a church, you philistines.'

Dane smiled at the memory as Mrs Morgan showed him into the comfortable sitting room at their home on the outskirts of Colchester.

The sight of the once ramrod-straight man shocked him. Morgan lay in a hospital-style bed and looked skeletal. The once thick black mane was now only thin wisps of iron-grey hair. A mask covered his mouth, a drip dispensed something into the back of his hand and oxygen bottles and bleeping machines surrounded him. A faint antiseptic tang pervaded.

'Good afternoon, Mr Dane, it's nice to see you again. I've been following your recent career with interest,' Morgan wheezed. 'Sorry I can't get up. But I'm poorly.'

'I'm sorry, sir. If this is inconvenient…'

'I've not got long to go by the sounds of things, so we'd better do this while I'm able. Besides, it's always a treat to see someone from the old days. Now what can I do to help you?'

Dane told him about the investigation and his visit to the bishop.

'I've followed the killings in the press,' Morgan said. 'An interesting and perplexing case, but one I'm sure you've got a handle on. I knew Colin Parr well, of course, but it came as a shock.'

'I believe you were involved in the George Wilson case after his conviction?'

'Did they show you my report?'

'Some of it, but someone has redacted the last page. Bishop Simpson doesn't know who did that, nor would he give me a copy.'

161

'You can have mine and my notes as well. What you've read is what I felt able to say without fear of contradiction, or litigation. That last page contained my conclusions and the names of four men we should have investigated further. My observations go much further, though, and make for very dark reading. The bishop at the time employed me, you understand, and insisted my report remain confidential. As I'm about to meet my maker, I'll bend things a bit. Particularly as it's you I'll entrust them to.'

'Thank you, sir. What did you find out?'

'Wilson was one of the most prolific and unpleasant paedophiles I ever dealt with. You'll know that, until recently, crimes of that sort rarely came to our notice. The odd victim stuck their neck out to make accusations, but nothing usually came from it. People like Wilson smiled and expressed regret at how unfortunate the person was. How they couldn't understand why they should say such a thing against him. And they got away with it, time and time again. Wilson and those like him were offending with complete impunity. Goodness knows how many young lives they damaged or destroyed.'

'But you identified others involved in the abuse?'

'Yes, although there was little evidence to support my suspicions. They covered their tracks carefully.'

'They're able to do that much more efficiently these days with the internet.'

'I'm glad I don't have to deal with that sort of abomination anymore,' Morgan said. Then a coughing fit seized him, and his wife rushed to help.

Dane felt helpless as Morgan heaved and struggled to breathe. It took several minutes before the coughing subsided.

'Please excuse me, but once it starts, it's difficult to stop.' Morgan panted for a few seconds, dabbing a handkerchief over his mouth, wiping the blood away.

'Are you all right to continue, sir?'

'Don't worry, it's all part of getting old and clapped-out. Anyway – where was I? Oh yes, I discovered a much larger group was involved. Wilson's guilty plea protected them. The four names are the people I'd identified.'

'Is Parr one of them?'

'No, why do you mention him?'

'The method used to murder both Parr and Wilson is identical, and it looks like they died within days of each other. There's little doubt that Parr abused children, both when he was serving and since his retirement. I recently discovered his involvement with an international organised crime group, trafficking children and young women into the country for the sex trade. And we found a huge cache of indecent material in his home.'

'Well, it just goes to show. He was a thoroughly unpleasant piece of work. I was the only chief officer who voted against his last promotion.'

'Why did you do that?'

'Because he was bombastic, crude and a bully, but at the time he was achieving the results we desperately needed.' Morgan gazed up at the ceiling for a moment. 'I found nothing to link him to Wilson or what happened to those poor children. Parr had an unpleasant wife if memory serves. I remember an occasion when she drank to excess and upset everyone with her behaviour.'

Dane smiled. 'I've met her, I can imagine. So, how about Graham Binks? Does that name ring a bell with you?'

Morgan nodded. 'He is on the list. He was the manager of the children's home where Wilson carried out several assaults. Another horrible little man. He threw me out of the children's home and accused me of trying to dump the blame on him. Because of his job, he and Wilson were on the Board of Visitors together and Binks investigated some of the early complaints against Wilson. He refused to answer my questions and became very shirty with me. I had no official standing, so he was within his rights not to talk to me. I spoke to some victims, though.'

'What did they say?'

'They just reiterated their experiences. I developed my suspicions against the men as a result of those conversations. There'd been a clutch of complaints against Wilson around the same time, all from children at the home Binks managed. None of them featured in the court case and no one pursued them, as I recall. The police caught their dirty man and locked him up, so they looked good. Social services wanted it all to go away because they'd been in the spotlight for too long. So, the church endured the blame for the abuse.'

'Did you hand your notes over, or make your suspicions known to anyone in the force?'

'Yes, I did. I was so appalled by what I'd uncovered that I handed everything to the head of CID, Colin Parr. He assured me that someone would deal with it, but I never heard from him again. Gill.' He smiled at his wife. 'Would you fetch a file marked Wilson from the cabinet, please?'

Mrs Morgan slipped out, returning a few moments later with a thick buff folder.

'This contains copies of my notes and everything I handed to Parr. I've always kept a copy whenever I give things to my senior officer. I urge you to do the same,' Morgan said.

'Don't worry, I do. I assume you didn't trust Parr?'

'Let's just say I passed him a potential time bomb. Child abuse is a tricky subject. No one likes to discover it's been going on unchecked or undetected under their noses. Wilson was locked up for a long time, even though he pleaded guilty. Most thought he did that because of his Christian beliefs and to purge his sins, but I'm not so sure.'

'What do you mean?'

'He wanted to protect the others in his circle. His plea prevented a more in-depth investigation and what I did barely scratched the surface.'

Dane could see the effort of talking was taking its toll on Morgan. 'You've given me enough to get on with. Thank you for your time and help. Would you like me to keep you informed of how I get on?' He grasped Morgan's thin hand as he got up to leave, receiving a smile of gratitude from Mrs Morgan.

'That would be kind of you. I've been told I don't have much longer, and these doctors are usually right. It would be nice if someone got to the bottom of that business.'

Dane returned to the incident room where he settled down to read through Morgan's comprehensive papers. He noted the three names besides Binks's and called Sally and the sergeants in to tell them what he'd learnt. He gave the list of names to Vonn and asked her to do the usual checks on them and find out where they lived now.

After the meeting, Polly from the press office rang him.

'You should know I've received a request for information about the enquiries you're making into the Italian mafia,' she said.

'Who made the enquiry?' Dane replied with a sinking feeling in the pit of his stomach.

'Angus Boyd.'

'What did he ask for?'

'Just for confirmation that you're investigating a link between the murders and the mafia in Naples.'

Dane slammed his fist onto his desk, furious that someone had betrayed him again. He'd briefed the entire team on his conversation at the National Crime Agency but left out the information about the mafia method of murder, although he'd recorded it all in his notebook. Thankfully that was never out of his sight now, so whoever leaked the information could only pass on what they'd heard. It seemed even more likely that the traitor was a member of the investigation team. *So, how do we trap them?* he thought, and had an idea.

Sobers and Dane met with the chief constable and Wix the following morning to discuss his plan to expose the person responsible for the leaks. They all agreed to it, and Dane signed out a pinhole camera from the Technical Support Unit. He'd used this type of equipment on countless operations in the past and knew where he would hide it.

Once the trap was in place, Dane visited the force archive and asked to see the original crime file on Wilson. The store man, an unpleasant retired police officer called Reeves, checked his records, sniffed then frowned and suggested Dane take a seat. Reeves returned half an hour later, looking perplexed.

'There's nothing relating to Wilson in here. According to my records, Colin Parr signed it out years ago and never returned it.'

'What about a James Patey? We cautioned him for rape while he was a juvenile.'

Once again, the clerk disappeared into the bowels of his domain and came back empty-handed.

'Sorry, nothing there in that name, but if he was a minor, the file would have been destroyed when he became an adult.'

'We shouldn't do that for a rape. Are you sure it isn't there?'

'I double-checked.'

'Mind if I take a look?'

Reeves looked offended. 'Don't you trust me?'

'It's not that, but there are too many files missing here for my liking.'

'Be my guest,' Reeves replied, and led the way through into the cavernous store.

Lines of metal archive shelves stretched into the distance. The building was the size of an aircraft hangar and the summer heat turned the interior into a sauna. Reeves showed him where Patey's rape file should have been. Dozens of cardboard boxes, each containing up to a hundred crime files, lined the shelves. The last resting place for closed investigations. Dane mused that even in this digital age of paperless offices, the police and courts still ran on paper.

Every case had a unique reference number and should be filed in order. Dane spent an hour riffling through the box files before he discovered what he was after, hidden eight boxes down from where it should have been. The folder contained a dozen sheets, but no record of who the complainant was. This can't be right, Dane thought, as he flicked through it. Even an investigation that only led to a caution would produce more paper than this. He noticed the name of the investigating officer and swore silently. Colin Parr. He'd covered this up as well. After two more hours searching for the Wilson papers, Dane gave up. He walked back to headquarters, his hands and shirt filthy from the dust, which made him sneeze. His secretary Angela made him a cup of tea, and as he cleaned himself up, he described his fruitless afternoon.

She glanced at him and smiled. 'If they tried him at the Crown court, won't there be a copy of the papers held in their archive?'

Dane leapt up and kissed her on the cheek. 'I don't know what I'd do without you. Get hold of the clerks down there for me, please, and see if they can dig it out.'

Later that afternoon, he left the court with a stack of papers under his arm and a triumphant expression on his face.

21

More than sixty detectives gathered in the briefing room at the incident office the next morning, and each investigation team ran through their respective lines of enquiry. They had a lot to do to improve the current situation of a complete dearth of hard evidence against any firm suspect for the murders. Dane knew he could rely on them to do the work. But a sadness lingered at the back of his mind. One of them was betraying them all.

The meeting had been running for an hour when his mobile rang. Dane took the call and held an animated conversation. He scribbled notes, becoming more and more excited.

'You should be in show business,' Sobers chuckled at the other end of the line.

'Thank you, that's significant. I'll be in touch,' Dane said, and broke the connection. 'Would you all excuse me for a few minutes? I must make some calls. Take a break and get a brew,' Dane said to the crowd of detectives who were watching him with undisguised curiosity.

Dane returned to his office and closed the door, but not the blinds, so everyone could see him on the phone and making furious notes. He used the last pages of the notebook and when they all reassembled fifteen minutes later, he had a new one on the table in front of him.

'I've received some very interesting information regarding the Italian connection and Parr. I can't go into any more detail right now. I'm hoping we'll soon have more that could provide the breakthrough we need.'

Dane could see they were intrigued and desperate to hear what this exciting development could be, and there would be plenty of speculation. He didn't enjoy deceiving them, but if it drew the leaker out, it would be worth it.

'Sally, how are you getting on with social services and their records of the children involved in the Wilson investigation?' Dane asked as they resumed the briefing.

'I've hit a brick wall. The problem is the head of children's care. She's refused to assist in any way.'

'Who's blocking you?'

'A lady called Chris Hogg.'

'Leave it with me.'

Afterwards, Dane phoned the director of social services and arranged for a meeting. He took Hayley with him and briefed her.

'I want you to handle this on your own. Once we've sorted the manager out, work from here until you've finished the research. Report to me and no one else. If you get a call from anyone, tell them you're still busy looking for Geraldine. If they persist, then notify me.'

'No worries. Have I got time for a fag?'

Dane checked his watch. 'No.' He laughed at the look of disgust on her face. 'It's bad for you, and I only have your best interests at heart.'

'Cobblers. You're a sadist. Let's do this, then you can leave me alone to kill myself.'

Corinne Lewis was the chief executive of social services and an old friend of Vicky's. She welcomed them into her spacious office as Dane introduced Hayley. 'What can I do for you?'

'My inspector has been trying to get some information from the children's department about historical records of complaints of abuse by children in care. But a manager won't allow us to examine them. In fact, she's become positively obstructive.'

'Well, it's a difficult area and there are confidentiality issues, plus there's the natural tendency not to share anything with the police.'

Dane heard a snort of impatience from Hayley but pressed on. 'I understand that, but I'm investigating the murder of Graham Binks. A paedophile who spent thirty years in charge of children's homes and finished at the Agnes Brown home in Maldon, from where he retired and took his pension. Soon after, he decamped with a sixteen-year-old girl who'd been in his care since she was twelve.'

'Ah, that's not the done thing.'

'We've linked him with an ex-cop called Parr and a defrocked priest. Both also recently murdered. We know all three of them knew the last victim.'

'I've been following your investigation. Are you sure they were all involved in the abuse of children?'

Dane explained what they'd uncovered, what he'd learnt from John Morgan and how Morgan had passed his concerns on to the police and the bishop.

'I suppose all that material has disappeared?' Corinne said.

'Yep, all gone. It's a shame Parr's dead because I'd have loved to lock him up.'

'But is this ring still operating?'

'We're not sure, but you remember Laura Hobbs? Parr paid three hundred pounds to a pimp for her. So, he was still involved in child abuse.'

'What do you need from me?'

'Sight of the documents from the Agnes Brown home when Binks worked there. A list of the children in their care and, if possible, where they are now. I'm trying to identify a link between what the kids suffered and the murders to start with. Patey spent his childhood in the system, so it wouldn't surprise mc to discover they were abusing him as well. We think he might have been working as a male prostitute and his clients could have included Wilson, Parr and Binks. If we find and speak to any of the youngsters from then and they disclose abuse, we'll deal with it. But my priority is the murder investigation. And to enable us to follow this line of enquiry, we must see the records. And I'd rather not go ten rounds with some bolshie manager whenever we ask for something.'

'Okay, who have you been getting the runaround from?'

'Chris Hogg. We don't need to take anything away. Hayley will come here. All we need is for her to access it, and once we've finished, you secure the records in case they're required for court.'

'She's a hard person to get on with – takes her responsibilities seriously. Give me a few minutes.'

As the door closed Hayley stood and paced the office. 'I have contacts everywhere, you know that. But these people are always the hardest to work with. It's almost as if they take pleasure in obstructing us.'

'They have to protect the people they look after, so some of it I can understand. At least Corinne is keen to help. Give this one a chance and smile sweetly.'

Corinne returned a few minutes later accompanied by a large, angry-looking woman with a shock of purple hair whom she introduced. Dane held his hand out but she ignored it and glowered at him.

'Ms Lewis has instructed me to assist you and I'll say from the outset that I don't like it.'

Having got that off her chest, she led them two floors down to a small windowless room with a single desk.

'You can work here. I'll have what you require brought to you.'

'May I call you Chris?' Hayley asked.

'No, it's Ms Hogg to you.'

'Fair enough. Where does someone go for a smoke around here?'

'Down the stairs and out through the fire escape. Be careful not to lock yourself out. If you do, you'll have to walk round to the main entrance.'

'Thanks,' Hayley replied.

*

Dane found a sheet of paper on his desk from Vonn Clyde when he returned to the incident room, saying she was having difficulty locating the men on the list but hoped to have a result for him by later that day.

Vonn had impressed Dane by the way she'd settled in. He'd noticed her working out on a heavy bag in the gym, punching and kicking with a furious intensity, but with poise and balance. He made a brew and sat down to read Morgan's report again.

Morgan had been a meticulous investigator and kept neat and copious notes of what he'd discovered. The Wilson case had, in its day, been sensational and featured in the national press for weeks.

Once Wilson's identity gained wider publicity, dozens more victims came forward, claiming the priest had abused them. This sudden influx couldn't be covered up this time, and the church was forced to admit a tragic failure in their collective duty of care. The official line was that Wilson was a single rogue abomination. Morgan had gone about his business methodically, speaking to some victims, although many more wouldn't see him. Those who talked described what Wilson did to them in their rooms at the homes. Others spoke of being taken to a house and raped. Most of them couldn't or, more likely, wouldn't identify those abusers. Morgan had picked up rumours about a sex ring operating from the Agnes Brown home but when he approached Binks, he received no cooperation. Binks was the manager at the time and accused Morgan of seeking to deflect the blame for Wilson away from the church and onto him. He refused Morgan permission to talk to any of the children. Morgan wouldn't be put off and discovered that a care worker, Alison Boyle, had complained about Binks's inappropriate behaviour. She followed up her complaint when nothing happened, but later lost her job. Morgan tracked the woman down and she told him that there'd been a few others besides Wilson who came to the home at night. She gave him three names and these with Binks made up his list.

Dane's phone vibrated with an incoming text message from Hayley suggesting a meeting. He tidied his desk, checked the covert camera was operating and left his notebook in plain view on his desk.

Hayley was waiting in what the landlord of the town-centre pub advertised as the garden. It comprised a picnic bench in the car park next to the dustbins where smokers could indulge. She had lined up a large glass of white wine and a pint of lager.

'How did you get on?' Dane asked after taking a sip of his beer.

'She threw a bit of a hissy fit after you left, moaning about us intruding on her turf.'

'She knows you have a direct line to her boss, does she?'

'Yes, we cleared that up. She won't be a problem.'

'What have you learnt so far?'

Hayley stubbed out her cigarette and pulled a notebook from her bag. 'The Agnes Brown was a mixed sex home that catered for up to twenty kids until it closed. Binks was there for seven years and during that period there were five complaints alleging abuse. The

Board of Visitors investigated them all and always decided there was no case to answer. Geraldine arrived there soon after her twelfth birthday and stayed until she left with Binks. James Patey was there at the same time as Geraldine.'

'Really? Now it all comes together. I'll lay money they abused him as well,' Dane replied.

'Fifteen other kids were there, including his rape victim. She reported the attack to the local police station and, according to the notes, Binks wasn't happy about her doing that. Patey had several other complaints made against him, all of which were internally resolved.'

'I suppose that means nothing happened?' Dane said.

'Yes.'

'Did you find the girls who made those complaints?'

'Their details are in the files, together with a psychiatrist's assessment of Patey. It seems he was a troubled child, desperate to be accepted by the others and loved by someone. All the other complaints related to him constantly trapping girls and touching them up. He even assaulted members of staff. There are records of him being subject to discipline measures that would include loss of privileges, like watching the TV or playing pool. Geraldine, on the other hand, appears to have been a model resident.'

'How about the other children?'

'It's all there. I'll track them down tomorrow.'

'It'll be good to talk to them all. We'll start with the girl who claimed Patey raped her.'

Dane told Hayley about the findings from Morgan's report and that Vonn had, so far, been unable to locate the three men he'd named.

'They're all recorded in the file,' Hayley said. 'People with regular access to the premises had to be vetted by the manager. It would be much more stringent now, of course. But those four names including Wilson and their addresses are there.'

'Okay, get me that information tomorrow, and don't let anyone else see it. It shouldn't be too hard to track them down.'

'Who do you think is leaking to the press?' Hayley asked.

'No idea. I've not worked with any of them before, so it's

difficult to gauge who would do something like that.'

'It won't be Sally. You can trust her. I've known her for ages, and she's chuffed to be working with you.'

'How about the sergeants?'

'Reece seems all right. Reg Phelan is a grumpy sod, but that's always been his default position, and I'm not that keen on Vonn.'

'Why not?'

'She's a strange one, and barely talks to anyone unless it's to do with work. Tom Jones asked her if she wanted to go to the pub and she went mad, accusing him of assuming she was some sort of trophy. Her words. It mortified poor old Tom. He's married and only asked her if she wanted to join the rest of them for a beer. Once she realised, she calmed down and apologised, but no one'll go near her now.'

'Don't you like her?'

'It's not that. She rubs me up the wrong way. There's something about her manner that makes me wary of her. And she's far too fit, obsessed with running and the gym, and she eats all that supplement rubbish. Can't be good for you,' Hayley stated and lit another cigarette. Dane choked on his beer and laughed. Hayley raised an eyebrow and blew smoke through her nose. 'What?'

'You're priceless.'

'I'll tell you something else, though. She is not a well lady.'

'What do you mean?'

'She doesn't eat junk food and is physically fit, but she swallows a lot of medication every day. She keeps it quiet and out of sight, but I've seen her and sometimes, usually first thing in the morning, she looks bloody awful.'

'I thought she looked unwell but hadn't noticed her taking tablets, so thanks for the heads-up. I'll keep an eye on her. Have you found Geraldine yet?'

'She's in Somerset, but we'll have to go down there and find her ourselves. The locals have tried to help, but she's not a missing person or at risk, so finding her isn't a priority for them.'

'Okay. Let's concentrate on the people she lived with at the home and having a talk with them first. Then we can drive down and surprise her.'

They parted, and Dane drove home to cook a lonely dinner. Vicky was still hard at work on the course. He'd just finished the washing-up and was thinking about an early night when his phone rang. He sighed and offered a small prayer, asking for this not to be another case, then saw Brian White's number and answered.

'I'm sorry it's so late, but I've got some news about your friend Dragon,' White said.

'What's that?'

'He's popped up in Naples and is keeping his head down.'

'Are the Italians going to arrest him?'

'They will when they find his precise location.'

'That's better than nothing.'

'They've promised to keep me updated, but it'll take time.'

'Thanks for calling.' At least he didn't have to worry about the Albanian trying to murder any more of his witnesses. Dane wondered if he'd ever see Dragon again, then went to bed. He had a busy day planned for tomorrow.

22

Alison Boyle was not keen to meet Dane, and it took him a few minutes to persuade her. She was in her late fifties, with a kind face that didn't extend to a smile of welcome, although she dispensed the obligatory cup of tea.

'What do you want, then?' Her barely concealed hostility surprised him.

'I'm looking into the complaints you made against Graham Binks,' Dane said.

'You're too late. He's dead.'

'I'm investigating that as well, and I believe what happened at that home has some significance to his death.'

'I didn't kill him,' she blurted.

'I believe you. But I'll need to know where you were the weekend he died.'

'That's easy, I was with my daughter in Spain. We only got back the other day. I can give you her number.'

'Thank you. That will be helpful. The main reason I've come to see you is I'm interested in what you saw at the home. That's what I wanted to talk about.'

'I did the right thing, and it cost me my job, and I've never been able to get another one with the council,' she said bitterly. 'And to rub salt into the wound, two years after I got the heave-ho Binks confirmed everything I'd said by running off with her.'

'So, what was going on?'

'Binks groomed that girl, Geraldine, from the minute she arrived. She was a tiny little thing and completely alone in the world and vulnerable. The other darlings gave her a hard time until he took her under his wing. She responded to him because no one had ever shown her any kindness before. I believed their relationship was unhealthy, and I notified the Board of Visitors and they spoke to her, but she denied everything. When I didn't shut up about my other concerns, they sacked me.'

'Perhaps you'd better start from the beginning.'

Alison had worked in half a dozen local-authority-run care homes during her career. She'd arrived at the Agnes Brown home

175

a year after Binks took over and joined a team of seven support workers. Two members of staff remained on duty overnight and slept on the premises. She preferred to do the day shift because of her husband's work and difficulties getting childcare. Some of the older children could go out in the evening on the strict proviso they were in by a certain time. Should they be late back, the policy stated the staff must report them missing to the police, although in practice that never happened.

'Binks instructed everyone not to call the police because they always returned when they were hungry, and the cops would frighten them. That was rubbish, because none of those kids worried about getting a stern telling-off from a copper. Binks didn't want them around asking questions. Anyway, I only had to do the occasional night duty, which pleased me but came as a surprise.'

'Why?'

'Because everyone in the business hates doing nights. If anyone asked to be kept off them, the others would moan like mad. But no one complained at that place.'

'Who did them then?'

'There were four people who did most of them. They all had second jobs, and you usually got a decent night's sleep there, so they were all making a lot of extra money.'

'Seems reasonable.'

'It does, and Binks would do at least two night shifts a month, which no other manager I worked for did. He even did it for me once. They'd put me down for three nights in a row and I asked to change it because I had childcare issues, and he took them. I was grateful, but now I know he had an ulterior motive.'

'What was that?'

'He was carrying on with the girl, and a night shift alone there gave him the perfect opportunity to spend time with her.'

'How did you know that?'

'I never caught them doing anything wrong, but she would follow him round like a puppy dog. That's not unusual. The kid receives attention and affection for the first time, and they respond to the person giving it. It happens to us all, but you've got to put a stop to it quickly, or it gets out of hand. You rarely realise yourself,

176

so we would all keep an eye out for it and if we saw a situation arising, we'd warn each other. I did that for Binks and he bit my head off. He said I was imagining it and to watch my step. That surprised me, but I recorded what we spoke about in the log. After that, she seemed to calm down, but her eyes never left him if he walked through a room. She adored him. Then when I checked a while later, the report had disappeared.'

'How could that happen?'

'We used a loose-leaf binder with template forms. If anything happened, we filled one out and it would go in the folder. I made a record of my conversation with Binks and what I'd said to him. It wasn't locked away, so anyone could have taken it, but it seemed suspicious that particular report should disappear when I needed it for my case. I told the hearing what we'd spoken about, but he denied the conversation ever took place.'

'Did any of your co-workers see anything untoward or make any complaints?'

'Not that I'm aware of. The staff there weren't a friendly bunch, and I'd never come across any of the others before. The day and night teams rarely had much to do with each other beyond the routine handovers.'

'Apart from the situation between Binks and Geraldine, what else made you unhappy?'

'A couple of things. You didn't see it on the day shifts, but on the few occasions I did a night, you'd always find the home's taxi driver hanging about the place, collecting or dropping kids off. He shouldn't have been in there, but he had the code to get in through the door.'

'How do you know that?'

'Because late one evening he appeared at the office. Made me jump, and frightened me, this strange bloke wandering in like that. I challenged him, and he laughed at me. He said I must be new, and he'd been dropping a couple of the kids back and fancied a brew. I kicked him out and reported it to the supervisor, but she told me he was okay because Binks had given him the entry code.'

'Do you remember his name?'

'Phil something, he was a great big fat bloke in his fifties. He ran his own private hire car and had the contract to drive the kids to and from school and tutorials.'

Dane checked Morgan's list. 'Could it have been Phil Joiner?'

'It might have been. I never heard his surname, but I didn't like the way he leered at the girls.'

'Anyone else?'

'There was the so-called handyman. Eric Lowe.'

'What do you mean so-called?'

'He'd wander round with his ladder, pretending to fix things. If anything more technical than fixing a plug or replacing a light bulb needed doing, they had to call in a contractor. But he was always creeping about, and he had access to everywhere, including the bedrooms. His eyes never left the girls, as if he were undressing them. If there was a group of them in a room, he'd turn up with his ladder and pretend to be doing something in there. I shooed him away on more than one occasion, and I told Binks about him.'

'Did any of the kids confide in you?'

'No. I tried to make friends with Geraldine, but she was so wrapped up in Binks that she wouldn't respond.'

Alison took a sip of tea as Dane made a quick note, then changed tack.

'What can you tell me about Jimmy Patey?'

'God, he was a horrible little creature! I shouldn't say things like that because he'd suffered a horrendous upbringing, but I couldn't stand him. The other children hated him and excluded him from everything. He used to hide in the girls' toilets and touch them up. He groped me once.'

'He must have got some help or seen a physiatrist?'

'He did, but it made no difference to his behaviour. Then a girl accused him of rape. She told Binks, who did nothing, so she ran off to the local police station to report it. He was spitting mad about that.'

'What was her name?'

'Julie.' She thought for a moment. 'I don't remember her surname. It's too long ago, another one with a miserable history. She and Geraldine and another girl, whose name I can't recall, were best buddies and always hanging out together. The police investigated and cautioned Patey, and nothing happened to him, he stayed with us. Then it got worse because later Julie accused him of not only raping her, but Geraldine and the other one as well. Binks quashed all that when the other two refused to back her up or make a complaint.'

'Did he report that allegation?'

'No, even though me and another of the workers said he should. Binks locked Julie in her room. We had to take food to her as she was screaming blue murder and banging on the door. That was against the rules, and I told Binks that unless he let her out, I'd report what he was doing. He ordered me to mind my own business, saying he had to maintain discipline, but I stood my ground and he backed down.'

Dane could barely believe what he was hearing. How could anyone treat a child in their care like that?

'Did you talk to Julie about what she'd been alleging?'

'I tried, but she pushed me away. She refused to engage with us because she said we were all in on it.'

'What did she mean, "in on it"?'

'No idea. But thinking about it, I'm sure something sinister was going on with the youngsters. They revealed nothing to me or anyone else. But they were obviously unhappy.'

'Is any child ever happy in such an environment?'

'Not really, but most of them are remarkably resilient and make the best of a bad thing.'

Alison was a gold mine of information and now she'd accepted he wasn't a threat to her, he tried another name from the list. 'Did you know a tutor called Gareth?'

Alison laughed out loud. 'He was no more a tutor than my cat.'

'Do you remember his surname?'

She thought for a moment and shook her head. 'I don't think I ever knew it. He started working there about nine months after I arrived. The story was he'd been employed to give the kids remedial lessons after school and assist with their homework.'

'Did he take them out of the home to do that?'

'I did hear that it was a regular occurrence, although I only saw it happen once, on one of my rare night shifts. He appeared with Eric and three of the girls, Geraldine, Julie, and their friend – what was her name?' She paused as her brow furrowed. She shook her head in frustration. 'Can't remember. I'll think of it in a minute.

179

Anyway, he wanted to take them out in Phil's taxi. I queried this because of the time when he came for them, and I asked why Eric was there. He said they were giving him a lift to the town. It sticks in my mind because I didn't like what I was seeing. He was quite rude and said Binks had organised it all. I rang Binks because it worried me. Binks shouted at me and ordered me to stop interfering. Then he spoke to Gareth, before they all left in Phil's car. They were all back at ten, but he wasn't happy, and Phil had the hump with me. I got the impression I'd ruined their evening. It was that sort of atmosphere.'

'What did the girls do?'

'They kept quiet and went straight to their rooms. I didn't do a single night shift after that, but I noted what I'd seen. It wasn't long after that when I made the official complaint. They investigated and a few weeks later, they dismissed me.'

'Who sat on the Visitors Board?'

'That vicar, the Reverend Wilson, chaired it. He talked to me as if I was a communist agitator trying to damage the children's lives. The rest of them were no better, the usual sort of do-gooder idiots who just followed Wilson and Binks. I said my piece, and they threw me out. Then, when Wilson got arrested, I contacted the police, but I never heard from them. I rang again a few months later, and a policeman visited me. A great big bully who told me that because I'd made things up about the staff, I wasn't to be trusted, so he didn't want my information.'

'Did he identify himself?'

'His name was Parr. I remember that because he scared the life out of me. My John threatened to complain about his behaviour. But he claimed he was friends with my husband's boss and if he wasn't careful, he'd have a word in his ear. He told us to keep our mouths shut or he'd ruin our lives. We believed him, so we kept quiet.'

This revelation stunned Dane. 'You're talking about Colin Parr?'

'That's how he introduced himself.'

'Can you describe him?'

'About six foot, heavyset, with grey hair and a beard. The most frightening man I've ever encountered.'

Now Dane understood why she'd been so hostile. If the meeting with Parr was her only previous experience with the police, it was no wonder. He could imagine Parr browbeating the Boyles, preventing damaging information from coming into the incident room. But he'd taken an enormous risk, obstructing a live investigation. Parr and Binks must have been desperate to keep everything about the care home quiet. Dane wondered what they'd promised Wilson for taking the rap.

'Is your husband here?'

'He passed away five years ago,' she replied sadly.

'I'm sorry to hear that.' Dane gave her a moment to gather herself and considered what else he needed to glean from her. 'Did all the children there go to the same school?'

'They all attended Woodland Grove School in Maldon.'

'How did they get there and back?'

'By bus.'

'So, why was a taxi driver needed then?'

'You tell me. Or the tutor. If they needed remedial education, they should have received it in the home from approved tutors.'

'Wasn't Gareth on the list of approved tutors?'

'No, and I found that out when I asked some friends of mine at the council, and they'd never heard of him. When I brought that up in the hearings, Binks got round it by saying that he was cheaper, so he saved money to spend on the youngsters.'

'How did he get away with that?'

'Because the management of those places was rubbish. They left it all to the house managers. There were no checks or inspections. People like Binks could do what they liked. I heard that someone looked into the situation with Gareth, but nothing came of it, and after Binks retired, he disappeared.'

'What do you believe they were doing?'

'I'm sure Binks and the others were abusing the children.'

'So why didn't you or any of your colleagues go to the police?'

'They encouraged us not to. Even though the council had a safeguarding policy, the thought of allegations of abuse being aired with anyone outside the organisation petrified the management. They much preferred to keep it all in-house and sort it out without having everything dragged through the courts and

181

the press. And remember, I took a stand and lost my job, and had that pig threaten me in my home for my troubles.'

Dane put up his hands to placate her. 'I'm not blaming you. You did your best. Why didn't the kids say anything about the situation?'

'Binks and Wilson had complete power over them. All they could do to stop the abuse getting even worse was to keep quiet. Julie asked for help, but they still shut her up and Patey got away with it. What could any of them do? They were powerless.'

'Do you know what happened to them?'

'No. I lost touch with the place after I left. But at sixteen, they would have been moved out to fend for themselves.'

'Can you remember the name of the third girl in that group of Geraldine's?'

Alison closed her eyes for a few seconds, then smiled and held her index finger up. 'Got it! Stephanie, that's it: Steph, Geraldine and Julie. They always stuck together.'

Dane nodded and underlined the names in his notebook. What she had described was heartbreaking. *How did those youngsters cope with being in the middle of such a nightmare?* But it strengthened his resolve to find and prosecute any of the abusers still alive.

'So, what are you going to do?' Alison demanded.

'If any of them are still around, I'll put them away for what they did.'

'Good. I shouldn't rejoice at the death of anyone, but all those men deserve what's happened to them. If you catch the others, I'll stand up in court and tell them what I saw.'

'Thank you. I would prefer them all in a cell and petrified at the prospect of a long time in prison. Death is the easy way out for them.' Dane left her with a handshake, which she turned into a hug after getting his further assurance that he wouldn't let anyone get away with it.

23

Alison's information opened a completely different slant on the investigation. Dane was now sure the killings were nothing to do with the mafia, or even people smuggling. The key to all this was far closer to home. He spent the afternoon reading the Wilson court file. It included copies of all the evidential paperwork the police provided to the prosecutors for the hearing, and there wasn't much of that.

Parr had been the senior investigating officer, and led an inquiry that was bland and perfunctory. The complainants' statements contained the barest of details about what they'd suffered. Wilson refused to answer questions when the police interviewed him. But when he first appeared in front of a judge, he surprised everyone, including his barristers, by pleading guilty to everything. As a result, he spared the victims the ordeal of reliving their experiences. The court gave him credit for that and reduced his sentence, but he still served ten years inside.

What shocked Dane was how little actual evidence the investigation team gathered, and they'd made no attempt to find more victims. Someone constrained the enquiry so it finished quickly and with the least possible fuss. It wouldn't stand muster today, and Dane would have been ashamed to be part of such a shoddy job. If the vicar hadn't pleaded guilty, Dane doubted there'd have been enough to convict him. This strengthened John Morgan's theory that Wilson took the fall to protect others.

He stood and stared out of his office window, pondering what he'd learnt. Parr was responsible for a massive cover-up of whatever was going on in the Agnes Brown home. To make matters worse, he'd got away with it right under the noses of all the senior officers. What a pity he was dead. He should have spent the rest of his days behind bars.

He rang Hayley. 'Have you got the addresses for the taxi driver and the handyman?'

'Yes,' she replied and read them out to him.

'What about the tutor?'

'I've still not confirmed his surname.'

'What are you doing this evening?'

'I'm taking Mum to bingo. We know how to rock in our house.'

'Sounds fun. I'm going to pop round and see them.'

'I can put her off.'

'No, don't do that. I'll only make sure they're still at the addresses and have a quick chat.' Dane glanced around and saw the office was empty, so retrieved the camera from its hiding place.

There had been several activations since he'd left it there. He wound the recording to the beginning, and with a deep breath, pressed the play button. The first shots were of him. Next came Reece Lewin and Reg Phelan, who stood by his desk looking through a policy book for one of the other investigations. Sally came in, an hour after the sergeants, and put some papers in his in-tray. None of them touched his notebook.

The next activation occurred in the middle of the previous night, and Dane swore with frustration. The footage showed the silhouette of a person standing with their back to the camera reading his notebook, before photographing the last couple of pages with a phone. Dane couldn't even discern the sex of the intruder. The door to the major incident room was always kept locked, but anyone who knew the numerical code could open it. The station was closed to the public and CCTV covered the outside of the building. The external doors were locked but could be opened in the same way as the incident office. Dane wandered around the building until he found the solitary security guard.

'I'd like to have a look at the CCTV of the yard for the last week, please.'

'It's broken. Has been for a month,' the guard replied.

This turn of events frustrated Dane, but it confirmed the traitor was one of his team. The information from his notes hadn't made it into the press yet, but he knew Boyd would use it soon. He rang Sobers and told him about the film.

'I'll get Technical Support to fit a more sophisticated system throughout the office. This is getting silly, but I'll sort all that out. You concentrate on finding the killer.'

*

Dane drove to a council estate outside Chelmsford and found the end-of-terrace property. The front garden was unkempt and littered with piles of dog mess. He picked his way up to the door

184

and knocked. It opened a crack, and a female face peered through it.

'Who are you? What do you want?'

'My name is Dane. I'm a police officer, and I'm looking for Phil Joiner.'

'He died, so you're out of luck,' she replied as the nose of a large Alsatian appeared between her knees.

'Are you his wife?'

'Yes, what's this all about?'

'I wanted to talk to him about his work as a taxi driver a few years ago,' Dane said, watching the dog as it struggled to squeeze between her legs.

'You'd better come in.'

He followed her into a shabby sitting room and perched on the old settee as the dog settled beside her and eyed him.

'What are you after my Phil for?'

'I'm investigating a couple of murders, and his name has cropped up. I'm interested in the period when he drove a cab and picked up some children at a home in Maldon.'

She nodded. 'That was a good contract, and he made a few quid there.'

'Who employed him?'

'The manager at the Agnes Brown, the one that got killed the other week. My Phil did a few bits and pieces for them. Then the manager cleared off, and they didn't pay him for the last few months' work. Things were hard after that. He was never in the best of health.'

'What did your husband do there?'

'He used to collect the kids in the evening. He wouldn't get home till gone midnight, one in the morning, that sort of time.'

'That's a bit late to be ferrying children about, isn't it?'

'Never thought about it, to be honest. So long as he brought the cash in, and it meant I had the evenings in here to myself, I wasn't interested. I could watch what I liked on the TV. If he was here, it would be football or fishing.'

'Did he say where he took the children?'

'No, and I never asked him.'

'Do you know Eric Lowe?'

'Oh yeah, we were all mates for years although I haven't seen him for a while. Now, that's strange, because a journalist was here yesterday asking about him and my Phil.'

'Did they give you their name?'

'No, she said she worked for a national paper and was following up on the killings of Binks and another bloke. And she asked about Eric as well.'

'Did you tell her where he lives?'

'No, I didn't like the look of her. She was banging on about some horrible things she said happened at the children's home. I knew nothing about that, and nor would Phil, he just drove the taxi.'

'Can you describe her?'

'Short, and in her thirties, I suppose, with long black hair.'

Dane thanked her and drove to Lowe's address. He parked about a hundred yards down the road and watched for a few minutes. There was a car in the driveway and a light shining from a ground-floor window, but no sign of movement. He approached the door and found it ajar; he knocked, and it swung open.

'Eric Lowe,' he called out. 'Police officer at the door.' There was no reply. Dane stepped into the hall. 'Is anyone in here?' he shouted, louder.

Dane crept along the passage and into the kitchen. The acrid stench of faeces filled the room and made him gasp. Then he heard a harsh, rasping, gurgling sound. A table and chairs were in front of him, with a sink beyond, below a window overlooking a garden. The noise stopped, but the smell grew stronger. An arch led to the right and into the sitting room. Dane peered carefully round the corner and saw a man lying on the floor. His body arched back like a bow, held fast by a rope stretching from the neck to his ankles. The eyes were bulging and his tongue, swollen and purple with congested blood, protruded between his teeth. The scene momentarily stunned Dane. Then he realised what was happening and lunged forward. He grabbed at the knot by the ankles, his fingers scrabbling, trying to undo it, but couldn't get purchase. Dane tried to pull the feet up to make some slack in the rope biting deep into the victim's neck. But that didn't work. Knife, he thought, as something hard crashed into the side of his head, knocking him sideways. Several heavy blows into his midriff doubled him over, and darkness overwhelmed him.

24

Dane slowly came to. He was sitting upright against the patio door with his wrist handcuffed to the handle. The glass was cool and soothing on his back, but his head was throbbing with such intensity it felt like it was going to explode. His vision swam and he tried to focus as the stench made his eyes water, turning his stomach. The man, who Dane assumed was Eric Lowe, had stopped moving. The rope had bitten deep into the soft flesh of his throat as his legs straightened out.

Dane hauled himself to his feet and gingerly ran the tips of his fingers along the side of his face which felt puffy and painful. A quick check round the mouth with his tongue confirmed there were no broken teeth.

He took stock of his situation. He must have disturbed the killer, who'd knocked him cold, probably with the wine bottle that was shattered around the corpse. A sudden bout of dizziness and nausea overwhelmed him, and he leant against the door. It took a few minutes to force his stomach to behave and keep his lunch down, and then he turned his attention to the handcuffs.

They were squeezed tight enough to prevent any chance of wriggling out of them. His pockets were empty, and he saw his mobile phone, keys and the little leather pouch with his lock picks on top of an occasional table ten feet away.

Dane checked his watch and calculated he'd been unconscious for about five minutes. The rear garden was long and surrounded by six-foot-high fences, with no other houses overlooking it. The curtains were pulled across the front window so there was no chance of someone seeing into the house from the street and noticing his predicament. The patio doors were locked and double-glazed, so almost soundproof. He tried pulling the handle out of the frame but soon gave that up. There was nothing within his reach solid enough to break the glass. Dane tried a couple of half-hearted kicks at the doors but all that did was hurt his foot and he swore aloud in frustration. *How could I be so stupid?*

His ears pricked at the sound of an approaching siren. But all hopes of a quick rescue were dashed as the emergency vehicle roared straight past the house and into the distance.

Dane looked longingly at the occasional table and stretched towards it but was several feet short. He felt dizzy and had to take a couple of deep breaths to settle himself.

'Come on, think,' he muttered, and rested his forehead against the cool of the glass.

When Dane trained for the Special Forces Unit he'd served with in Ireland, the instructors frequently posed seemingly impossible problems for the students to solve. It was known as doing an A-Team, after the American TV show depicting a team of former soldiers who always escaped no matter how fiendish the obstacle. The purpose of the exercises was to encourage the students to think out of the box. Use what they had available to improvise and solve the problem.

The situation Dane now found himself in was just such a moment and he could almost hear his instructors telling him to 'get a wiggle on' or 'pull your bloody finger out'.

The problem was obvious: he was locked to the door and needed his keys or lock picks to escape. The solution seemed simple. Get them from the table. He couldn't go to them, so they would have to come to him. How to achieve that?

After a moment's thought Dane looked down then pulled his belt off. He gripped the very end of it and stretched towards the table. With a flick of his wrist he tried to lasso the table but was still a foot short. He removed a shoe and tied it to the belt buckle: still not long enough. With both shoelaces tied together end to end and then to the shoe, Dane finally had an implement that could reach the table. Now all he had to do was whip the shoe round its leg and gently pull it towards him. This proved easier said than done. The table was about two and a half feet high, with a flat round surface a foot in diameter. It had a single leg that went to a small plinth close to the floor and didn't look terribly stable. He would have to be careful not to knock it over, and once snared would have to gently tug it across the carpet. He took a breath and flicked the shoe towards his target.

Fifteen minutes later and after a dozen attempts, Dane was still locked to the patio doors. His frustration grew with the intensity of his headache. His arms were aching, and he hadn't come close to securing the table once. He rested for a minute then stood and got into position.

Dane swung the belt and lobbed his contraption then watched in dismay as the knot holding the shoelace to the belt buckle unravelled and the shoe, now free of restraint, sailed straight into the table, causing it to rock then topple over. Dane saw his keys and lock picks fly in one direction and the phone bounce off the armchair and land on the carpet, still tantalisingly out of reach.

He slumped to the floor and glared at the phone. The screen had illuminated after it fell, and a thought suddenly occurred to him. 'You idiot,' he groaned and stood before saying in as clear a voice he could muster, 'Hey, Siri.'

Five minutes later Dane heard another siren, followed by the sound of tyres screeching as a vehicle pulled up outside.

A few seconds after that a voice called out, 'Is anyone there?'

'Yes, in here, in the sitting room,' Dane replied.

Two uniform officers appeared in the kitchen and stopped dead in their tracks at the sight in front of them. 'Bloody hell,' the lead officer exclaimed.

'Get me out of these handcuffs and watch where you put your feet,' Dane snapped.

As the bobby fumbled with his keys, he looked at Dane's feet then over at the shoe lying next to the table.

'Don't ask,' Dane said.

'You don't look too good, sir, come and sit over here,' the second officer suggested, pointing to a chair at the kitchen table.

'Not in here. This is a crime scene. You two wait outside for the ambulance and guard the front door. I need to check upstairs first.'

Dane replaced his shoes and then stumbled up the stairs and checked the three bedrooms. The largest had a double bed and was where Lowe had slept. The second room contained just a wardrobe, and the third was a home office, with a computer on a desk and bookshelves stacked with hundreds of slim photo albums, an all too familiar set-up. Once Dane was certain no one else was in the house, he made his way downstairs to find two paramedics waiting patiently to gently assist him into the ambulance.

The next thing Dane knew he was lying in A&E at the local hospital. Whenever he moved, he felt sick, so he laid back, closing his eyes. For the next few hours Dane was vaguely aware of being shunted around by a porter to different departments. They took his blood and put him through a scanner before depositing him in a side room.

A doctor told him he was suffering from concussion, bruised ribs and a lovely black eye. Given his recent history of being shot in the head they'd decided to admit him for observations.

Sobers and Wix were allowed five minutes to visit.

'Are you incapable of investigating anything without getting yourself bashed up?' Sobers asked, looking concerned at the sight of his friend flat on his back.

'I'm suffering from a monumental headache, so be gentle with me, please.'

'What on earth were you doing going there on your own?' Wix interjected. 'Are you mad?'

Dane explained his reason for going to the house and about his visit to Mrs Joiner and what she'd revealed about her visitor the day before.

'That person might be our murderer, or at least be involved. Lowe wasn't dead when I arrived, and I was trying to release him when whoever it was whacked me. Joiner has seen her, so we must protect her,' Dane said, getting agitated.

'Don't worry, Hayley is sorting that out,' Sobers said.

'Could it have been Dragon?' Wix asked.

'No. If it was him, I'd be dead,' Dane replied.

They left him alone with his pounding headache. Every time Dane closed his eyes, the sight of Lowe's bulging face appeared. That vision and the knowledge he'd not been able to prevent his death bothered him, and his mind churned through what had happened.

Who was the woman? Was she the murderer? If not, what was her involvement? Mrs Joiner's description fitted the person seen outside the Parr house the night he died. But so did Dragon and Patey. She'd taken a risk visiting Mrs Joiner unless she really was a journalist. Perhaps she was working with Boyd following up on something new from the incident room. Whoever attacked him was strong. They'd smashed the bottle across his head and then dragged him unconscious into a sitting position and cuffed him to the door. Could a small woman manage that alone?

Dane could only doze through the night. Every hour he was roused by a nurse who checked his pupils, pulse and blood pressure. By daybreak he was worn out. At least the headache was subsiding, and he fell asleep until the doctor returned to give him another check-over.

'How are you this morning?'

'Groggy, frustrated and knackered.'

'That's only to be expected. It is a mild form of torture being woken every hour, but it's necessary. Is there anyone at home to take care of you?'

'My partner will be there.'

'You're definitely on the mend if you can drop a fib in that quickly. I've already spoken to Vicky who told me she's away until tomorrow.'

'So, why ask me?' Dane snapped.

'I wanted to confirm you were awake enough to give me the runaround. We'll watch you for another day. The worst of the symptoms will have passed by then and it'll be safe to send you home.

'Thanks, but I'm discharging myself as of now.'

'Well, I can't stop you doing that, but it's an ill-advised thing to do.' The doctor replied and opened the door to wave Sobers and Hayley in. 'Talk some sense into him, please, he's decided to leave against my recommendation.'

Hayley shook her head, concern etched on her face. 'You don't have to do this. Take the time to recover properly. It'll only be for a couple of days.'

Dane waved her concerns aside. 'How are you getting on with finding Geraldine and Gareth?'

'She's in Weston-super-Mare. Everything points to the pub she rang. It's run by a man called Salvatore Piazzi with his wife, Stephanie. And I'm no further with the tutor.'

191

Stephanie. He'd heard that name very recently. He tried to concentrate and closed his eyes for a moment. Yes, Alison had said a Stephanie was Geraldine's friend, and she'd mentioned another girl. There'd been three of them, but he couldn't remember what Alison called her.

'Piazzi doesn't sound like a Somerset name to me,' he said.

'He's a British citizen and has held a liquor licence for years.'

'We need to go and speak to them.''

'You should wait to get the all-clear from the medics first,' Sobers said.

'This can't wait. I'll be okay walking around and asking a few questions. I'm going home in a minute for a shower, and then Hayley and I are off to Somerset. I suggest we put it about that I'll be off sick for a few days and Hayley applies for some leave to care for her very sick mum.'

'Why?' Sobers asked.

'Because we need some space to operate. If I'm out of the picture, the traitor in the office won't be watching what we're up to. I don't want details of our visit to become public knowledge.'

'That reminds me. That phoney message was published this morning under Boyd's byline. He also knows about the attack on you and that Lowe died while you were there,' Sober said.

'I suppose he's saying that I was incompetent in letting the man die?'

'Something like that.'

'Okay, we can't afford any more information to find its way into Boyd's hands. I'm certain this case revolves around that children's home. Someone is bumping off people involved in running the place and abusing the kids. This is all to do with revenge. We must talk to Geraldine, and Stephanie if she's the woman I think she is, because they're the key.'

'What about Gareth?' Hayley asked.

'Tom Hanson can take over the search for him,' Sobers said. 'What do we do about the leaker?'

'That can wait. If I'm not in the office, Boyd won't hear anything juicy. He's only interested in stories about me, and I have a plan to use Jane to draw him and the traitor out.'

'I've not seen Jane recently,' Sobers said.

'She had to go home to deal with some personal issues. She'll be back in a couple of days. The priority now is to speak to Geraldine and Stephanie, and then find Gareth.'

Hayley drove him home where he had a long, hot shower, and a tense telephone conversation with Vicky.

'I promise I'll be careful, but we must find the woman,' Dane said.

'It doesn't have to be you. There are others who should do this,' Vicky replied.

'You know what I'm like,' he whispered. 'There are people dying and more at risk unless we stop them. Hayley will take care of me.''

'If you kill yourself, I'll bloody murder you.'

*

Dane snoozed as Hayley drove them on the four-hour trip to Western-super-Mare. He woke when they stopped for a break and swayed as he stood at the urinal. Was I a little hasty leaving the hospital, he wondered, before dismissing the thought. There was no way he could have stayed there, doing nothing. Hayley was waiting in the cafeteria with mugs of tea, and he received a text from Sobers with the e-fit image Mrs Joiner had produced of the woman who called at her door. The round face of a dark-haired woman stared back at him. Dane didn't put too much store in these computer-generated images. It was rare for them to lead to the arrest of a suspect. He showed it to Hayley.

'What do you think?'

'They all look the same to me. I've never seen one that catches the likeness of the actual person,' she replied, and popped out for a smoke.

Dane stared at the picture, and then slipped the phone in his pocket. His head was still pounding and his ribs were sore, so he sipped his tea and swallowed some painkillers. They set off again and two hours later pulled into the car park at the rear of the ugly concrete police station in Western-super-Mare.

Chief Superintendent Grainger greeted her visitors from Essex with a quizzical expression. The tall, statuesque black woman and a white man who appeared to have just climbed out of a boxing ring were clearly not what she'd been expecting.

Dane told her about the investigation. 'I believe Geraldine is staying with the people running the pub, and I need to talk to her and the friend she's with.'

'The Tavern is a popular venue in the town. There's a bit of drug peddling and the odd report of violence, but that's it,' Grainger declared, and called in Constable King, the local licensing officer who knew the landlord.

'It was me who visited and spoke to the couple who run the place,' King said. 'They both denied any knowledge of her, but I've a source who told me there's a new barmaid there.'

Armed with a picture of Geraldine, King left to visit the pub. Dane and Hayley booked into their hotel and grabbed something to eat. When they returned to the police station, King was waiting for them with a wide grin.

'She's working behind the bar. There's a band playing this evening, and the place is already heaving.'

At a quarter to eleven, Dane and Hayley slipped into the seaside pub with its three bars and large garden at the rear, full of smokers. The place was still busy, with a six-piece band belting out music being enjoyed by the young audience. The bars were crowded with punters clamouring to buy their final round of drinks before closing time.

Dane saw Geraldine and watched as she pulled pints and passed them over to the customers. She appeared happy and relaxed. Another woman, about the same age and height although much heavier than Geraldine, was working beside her and there was a big man with a black beard circulating and collecting the empty glasses.

Dane waited until the crush eased before sidling up to the bar. Geraldine was at the till collecting a customer's change, which she handed over before turning towards him.

'What can I get you?' she said with a smile that fell off her face when she realised who was standing there.

'Hello, Geraldine. I'll have an orange juice, and a gin and tonic for Hayley, please.'

25

Geraldine stepped back as if she'd seen a snake waiting to bite her. 'What are you doing here?'

'We need to talk to you,' Dane replied. The woman at the other end of the bar spotted what was going on and marched up to stand in front of Geraldine. 'I assume you're Stephanie?' Dane asked.

'You people never give up. I told you she doesn't want to talk to you. Toto, Toto, help us over here,' she shouted.

The bearded landlord moved with surprising speed and grabbed Dane by the shirt collar and slammed him against the wall, making him grunt in pain.

'You're not welcome. Now clear off before I hurt you,' he growled in Dane's ear.

Hayley grabbed Toto's free arm and twisted it into an armlock, causing the big man to yelp and let Dane go. Before he could recover, she'd spun him round and into the bar, kicking his legs from under him and pinning him down. Then she shoved her warrant card in his face.

'Police officers. Stay there and shut up before I forget I'm a lady.'

Dane turned to Geraldine. 'I don't have time to waste dancing around with the three of you. We've got to talk, and where we do that depends on how you behave in the next ten seconds.'

'You're not the press?' Toto grunted, his face pressed into a puddle of beer.

'We're police officers. When were they here?' Dane replied.

'This morning. He tried to barge in, but Toto told him to stay out,' Stephanie said.

'Did he give his name?'

'No. And I didn't ask. I'm sorry, if I'd known you were coppers, I wouldn't have done that,' Toto said.

'Don't worry about it.' He glanced at Hayley and grinned. 'Easy, tiger. You can put him down now. We'll sit over in the corner while you close.'

Dane sipped his orange juice and winced at the pain in his side as they waited.

'Are you all right?' Hayley asked, concern etched on her face.

'Yeah, chest is sore, though. It didn't help him grabbing me.'

Twenty minutes later, the two women joined them.

'What do you want with us?' Stephanie said. 'She's given you her statement, so what more can you possibly need?'

'A lot has happened since we last spoke to Geraldine. More people have died and we've found out what was going on at the Agnes Brown home.'

'You only want to blacken Graham's name,' Geraldine replied.

'His reputation has nothing to do with this. Five people are now dead, and they're all connected to that place. I'm sorry to have to rake it all up again.'

'We'd rather forget that time,' Stephanie snapped.

'I can understand that, but I've a job to do. I need your help to do it.'

Toto joined them and stood protectively behind Stephanie. He was about forty and his jet-black hair and beard gave him a piratical look. Dane doubted many customers tried to take advantage of him.

'You have an unusual Somerset name in Piazzi. Where're you from?' Dane asked.

'London. Clerkenwell,' he replied, his South London accent unmistakable.

'So how did you get it?'

'It's Sicilian, and I got it from my father, who got his from his papa and so on. We maintain the old traditions, so the family still use Sicilian first names too. Kevin Piazzi wouldn't work, would it?'

'No, I guess not, and there's nothing wrong with keeping to your heritage.'

'I'm British through and through and proud of it. But if England plays Italy, it's difficult to decide who to cheer for.'

'Yes, I suppose that would be a problem. Have you got any kids?'

'No, we haven't,' he replied, looking at his wife.

'I can't have them,' Stephanie announced bitterly. 'Another legacy of my childhood in those care homes and why I don't want to be reminded of it.'

Dane sat back in his chair and looked at the three people in front of him.

'I'd rather not make you relive any of it. But I need to understand the relationship between those who've died and the home. There'll be more deaths unless I can stop whoever's doing this.'

'They all deserved to die for what they did to us. I'm not bothered if another couple of them go the same way. Why should I lift a finger to save them? They ruined my life,' Stephanie snapped and sat back, her fists clenching in anger.

Dane glanced at Hayley, who said, 'All of them should have paid dearly for what they did to you. But killing them is too easy. Prison would be a better punishment. And I don't believe you mean what you said. You've made a life for yourself despite everything that happened to you, with a husband and a thriving business. And you've taken Geraldine in and are caring for her. You're a decent human being and you shouldn't lower yourself to their level by turning a blind eye to murder.' The atmosphere changed instantly, and Dane knew Hayley had said the right thing.

Stephanie turned to Toto and took his hand. 'What about you? You've had to take the brunt of it all these years.'

'It's up to you, love, but it can't hurt to talk. You've got to deal with the demons somehow, so why not do it this way?'

'You always say that, and you're right, but it's not that easy.' Stephanie turned to Geraldine. 'What do you want to do? You've suffered the most.'

'I'll do whatever you think is best,' Geraldine whispered, looking down at her feet.

'See what Binks did? She's not an idiot, but he treated her like one for the last twenty years. He smothered her individuality, she'll do nothing on her own initiative,' Stephanie said.

'Oh, he wasn't that bad. He loved me.'

Stephanie snorted with derision. 'What more do I have to say?' She looked at Dane and Hayley. 'I don't know about this. I've been dead set against even seeing you, let alone talking to you.'

'Your information might benefit others who suffered there with you. Apart from helping us catch the killer, it could bring them some closure. Remember, it wasn't only you two they brutalised.'

'Gerry told us you saved a girl from a similar situation. Is that true?'

'Yes. She's thirteen years old, and Parr raped her not long before someone murdered him.'

Stephanie looked at her watch. 'It's late and we're all exhausted. We will talk to you, but I've got to sleep.'

The two women agreed to come to the police station the next morning to be interviewed.

Dane slept with the help of the painkillers, but his chest still felt sore, and it hurt to breathe when he got up. His black eye was fading and the bump on his head had gone. A hot shower, a decent breakfast, more tablets and the short walk from the hotel to the station made him feel much better. At eleven, Toto pulled into the parking area and dropped the women off.

'Sorry we're late, but it took longer to sort the pub this morning, and that reporter was at the door pestering Gerry. He's followed us here,' Stephanie said.

Hayley left the room as Dane organised some tea. She returned a few minutes later and signalled for Dane to follow her.

'It's Boyd. He's in the car park over the road.'

'It's going to be boiling hot soon, and he can fry for all I care,' Dane replied.

'How did he find her?'

'We found them, didn't we? He's a pain, but he knows how to track people down. I'll give him that.'

Dane asked Stephanie, who insisted he call her Steph, to describe her experience at the home. She hesitated, took a deep breath then recounted being orphaned at six, and with no other family, placed in care. Losing her parents and the subsequent upheaval throughout her miserable childhood seriously affected her. By her own admission, she'd not been an easy child to look after and was moved round a lot before arriving in Maldon soon after her twelfth birthday. Geraldine followed a few months later and a few weeks after that, their friend Julie appeared. They were all about the same age and became firm friends.

Julie, of course, that's the name Alison mentioned.

Julie came to Agnes Brown from Basildon with a deep hatred of the care workers whom she blamed for her predicament. The three girls were about the same height; Julie was thin, Geraldine doll-like and Steph heavier, even in those days. Within a month of their arrival, the grooming started.

Binks took them out on regular trips to the seaside or funfairs, where he'd spoil them. They all loved the attention, and none of them had ever been happier. After one of these excursions, he diverted to a house. Inside, they found three men, who plied them with drinks until they were semi-conscious and helpless as the men raped them. Binks ordered them to keep quiet and threatened dire consequences if they revealed anything about it to anyone. Julie had sobbed the entire night and told them she'd hoped she'd left that sort of thing behind in her last home. They were taken to the house twice a week after that and dozens of men abused them. The handyman and the fat taxi driver were among that group. A new face appeared one evening and dragged Julie away, and they listened to her screams. She could hardly walk for days after he'd finished, and she identified him as the police officer responsible for getting her moved to Agnes Brown. Binks called him Colin. Together, they reinforced the threats to the girls to keep quiet. The girls were convinced that if they ran away or said anything, Colin would find them, and no one would believe them. So, they kept their mouths shut while enduring the abuse and trying to support each other.

Binks laid claim to Geraldine, and the tutor took a fancy to Julie. They only knew him as Gareth. The vicar was a regular, and soon seven girls and four boys were being taken to the house every week.

Patey became a particular favourite of Parr's, but Steph was passed around the other men. One evening, a newcomer arrived. Older than the others, he was very well dressed, wearing a pinstripe suit and a silk tie.

'He liked to wrap it round my neck and tell me to enjoy the

sensation of silk against my skin as he pulled it tight. I'll never forget how smooth it felt.' Steph shuddered. 'He had a funny burning smell, coming from the pipe he was always smoking. It stank horrible. One night after they'd finished, they all gathered in the front room, drinking. The man with the pipe suggested it'd be fun to watch Patey doing it to us three. So, they held us down and encouraged him to rape us, one at a time.' Steph paused as Geraldine started sobbing and put her arms round her.

Dane felt his stomach churn as he listened to this horror. He glanced at Hayley and knew she would be boiling mad. 'Didn't Gerry belong to Binks?' Dane asked.

'Yes, but she'd misbehaved, so she had to be punished. Julie fought like mad and pushed Patey off. Parr knocked her unconscious, so she didn't know what happened next.

'By this time we'd all had enough, and we discussed what we should do. Julie said she was going to run, and we agreed to go with her. But Binks found out, and we paid for that as well.'

Geraldine let out a wail. 'I didn't mean to tell him. I'm so sorry I did that.'

Steph hugged her tight. 'No one blames you. It doesn't matter now.' She peeked at Dane over Geraldine's head and raised her eyebrows before continuing.

'A few weeks later, Patey trapped Julie in the girl's toilet and raped her again. She ran straight to the local police and reported it. Guess who turned up to investigate. Parr. Of course. Patey got away with it, and they made an example of Julie and forced us to watch. Binks said that would happen to anyone who dared say anything.' Tears were streaming down her face.

'Shall we take a break?' Dane suggested.

'No, I need to finish this.' Steph drank some water and composed herself before explaining how the abuse continued until Wilson was arrested, when things changed. They didn't go to the house for nearly a year but were continually warned to keep their mouths shut. Parr oversaw the police enquiry, so it was impossible for them to say anything, even if they'd wanted to. Once Wilson had gone to prison, the abuse started again. The funny-smelling stranger, who the others called Stephen, remained a regular. All the men, including Parr, treated him with some deference.

'Can you describe him?' Dane asked.

'He always wore either a suit or a sports jacket, a tweed one, with a gold chain from his lapel into the top pocket of the jacket. About six foot tall with sandy-coloured hair and a ginger moustache. He had a deep, gravelly voice, as if he'd been smoking all his life.'

'You have an excellent memory.'

'I'll never get the image of that animal out of my head,' Steph replied bitterly.

As they got older, the men lost interest in them, preferring younger girls from the home. The authorities placed Steph in a council flat on her sixteenth birthday.

'What happened to Julie?' Dane asked.

'I heard she ran away, and that social services were looking for her. Gerry and Binks left together when he retired. I met her by chance about ten years ago in Borough Market in London,' Steph said. 'I recognised her immediately and invited her to my place, and she spent the evening with me and Toto. She told us she lived up north and had come down for a job interview. She didn't want to swap numbers or stay in contact, which upset me, and I haven't seen her since.'

'What's her surname?'

'Miller, Julie Miller.'

Geraldine confirmed everything Steph had told them, although she was still loath to speak ill of her husband. She insisted he'd loved her and only wanted to keep her safe.

Steph described how after leaving the care system she moved around until ending up in London. She found work on a stall in Borough Market where she met Toto. He'd been working for his dad. His family had taken her in, and they married a year later.

'Toto's supported me through everything, putting up with my tantrums when I have a meltdown because I can't have kids. He's always been here for me when the nightmares started again. I told him what I'd been through as a kid, and he hugged me and said they'd get what they deserved.' She stopped, horrified at what she'd let slip. 'He meant nothing by it, though. He might look like a thug, but he'd never hurt a fly.'

'I'm sure he'll be able to prove he was here when all the murders took place.' Dane made a mental note to check.

'When did you first come down here to visit, Geraldine?'

'A couple of years ago.' Geraldine explained that Binks had found out she'd been in contact with Steph. 'At first, he was mad at me and told me to stop. But then he suggested I come down and visit occasionally. By then I'd learnt to drive, and he stayed in most of the time. So I visited, only a couple of times. I think that when he knew I'd come back to him he was happier for me to get away more often. I'd grown too old for his tastes by then and our sex life stopped. He wanted the place to himself for a few days, probably something to do with the computer.'

'Can we wind back a bit? Where did you go after he retired?'

'We lived in lots of different places. He was always worrying they'd find us, so we were always moving. I would do the shopping sometimes, but mostly I stayed in, and he warned me not to answer the door if he wasn't there.'

'Did he work?'

'He had a few jobs, so we had enough money to live on, and he changed the car a lot. We spent three years in Italy, and I hated it. I couldn't understand the language so I wouldn't go out on my own. We lived in a big apartment block on the outskirts of Naples, close to Pompeii. I know that because Graham took me there once.'

'What did he do there?'

'I'm not sure. He didn't tell me very much, something to do with his photography I think, but he never said.'

'Tell him what really happened, Gerry,' Steph said. 'You don't have to protect him.'

She hesitated, her eyes wide with fear, as Steph took her hand. 'He told me I was never to say.'

'He can't hurt you now.'

She glanced nervously at Dane and Hayley then looked down at her hands in her lap. 'Graham took thousands of pictures of me,' she whispered. She looked up and with tears running down her cheeks continued. 'He would make me pose and do disgusting things to myself.' She started to sob. Steph put her arm round Geraldine to calm her, and Dane glanced at Hayley.

Her face was deadpan. 'Would you like a drink of water?' she asked.

'Yes, please.' Hayley left the room.

Dane's mind raced as they waited. He didn't like having to ask these questions and make these two women, victims, relive their experiences, but it had to be done. Hayley returned with three bottles of water.

'I'm sorry to drag all this out, but it is important. Did he photograph you with other men?' Dane asked.

Geraldine bowed her head, staring at the floor and wringing her hands. 'Lots of them. Graham would dress me in schoolgirl's clothes and his friends would come, and he would take the pictures while...you know.' She paused for a moment. 'You must think I'm awful for doing that, but I had to,' she whispered, so low he strained to hear her.

'You're not a bad person, Gerry, you never have been. You're a victim,' Dane replied. 'When did he stop taking pictures of you?'

'About a year after we moved to Italy. He said I was too old and fat and he needed a new model.'

'Did he sell the pictures?'

'That's how he made money. He uploaded all the photos he ever took and sold them on that computer. Once he stopped using me, his Italian friends came with three much younger girls to the apartment. I had to wait in a bedroom while they worked.'

'When did you come home?'

'Two years ago. I didn't know where we were going until we arrived in England. He hadn't even told me he'd bought the house.'

'How did you travel here?'

'By car, it took ages.'

'Did you drive all the way in one go?'

'No, we stopped overnight with a friend of his in France. I'd never met her before, and she was drunk when we arrived. We stayed the night and left before she woke up the next day.'

'Who was she?'

'He called her Joyce, but she didn't talk to me. We got there late, and they were talking for hours while I sat in our room. The next morning, I found her passed out on the settee with two empty vodka bottles on the floor beside her. And she'd messed herself. Once we'd settled in Clacton, a builder converted the attic, and two men I recognised from Naples turned up and set up his computer gear. Graham spent hours up there working on it, but I didn't go up. I wasn't allowed.'

'She only told me about Italy the other day,' Steph put in.

'He told me it was a secret and if I said anything to you, he'd stop me from coming to see you.'

'Who visited your home in Clacton?'

'Gareth, the tutor, was one of them. I recognised him straight away and got a right shock when I saw him. But he didn't even acknowledge me as he climbed into the attic with Graham. Patey turned up and leered at me, no doubt remembering what he'd done to us.'

'Did he photograph girls in there?'

'No. He'd stopped doing that. Whatever he was working on, it had to do with the computer.'

'How about his friends from the photography club? Did they visit?'

Geraldine looked sheepish. 'I made that up. I'm sorry. The only people who ever came to the house were interested in what he had in the loft.'

'When you were at Maldon did you all go to the same school?'

'Yes, but we left before we did any exams,' Steph replied. Dane pulled a photograph from his pocket. 'Who are these young people?' he asked, showing it to them.

'That's us. Where did you find these?'

'On the wall in Patey's flat. I assume he's the boy, and the others are you three. Which is which?'

Steph pointed out her, Gerry and Julie. 'We must have been about thirteen when they took these. Well into the time they were abusing us. Perhaps he kept them as a memento of the first people he had sex with.'

Dane considered what he'd heard and looked over at Hayley, who shook her head.

'Thanks for your help. It can't have been easy for you, but it's made a few things much clearer. I intend to find Gareth and the man called Stephen and prosecute them.'

'I don't think Stephen was his real name. Apart from the men from the home, I'm sure everyone else used fake names,' Steph said.

'That wouldn't surprise me, but we will find him, and when I do, would you give evidence against them for what they did to you?'

'You won't be able to do anything now. It's been too long,' Steph said.

'We're better at dealing with these offences these days. With what you've told me, we'll have a strong case against them for rape and child abuse.'

'We'll have to talk about it. It might help, but it could just as easily have the opposite effect, and I don't want it to hurt Gerry.'

'Hayley could sort out some counselling for you both?'

'I've looked into it in the past but we couldn't afford it.'

'I know some useful people. I'll organise all that for you,' Hayley said.

'What should we do about that reporter?'

'Ignore him and bar him from the pub. He'll soon get the message and clear off. Please don't tell him you've spoken to us personally. I'd rather he didn't know we were here. When did you last see or hear from Julie?'

'Not since I bumped into her that time in London.'

'What did she look like?'

'She's about the same height as me, slim, and she looked well. Her hair was dyed red and cut really short, like a man's crew-cut. I only just recognised her. All she said was she'd got her life in order and had a good job, although she lived on her own.'

'What colour are her eyes?'

'Brown.'

Dane's interest was piqued. Julie could look completely different now, she could even be dead. But if she hadn't changed that much physically, she could fit the descriptions of the person seen leaving Parr's home, visiting the storage company in Southend and calling on Mrs Joiner. She'd been brutalised by all the victims so had a good reason to want revenge. But he had to be careful. All the other children abused at that hellhole of a home had just as much motive.

'Can you recall the names of the other children abused at the home?'

They both shook their heads. 'It's so long ago, and I've spent all this time trying to forget,' Steph said.

'I can't remember a single name,' Gerry added. 'That's sad, isn't it?'

'I suppose it is, and speaks volumes for what they did to you.'

There was nothing else to ask, so Hayley rang Toto and he collected them from the rear of the station.

Boyd was still in his car, looking hot and bothered as he baked in the full sun. They left him to broil.

26

Dane made them a mug of tea and joined Hayley who was in the backyard of the station leaning against the car smoking. He felt exhausted and had another headache, so found a couple of paracetamols in his bag and swilled them down with some tea. A puddle of acid worked in the pit of his stomach as he pondered what they'd been told. He'd been lucky and enjoyed a good childhood. Even with the grief over his sister's death and the years of strain in his relationship with his father, he'd never been abused or neglected. He couldn't conceive of what it must have been like for those kids. There is a wealth of psychobabble about why some men want sex with prepubescent children. They all know what they're doing is wrong, but usually only accept that after someone catches them red-handed. Once in custody, some will plead mental illness to try and wriggle out of their criminality. That those involved in the abuse at the Agnes Brown home were in positions of power and had been caring for the children made it worse.

Hayley stalked to the overflowing ashtray screwed to the wall and angrily stubbed out her cigarette, then put another in her mouth. As she pulled her face up from the lighter, Dane saw the tears streaming down her face.

'What's up? Got a bit of grit in your eyes?'

'Yeah, sorry,' she replied, then sniffed and wiped her nose with the back of her hand. 'I'm so angry. How can this still be happening in a civilised society?'

'It's nothing new. People have been abusing kids forever, and we can't fix the world on our own. But we are doing something in our own little corner of it and I'm determined to nail those creatures for what they did. But first we've got to find our killer before they strike again. When we get back, I want you to concentrate on finding Julie.'

'What about Gareth and Stephen?'

'Leave them to me.'

'Do you think she could be the killer?'

'It's a possibility and one we've got to consider. She would certainly have a very strong motive, and who could blame her? But could someone described as being so slight be strong enough to control the victims? They were all bigger than her. Even the vicar.'

'If you have the will a woman can do anything. And remember that Parr and Lowe were both zapped with a Taser, which is always a good equaliser in a fight.'

'That's an excellent point. And as Dragon is unlikely and Patey certainly ruled out, there are no other candidates at the moment.'

'Do you want me to stay out of the office?'

'Yes, until we've resolved who the leak is. I don't want anyone knowing what we've discovered or what you're up to. So, you stay with the delightful Ms Hogg in social services, and I'll concentrate on the others.'

As they drove home Dane rang Sobers and told him what they'd discovered. Several covert cameras were now recording what was happening in the incident office, with three people from the complaints department monitoring the tapes. So far, they'd observed nothing suspicious.

*

The bruise around Dane's eye was fading to a revolting, yellowish hue as he set off for work the following morning. Sally met him with an update and confirmed the forensic examinations of all the scenes were complete. Lowe owned hundreds of photo albums, which contained the same catalogue of images as the other scenes. The computer was being downloaded and searched by the High-tech Crime Unit and the NCA.

There was a knock on the door and Dane looked up to discover Jane Mitchell smiling at him. 'Hello, nice to see you. Have you sorted everything out?'

'Yes, thank you. I heard what happened. Do you mind if I rejoin the team?'

'Be my guest,' he said. 'Go with Sally and she'll bring you up to date. We'll chat later.'

Dane rang Inspector Harding. 'Are there any contact lists of private emails on any of the computers we've seized?'

'They only use their machines to store the images and they've been careful to erase their internet history religiously every hour. They know that if we follow them through cyberspace, they'd be in trouble. Whoever set their systems up are experts.'

Dane checked the search records of all the scenes to see if any diaries or address books were recovered from any of them. There had only been one, from Patey's flat, and he asked Reece Lewin to retrieve it for him. Twenty minutes later he was still waiting, so strolled down to the store where he found the sergeant wading through a pile of boxes containing exhibits.

'It's not in here. But I remember seeing it. It must be here somewhere.'

'Has someone misfiled it?'

'That's unlikely. I'll find it if I have to tear this place apart.'

Dane left him to it and returned to his office. It was a small, slim address book that could easily get stuffed in the wrong envelope or box. But it seemed a strange thing to go missing, especially as it was the one exhibit he wanted to research. He picked up the documents relating to the mobile phones belonging to the victims. The analysts had been through them and found a couple of examples of numbers in common.

Patey had called both Binks and Parr regularly in the year leading up to their deaths. There was no record of Binks calling Parr, or vice versa. Binks contacted Lowe, and Dane suspected that, if he checked before Joiner's death, he'd find the same there. He studied the calls made and received, and a thought struck him. These abusers were still active at the time of their murders and kept in contact with each other. In that case, there might be a history of calls between them and Stephen and Gareth. Their numbers could be among those they hadn't identified from the call sheets.

He sat down with the analysts and together they worked through the lists and came up with thirty they considered worth checking. They applied to get the subscriber information and the Telephone Unit promised Dane they'd do their best to get a result for him the following day.

Dane glanced out of the window and spotted Vonn returning from her run, dressed in fluorescent yellow today. She jogged through the car park, warming down until she stopped and bent over, holding her knees. When she came into the office to collect her bag, Dane was once again struck by how unwell she looked, even with the glow of exercise about her.

'Are you feeling okay?' he asked.

'I'm fine, thank you,' she declared, then ducked into the changing room. Dane made a note to mention his concern to Sally, keen not to repeat his failure with Debbie Evans.

Vonn informed everyone at the evening briefing that she'd just found the elusive Gareth's full name.

'He's Gareth Neil. I picked that up from the social services files. Took me a few minutes to fight my way past the rude manager down there, but worth the effort, although I'm still looking for his current address.' She turned to Dane. 'I didn't leave you a note, boss, because you were away.'

They all listened intently when Dane told them where he and Hayley had been for the last couple of days and the reason for him keeping quiet about it.

'You must all realise that someone here is leaking information to the press. Whoever is doing this is disrespecting their colleagues as well as me and the force. I would ask them to own up. If they force me to waste valuable time and effort hunting them down, things'll go harder for them. It isn't Jane, so those of you looking sideways at her can get that idea out of your heads. In the coming week, we're concentrating on finding and interviewing the former residents of the children's home. If anyone reports abuse, we take their complaints. We must also find Gareth Neil because he's at risk. And I want him to go to prison for what he did.'

The meeting broke up and the teams drifted away to their desks, with a lot of muttering and the occasional glance towards him, but no one admitted to being the leak.

Dane changed into his running kit and headed for the gym for a gentle jog on the treadmill. As he started the machine, he noticed a mobile phone on the floor beneath a stack of weights. He hopped off and picked it up, pressing the last number dialled, and Boyd's appeared. Someone had called it less than twenty minutes before. It was a cheap pay-as-you-go burner phone and had only been used to contact the journalist. 'Got you,' he muttered, and put the handset back where he'd found it.

Dane finished his run and after a quick shower sauntered to his desk. Most of the officers were still there, finishing their work for the day. Anyone who worked in the station could use the gym, and it was always busy. Jane came in and distracted him as they chatted about what she'd been doing. He told her about the trip to Somerset but left out the information about Stephen. He hadn't mentioned it to the rest of the team, either.

'Boyd has been on to me again,' she announced.

'What's he after?'

'He says he wants to confirm aspects of what he thinks are the makings of a hot story. I told him to get stuffed.'

'Would you like to do a piece about what we are actually doing and include an interview with me with direct quotes?'

'I'd love to, but wouldn't that be against what we agreed?'

'Let me run it by Sobers and Wix. I want potential victims from the home to come forward. I can't rely on the press to put the complete message out. If we discuss the direction of the investigation and the appeal and my aim for it, could you get it published?'

'I know someone who'll publish it in a nanosecond. But I must ask you this. Are you using me?'

'Of course I am. To publicise the message as I want it to go out. But that's it. I wouldn't expect you to do anything else for me.'

'And I'll interview you and quote you directly?'

'Yes.'

'Is this something to do with exposing Boyd's source?'

'How could it be? I need to catch whoever the leak is, but how would you doing this help me do that?'

Jane stared at him and pursed her lips as she pondered the offer. 'I have a sneaking suspicion I'm being used to expose the traitor and I have a problem with that.'

'We're going to have a press conference where I'll make the appeal. Then we can sit down for an interview, that's all. And when this investigation is all over, I'll give you the exclusive on what happened in Ireland and the attacks on me last year.'

Her eyes lit up, but then she looked sideways at him. 'You're up to something. But okay, you're on.'

'I'll clear this with Wix in the morning, then we can get moving on the article.'

*

Dane met Hayley later in her customary spot in the pub garden, puffing on a cigarette. 'What have you found out?'

'Not a lot that's of any use to us. They transferred Julie Miller to the Agnes Brown from Basildon when she was twelve. According to the documents she'd been a disruptive child at Basildon and constantly went missing, so they moved her away. The manager reported she was a nightmare and caused the local police no end of trouble. Her record at Agnes Brown reads the same, although as we now know she was being brutalised so that isn't surprising. Binks wrote most of the reports there, so they're probably not accurate. The allegation of rape and the other accusations are all there, but he brushed them aside as the ravings of an attention-seeker. When she reached sixteen, social services planned to place her in secure accommodation. She got wind of that and disappeared. They put out a national alert, but nothing came of it. I've checked her name and date of birth through every database I can think of, but I can't find her. It's almost as if she ceased to exist.'

'Perhaps she did. Maybe they murdered her.'

'I considered that, but remember, Steph saw her looking fit and well years later, and it's relatively easy to create a new identity. If she just wanted to get rid of Julie Miller and become someone else, she could have done. I'm going to look at her records from Basildon in case there are any connections. It's a long shot, but I'm running out of options.'

'Okay, thanks for the update. And I've agreed to do an interview with Jane,' he said and explained what he had in mind.

27

Dane had an early finish for once. The pain from his ribs had subsided and the headaches stopped, but after the excitement of the last few days he was feeling worn out. He called Vicky, and they had a long chat. He told her about their trip to the West Country and how Wix had seemed to ease off him in the last week. Vicky admitted she'd got into the battle rhythm of her course and was now enjoying the challenge. As they nattered, he realised how much he missed her. He couldn't wait until they could spend their evenings having these conversations when curled up on the settee together.

No sooner had he put the phone down to her than it rang again. It was the divisional commander in Weston-super-Mare.

'I've had an irate, frightened journalist called Angus Boyd in my office. He's reported that three masked men kidnapped him earlier this afternoon and he's adamant they were from the Italian mafia.'

Dane burst out laughing. 'Oh, that's priceless. What happened?'

'He alleges he was sitting in his car minding his own business when they jumped in. They ordered him to drive to a remote spot on the coast where they threatened him. He insists this is all to do with your investigation, and you're looking into the mafia. Are you?'

'No, I'm not. There is a crossover between the murders and one of the NCA's international operations, but that's as far as it goes. Boyd's been in Weston, trying to interview a victim's wife. Did they injure him?'

'No. But we had the police surgeon check him to be on the safe side. There are no witnesses.'

'How did he get away from them?'

'They forced him to drive back to the town centre where the three of them got out of the car and left him.'

'Strange kidnap. I can assure you the mafia hasn't come to Somerset to put the frighteners on Mr Boyd. What's he going to do?'

'He's leaving tonight but insisted on lodging the complaint and that we investigate it.'

'Well, good luck. It's nothing to do with us here.'

Dane chuckled as they finished the call, then had a thought and rang the Tavern pub. The hubbub was evident in the background when Toto answered.

'Hi, it's Christian Dane here. How are they?'

'They're doing fine, thanks. Steph is pleased she spoke to you. She says it's like it lifted a big load off her. Gerry's the same, but it'll take a bit more than a chat for her to escape her demons.'

'You're probably right, but I'm glad they're okay. Has that journalist given you any more trouble?'

'He tried to talk his way in here last night, but I gave him a final warning and he hasn't been back since.'

'I'm pleased to hear that. How many brothers do you have?'

'Why do you ask?'

'Just curious. If I guessed at three, would I be close?'

'Four, and two sisters. We like big families.'

'Are any of them visiting you at the moment?'

Dane heard Toto's sharp intake of breath. 'Erm…'

'Listen, Toto. That journalist has been into the local police station alleging the mafia kidnapped and intimidated him. He's so scared he's leaving town, so it worked. But tell them not to do it again. If they get caught, they'll go down.'

'I don't know what you're talking about,' Toto replied.

'Good. Take care and give my regards to Steph and Gerry.'

*

In a meeting with Wix and Sobers the following morning they readily agreed to his suggestion of the article by Jane and the press conference. Afterwards, Dane joined Hayley in the canteen.

'How are you getting on?' he asked taking a bite out of his sausage roll.

'I looked through Julie's file. She came from Canning Town originally, no parents or other family, and she arrived in Basildon soon after her eleventh birthday. About a year after that, she started running away and on one of those occasions got caught

214

shoplifting. I checked and they gave her a caution, so we destroyed her fingerprints when she turned seventeen. The manager there hated her because she caused him work and he hinted she was sexually active.'

'Is there any record of them following up on that?'

'No, of course not. And there's no evidence to support that assumption. He threw it in to make it easier to move her somewhere else. There's also mention of Parr as someone who gave advice on how to deal with her. A week after, they shipped her out to the Agnes Brown.'

'What are the dates for all this?'

Hayley checked her notes and told him.

'That's when I worked in Basildon. I wonder. Wait here for me.' Dane went to the headquarters registry and asked for a couple of his old pocket notebooks and returned with them to the canteen. He flicked through them, then, with an exclamation, banged one down on the table, turned it to Hayley and pointed to several entries.

She read them and looked up in surprise. 'Christ, what a coincidence.'

The entries recounted a meeting Dane had at the Basildon children's home, the third time he'd been there that week after earlier he'd picked up reports of a missing girl named Julie Miller. He'd previously discovered her in the dustbin area behind the nearby shopping centre, where he thought she'd been hiding from someone. After he took her back, she disappeared again a few days later, and he scoured the town until he found her. She'd refused to say anything to Dane about why she kept running away or who she had been with. He'd reported this to the manager, and advised they check her physical welfare. He told Dane to mind his own business, so he submitted a duty report to his boss, explaining his concerns for the safety of the child.

'That report got Parr on my case. My chief inspector backed me up and there was an almighty row. I saw her once more when I was shopping in the town centre with my ex-wife. I spotted her hiding behind a shop.' He leafed through his pocketbook to the entry. 'I tried to persuade her to talk to me, but she wouldn't. I remember now. I was concerned someone was forcing her into thieving or something worse. She refused to come to the station but promised to contact me if she needed help and I slipped her five pounds.' He pointed to the date. 'They moved her to Agnes Brown three days later. Now I remember wondering what had happened to her. And I didn't recognise the name when Steph told us, either.'

'Don't be so hard on yourself. You can't expect to recall every incident from all those years ago,' Hayley said.

'Remember what Steph and Gerry said? Julie thought she'd left that sort of abuse behind her. Then Parr arrives and brutalises her the first time they see him.'

'It's not your fault.'

'If only I'd paid more attention – or pushed her more.'

'You did everything you could. I don't know any other officer who'd have done so much for a kid like her. Nothing you did would have stopped them getting rid of her, and Parr and Binks took their opportunity.'

Dane recalled a tiny dishevelled and frightened little girl but doubted he'd recognise her now. 'Come and watch the presser and sit in with the interview with Jane. You might be able to add something.'

The press conference lasted half an hour and Dane made his appeal for former child residents at the Agnes Bowen to come forward before sitting down with Jane. The editor of a national paper had promised a full-page splash the following day.

As they were finishing Sally rang him with news. 'Vonn has just called to say she's found Neil's home address.'

'I'll go there with Hayley straight away. Tell Vonn well done from me.'

'She's gone out for a doctor's appointment. She didn't look well.'

'Did she say what was wrong?'

'No. You know what's she like. I'll keep a close eye on her.'

'Thanks, I'll ring you after we find Gareth.'

Dane called Hayley over and asked her to go and get the car. 'What's happening?' Jane asked.

'Hayley and I are off to see if we can't track someone down. Do you want to tag along?'

'Love to. But I'd better write this. I'm on a deadline and I can't miss it. I'll talk to you later and you can tell me how you got on.'

The small block of flats on the outskirts of Chelmsford comprised twenty apartments with private parking and a security-controlled entrance with an unmanned concierge desk inside the foyer. He rang the bell for Apartment 17 but received no reply. He tried twice more before trying No. 15 and they were let in.

An elderly lady who introduced herself as Mrs Shaw greeted them on the top floor and confirmed that Mr Neil was indeed her neighbour. There was no reply when Dane knocked on his door, so she invited them in and offered tea and homemade cake. Hayley asked about her neighbour.

'Oh yes, he was here before I moved in. He likes to keep himself to himself. But he's a nice young man and does a bit of shopping for me.'

'Have you seen him recently?'

'No. It's been a couple of weeks since we last chatted.'

'What does he do for a living?'

'I don't know. He's never mentioned it.'

'Has he many visitors?'

'A young woman called on him yesterday.'

'Have you seen her before?'

'No, and she was a lot younger than the usual people who visit.'

'Can you describe her?'

'She had her back to me, but I would estimate in her thirties. With long brown hair. And quite short, but I didn't see her face because she walked towards the lift.'

Back on the landing, they considered their next move. 'Perhaps we've turned up here on the odd occasion he's gone to work,' Hayley suggested.

'The neighbour hasn't seen him, and a small female fitting the description of the woman who called on Mrs Joiner bangs on his door. That's too much of a coincidence for my liking. Let's go in and make sure everything is okay.'

He knelt and peered through the letterbox. A draft excluder blocked it, but he still detected a pungent odour coming from inside. Dane grimaced as he stood and selected a lock pick.

'I think we can justify entering here.'

The door opened behind them, and Hayley turned to see Mrs Shaw. 'Should you be doing that?'

'We're concerned about his welfare.'

'Oh dear, I hope he's all right,' she replied and stayed to watch the excitement.

It took less than a minute to open the door and Dane paused in the doorway. A short passageway led to a well-appointed sitting room, two bedrooms, a bathroom, and a kitchen. The larger bedroom contained a double bed with wardrobes and drawers, and the second, a desk but no computer and the single wooden bookshelf was empty. The smell was coming from half a dozen supermarket carrier bags full of rotten produce. It looked like someone had returned from the shops, dropped them and left in a hurry. Dane found a till receipt in one of the bags, and then stood for a few moments looking around. A copy of the local paper was on the table. The front page reported the discovery of Wilson's body. The paper was dated the same day as the receipt in the bag.

He showed it to Hayley. 'Perhaps he thought he was next,' she said.

28

Dane leant against his car and took the opportunity for some fresh air while he made a few calls. Sally had dispatched six officers to join him, armed with a search warrant

The Scenes of Crime team arrived, and under their watchful eyes he retrieved the till receipt and diverted two investigators to the local supermarket. The rest of the detectives started banging on the doors of the other apartments to interview the occupants. They completed that task by mid-evening. One lady from the second floor recalled being followed into the lift the day before by a young woman. She gave an excellent description that matched the person Mrs Shaw saw.

'That explains how she got in,' Dane said.

A search of the drawers in the desk revealed details of a vehicle and a mobile phone owned by Neil. Dane called the number, but it was switched off.

The officers returned from the supermarket with a clear picture of the man who'd purchased the shopping, and Mrs Shaw recognised her neighbour. They had footage of him leaving the car park in the vehicle they'd learnt about, and a check on the police national computer confirmed Gareth Neil was still the registered owner. Dane and Hayley drove back to the incident room, which was buzzing with activity as everyone worked on their phones and computers. Sally was in her office and Vonn was at her computer.

'I checked with Automatic Number Plate Recognition and Gareth's car was pinged at Dover ferry port eight hours after he left his flat, and there's no record of it since,' Sally said.

'At least we know he was alive and well then. If he stays out of the country, then he should be safe from the killer. I'll contact the NCA and ask them to keep their eyes out. He might turn up at one of the places being watched. Have you got anything else for me, Sally?'

'Your appeal about the children's home was broadcast on the evening news, and we've already received several telephone calls from people who claim they were at the Agnes Brown home.'

'Do they sound legitimate?'

'Yes, and several are promising. They were living there at the same time as our three and one has already declared she was abused,' Sally said.

Dane saw Vonn at her desk and called her over to congratulate her on finding Neil. 'Sally tells me you've been to the doctor. Is everything all right?'

'I'm fine, thank you. Just a check-up,' Vonn snapped and bustled away.

'She's touchy,' Dane remarked to Sally.

'No more than usual. She prefers to keep herself to herself and doesn't mix at all with the rest of the team. But she's an excellent worker,' Sally replied.

Jane appeared with a broad smile. 'I've finished the piece, and my mate is going to run it tomorrow morning.'

'Can I have a look, please?' Dane replied.

'Yes, but you can't change anything. I've done what you asked, but what's written is what he will publish.'

'I wouldn't dare to edit you. I only want to read it.'

She handed him the article with a pensive look and sat down to gauge his reaction. Dane passed each page to Sally and when he'd finished, he looked up and smiled.

'Brilliant, thank you for doing this. This will make a big difference.'

Jane was true to her word, and her exclusive filled a full page the next morning. Dane read it over his breakfast and was delighted. It was exactly what he'd hoped for and he couldn't help the smile that creased his face as he left for work.

A large envelope was waiting on his desk when he arrived. It contained the results from the checks of the numbers on Parr's and Binks's mobile phones. As Dane pushed the sheaf of papers back into the envelope, he noticed the flap felt sticky. On closer inspection, he realised someone had steamed it open.

Sobers promised to check the camera footage but soon called back with bad news.

'Nothing on the tapes, I'm afraid. Whoever opened your envelope got hold of it before it arrived at your office.'

More frustration which became worse when they gathered for the morning briefing and Sally informed him that Vonn had gone off sick.

'She sounds terrible. I'll make sure she has everything she needs. In the meantime, I'll take the lead on the interviews of the people calling in. We've had another five in the last hour.'

'Thanks for letting me know. I hope it's nothing serious.'

Sobers called to tell him that the traitor's phone was being used. After finding it in the gym, Dane had persuaded Sobers and Wix to get a live trace put on it. Now when it was used, the intelligence cell monitoring the camera was informed.

'Where are they?' Dane replied, looking round the incident room.

'In the same building as you. That's as accurate as they can be. The call's ended, but it was an incoming from Boyd.'

Dane appealed to Sobers. 'Are you sure we can't get a full voice interception on this phone? We know they're committing a criminal offence.'

'The surveillance commissioners won't give us the authorisation. They're petrified at the thought of tapping a journalist's telephone. I'll talk to the chief, but don't hold your breath.'

Dane shook his head in frustration. He sat back and considered his options for a few minutes and then came to a decision. He walked half a mile to a pay phone and called John Lord. 'I need your help with that persistent leak I told you about.'

'What would you like me to do?' Lord replied.

Dane was back at his desk working his way through his bulging in-tray when Sobers rang him. 'They're talking again.'

'Any idea where they are?'

'Still in the building.'

Dane's mobile buzzed. 'I'd better take this. I'll wander round and see if I can spot them.' He hung up, and then opened the line to Lord.

'Your mole is on the top floor. Boyd is screaming at him for giving him worthless information and has threatened him with exposure unless he pulls his finger out. Hang on… Okay, the man your end has promised him something juicy and they're meeting later, and they've just finished the call.'

Dane could see that no one in the main office was using a mobile phone so he approached the gym and, as he reached it, Reg Phelan emerged. He looked startled to see Dane but recovered quickly. 'Morning, boss.'

Dane peeked through the glass door and saw the room was empty. It had to be Phelan.

'That's your man,' Lord declared in his ear.

'Thanks for your help, John. We'll go to the next phase.' With a grim smile, Dane returned to the office and called Sobers.

'It's Phelan. Can you send a surveillance team over here because I think he might go to meet his contact soon?'

'I'll try, but they're deployed elsewhere. Are you sure?'

'I clocked him on the phone, and I overheard him mention a meeting as he bumped into me.'

'It could be something else.'

'That'd be too much of a coincidence. They were talking and the only person on the team on a mobile was Phelan. What more do you need?'

Sobers sighed, then said, 'All right, I'll get the surveillance to you. It might take a while, though.'

'If he goes out, I'll follow and keep you posted. How's that?'

'Yeah, do that.'

Dane watched the sergeant as he worked at his desk. Half an hour later Phelan looked in on Sally before leaving the building. Dane rang Lord, who promised to monitor Phelan's movements.

Dane was soon speeding south on the A12, directed by Lord who confirmed that Phelan was a couple of miles in front of him. He'd informed Sobers and the surveillance team were being sent to catch him up.

As Dane approached the Brook Street junction at Brentwood, Lord advised him Phelan had stopped outside a nearby hotel. Three minutes later Dane slid into reception and spotted Phelan sitting alone in the bar. Dane found a spot from where he could watch without being seen and saw Boyd arrive and join the sergeant. The pair bent their heads together for a few moments before Phelan handed over a large brown envelope. The journalist looked around before pulling a sheaf of papers half out and flicking through them. He nodded and slid them back before putting the envelope into his shoulder bag. The two men had another hurried and tense conversation before Boyd passed a thick, white envelope to Phelan.

Dane had seen enough. Just then three surveillance operators arrived. He waved them over and together they went to the table.

'Hello, Reg, what are you doing here?'

Phelan looked around, and the blood drained from his face at the sight of his boss. 'I-I…' he stammered.

'Don't bother. You're under arrest for corruption and misconduct in a public office. And the same goes for you, Boyd.'

More officers joined them as Dane hauled Phelan to his feet.

'Why?' Dane said.

'I'm saying nothing,' Phelan whispered as he was frisked. The white envelope stuffed full of twenty-pound notes was removed from the inside pocket of his jacket.

'Take him out of my sight,' Dane growled, and turned to Boyd.

'You need to be extremely careful. I am a member of the press…' Boyd blustered.

'Don't waste your breath,' Dane snapped and opened the journalist's bag.

'That contains journalistic material.'

Ignoring Boyd's protests, Dane removed the brown envelope, which contained copies of the telephone records. 'This is stolen property, and crucial evidence in a murder investigation. So, your usual get-out-of-jail-free card won't wash.'

Back at the station, the incident room was full of detectives sitting in stunned silence. Dane had ordered everyone in and Wix and Sobers were standing at the back. He explained what had happened that afternoon and why DS Phelan would no longer be serving with them.

A voice muttered, 'Bastard.' Dane saw it was Tom Jones, his face puce. 'I'm sorry, boss, but I trusted him. It was me who told him about our trip to France. I thought he was interested in what we'd been doing, but he was betraying us all.'

'None of this reflects badly on any of you. Everyone in this room has acquitted themselves well in the last few weeks. No one has anything to be ashamed of.'

Dane recounted their recent investigations into Gareth Neil and, for the first time, told them about the mysterious Stephen. They listened in silence as he described him and his involvement in the abuse.

'Hayley and I will follow up on him while the rest of you interview the people who've been coming forward. Remember, they're likely to be victims and extremely vulnerable, so treat them all with compassion and respect. We still have to identify and find the killer. Who has probably got Gareth Neil and Stephen in their sights. But I want them locked away for what they did to those kids. They won't get the easy way out.'

After the meeting finished, Dane returned to his office with Sobers, Wix and Sally.

'I need a replacement for Phelan.'

'Can't you manage with the two you have?' Wix replied.

'No. Vonn Clyde has reported sick, and Reece can't do everything on his own. I'd like Bob Soanes. He's the uniform sergeant who set this entire investigation running because he spotted something was wrong at the Florida Motel, and he's an excellent detective.'

'I agree, Bob's the right candidate. I'll organise his posting as soon as possible,' Sobers said.

There were twenty-five names and addresses on the list from the Telephone Unit. These were numbers the mobile phones belonging to Parr or Binks had contacted on at least two occasions. They set out early the following morning to start by visiting the four men named Stephen. If none of them turned out to be who they were after, then they'd visit all the others. Their first port of call was a house on the outskirts of Colchester where they found a man in his late fifties.

'Mr Stephen Wayne?' Hayley asked.

'Yes.' He looked startled and peered at their identification. 'Will this take long? I'm just on my way to work.'

'We're investigating a series of murders, and your name has come to our attention because our victims contacted you.'

'Well, I'm an estate agent, so I receive dozens of calls every day. You'll need to be a bit more specific.'

'Do the names Colin Parr or Graham Binks mean anything to you? They both rang you in the last few months.'

Wayne looked confused. 'What number are you talking about?'

Hayley recited it. 'That's my work phone, and it's always ringing.' As Wayne spoke the Star Wars theme came from his pocket and he smiled. 'See what I mean? Why don't you follow me to the office and we can sort this out for you.'

It took less than an hour for Dane and Hayley to satisfy themselves that Parr and Binks had been enquiring about a three-bedroom rental property outside Colchester. The estate agent was helpful, and there was no reason to suspect him of being involved.

It was mid morning before they arrived outside their second destination, a semi-detached home in the shadow of the enormous water tower in Hertford. An angry man in his mid sixties and several inches shorter than Dane answered after the third prolonged ring of the doorbell.

'What do you want?'

'Are you Mr Stephen Taylor?'

'I am, and I'm extremely busy.'

Dane introduced himself. 'We're investigating the murder of several men in Essex and two of those victims have contacted your number.'

'I suppose you mean Colin Parr and Binks, do you?'

'That's right. May we come in and ask you a few questions?'

'No, it's not convenient and I have nothing to say to you. Graham and I worked together for the social services, and I met Colin through him. We became friends and often played a round of golf together. I haven't seen either of them for months. And I have no idea who murdered them. So, push off and leave me alone,' he announced and slammed the door in their faces.

The man's rudeness infuriated Hayley, who was about to ring the bell when Dane stopped her. 'Don't worry, I'm not that bothered about him now. He's not the tall man we're after.'

They found one more Stephen that day, and he wasn't their man either.

On their return to the office, Sally met them with some news. 'Gareth Neil had only arrived back in the country the morning he was in the supermarket. He'd been in Rome.'

'I wonder where he is now, then,' Dane replied and described their day tracking down the Stephens. 'This'll take a while. How're you getting on with the witnesses who are ringing in?'

'We spoke to three people yesterday. They were in the Agnes Brown home during the relevant period and all have reported abuse.'

Dane and Hayley spent the next three days on a fruitless road trip around southern England meeting the people on the telephone list, but none of them were who they were after.

Jane came with them on the fourth day and watched as they called on and interviewed another three potential Stephens. Hayley had just driven round a bend at the end of a long stretch of road when Dane asked her to pull over and park in a small dirt lay-by.

'What's up?' Jane said.

'I've had a feeling someone's watching us,' Dane replied.

'I haven't spotted anyone,' Hayley replied.

'Nor have I, to be honest. I just have this sense that someone's there.'

They sat in silence for a minute and watched the next three cars that passed them.

'Are you two winding me up?' Jane said.

Hayley turned around in her seat and looked at the journalist. 'I assure you we're not. I've seen the boss do this before and he's usually been right.'

'What? You just feel like someone's there?'

'I get a sensation on the back of my neck. I know it sounds bonkers, but it usually indicates someone's watching.'

'Have you always been able to do that?'

'It developed when I was in Ireland, and I've never lost it.'

'You're spooky.'

'I have been told that once or twice. But I ignore the feeling at my peril, as I discovered last year when I was shot.'

'What do you mean?'

'When I tailed the suspect for the five murders I investigated last year, I knew someone was following me and I didn't pay enough attention. The feeling was right because the man who nearly killed me was right behind me that day.'

'Had it happened before?' Jane said.

Dane was silent for a moment then smiled. 'This is not for publication, got that?'

Jane nodded vigorously, her eyes shining.

'On one of the first live operations I worked on in Ireland I was following a known gunman. The team had been behind him for a couple of hours when he led me through a couple of turns in the middle of an estate in Belfast. It wasn't a republican area so not a particularly high risk, but I had this growing sense that something wasn't right. He went down a side street and I was about to follow when the hairs on the back of my head stood on end, and I felt this strong tingling sensation. I just knew someone was watching me.'

'What did you do?' Jane asked.

'I didn't take the turn. I walked straight on and aborted the operation. The cops were informed later it had been a set-up. If I'd have followed, I'd have walked into an ambush. There'd been spotters watching the gunman's back. So, that's why I always take the feeling seriously.'

'I can see why. What was it like working under those conditions? I'm tempted to ask if it was exciting?'

'It was sometimes. Most of the time it was tense and stressful. You knew if you made the smallest slip you could die.'

'But you were always armed, weren't you? You could fight back?'

'Yes, we were but that didn't always save you. Look what happened to me that day in Derry. I was nearly shot with my own weapon.'

'Have you carried a gun since joining the police?'

'I served on two units where I had to train in firearms. But I haven't done anything like that for years now.'

'But you were still able to shoot straight last year.'

'Learning to fire a gun is like riding a bike. If you're taught to do it properly you never forget,' Dane said, then smiled. 'I think that's quite enough about me. We should employ Jane for her interrogation techniques, eh,' he said to Hayley.

'Yeah. I've never heard you open up like that before,' Hayley replied and nodded to Jane.

'First time for everything. I haven't felt any tingling for the last few minutes, so if someone was there, they must have gone home. Come òn, let's head to the office,' Dane said.

Sally was waiting for them, barely able to contain her excitement. 'We have firm evidence of child abuse from three women and a man. They all identify Parr, Binks and Wilson as their principal abusers and describe Gareth Neil and the mysterious Stephen. They were all petrified of him – he sounds a vicious piece of work.'

'Well done. We've had no luck so far, although there were two men we visited this afternoon who'll need some more looking at. One of them fainted when we appeared at his door.'

'He was a revolting little creep,' Hayley muttered.

'Is there any news on Vonn?'

'I popped round earlier and she looked awful. I think she's much worse than she's letting on.'

Dane rang her, and she answered in a weak voice.

'How're you feeling?'

'Not good. I've been puking all day and I'll leave the rest to your imagination.'

She sounded drained, so he didn't push her. 'Is there anything you need?'

'No, thank you, I have the television and a couple of good books to keep me entertained. How's the investigation doing?'

He told her what they'd discovered, and the news seemed to cheer her up a bit. 'I hope you're back with us before too long. Look after yourself.'

Dane rang the pub in Weston and spoke to Steph. 'You remember I asked you to think about giving evidence in court if we catch them?'

'Yes, but it's a big step for us both to consider, especially Gerry. She's doing well here, and I don't want to jeopardise that. Would you thank Hayley for organising the counsellor?'

'I will, but please think about what I said. The more victim testimony we can provide to the court, the better.'

'We are talking about it, and we'll give you a decision soon, I promise. Have you found Julie yet?'

'No. It looks like she doesn't want to be found.'

'That doesn't surprise me. And if she knows what's been happening, she'll rub her hands with glee.'

Dane spent his evening mulling over the day and what Steph had said. He was sure the men he was meeting were customers of Parr's and Binks's, all loathsome little creatures who were petrified at the sight of police officers on their doorsteps. They were all married and living a comfortable life with their wives and children around them. Each had a sordid secret, and he hated them all for the hypocrites they were. The tingling sensation returned as they did their rounds, visiting the last four. He was certain now they were being followed, but again, saw no one.

Sobers rang to inform Dane the CPS had sanctioned charges against both Phelan and Boyd. They were due to appear in court for their first hearing later in the week.

'Did Phelan offer any explanation?' Dane asked.

'He said he has serious, unmanageable gambling debts, and owes money to some dangerous people. Boyd found out somehow and threatened to expose him if he didn't pass him the information. In return, he paid him.'

'And what did Boyd say?'

'Nothing except to lay all the blame on Phelan, so they'll rip each other apart in court. I've no sympathy for him, and nor should you.'

'I haven't,' Dane replied, and told Sobers the latest from the investigation.

'So, you still haven't tracked down Stephen.'

'No, and we've exhausted the list. Sally and her team are building a powerful case against him so we must locate him.'

'What's next?'

'Mrs Parr, to see if she'll identify him.'

'Good idea, consider the trip authorised. Keep me posted.'

Brian White answered the call and from the dialling tone, Dane realised he was abroad.

'Hi, it's Dane.'

'What can I do for you?'

'I need to speak to Joyce Parr again and it's urgent.'

'Give me ten minutes,' White replied, and hung up without further explanation, which struck Dane as odd.

True to his word, he was soon back. 'There's a flight from Stansted at eleven thirty tomorrow morning. Can you be on it?'

'Of course. What's happening?'

'Can't explain now. Will you be bringing anyone with you?'

Dane gave him Hayley's details.

'If you both go to the Special Branch office at the airport, they'll smooth you through to the plane. I'll meet you in Bergerac.'

*

They landed in France the following afternoon and the immigration agents waved them past the queue to White, who was waiting beside a police car. As soon as the doors closed, the driver took off, a cloud of gravel spewing out behind them as he flicked on the blue lights and siren.

'What's going on?' Dane said.

'Sorry about all the cloak-and-dagger stuff. We were on the verge of making a series of arrests yesterday when something unexpected happened. A covered lorry arrived at the Parr place. It contained twenty women and children. They're all being held in the garage. When they move, the plan is to rescue them and arrest everyone in the house.'

'That explains the rush. But why bring us out here? We won't be able to talk to her for days.'

'There are a couple of men staying with her. The gendarme commander wants to see if you can identify them, and he's prepared to let you speak to her. It'll be helpful to all of us.'

They eventually turned onto an unmade road that went up a steep hill, passing a large property where children were riding horses round a paddock. Half a mile beyond, they arrived at the farmhouse across the valley from the Parr property that Dane had admired on his last visit. The police had commandeered the house and turned it into a command centre. A dozen black-clad cops were lounging beside their patrol cars parked in a barn. In the kitchen, more officers were sitting in front of four monitors displaying the Parr residence, each from a different angle. They had the place surrounded.

A tough-looking gendarme officer rose and shook hands with his visitors. '*Bonjour, Commissaire, je suis Colonel Patrick Paul, l'officier responsable.*'

'He doesn't speak much English, so I'll have to translate,' White said. 'He'd like you to have a look at the people by the pool.'

Colonel Paul led them into the sitting room and pointed to binoculars on tripods trained out of the window. Dane settled down and focused on the buildings half a mile away on the other side of the valley. The sun was beating down, and the heat rebounded from the landscape. A shimmering haze in the air made the buildings in the distance look like they were wobbling. Two men and Joyce Parr were sitting next to the pool. She had a glass in her hand, and they were all deep in conversation as another man appeared and sat beside her. Even from that range, and despite only having seen him on CCTV footage, Dane was sure one of the men was Gareth Neil. The others had their backs to him, but the shaven head and slight stature of one was familiar. He turned, exposing his profile and the black beard, which had grown considerably since Dane had last seen him.

'The fellow next to Joyce is Neil. On the left, with his back to us, is Dragon Hyka, but I don't recognise the other guy.'

White translated that to Paul, who grinned and clenched his fist. *'Bon,'* he said and left the room.

'They understand how dangerous Dragon is, don't they?' Dane said.

'This lot will take care of him.'

'What do we do now?'

'We wait,' White replied, and settled down beside them.

A young officer brought them coffee and sandwiches as they watched. Dane panned around with his binoculars and studied the property. The pool was on a long patio with a retaining wall around it. The land fell away outside the curtilage for about two hundred yards through heavy scrub to the road in the valley. At the corner of the patio was a brick shed which, Dane assumed, housed the filters and pumps for the pool. Joyce Parr got up to recharge her glass, and it was interesting to watch the pantomime of gesticulations from the group as they conversed. After half an hour, the unknown man stood up and disappeared inside, reappearing a few minutes later for a brief conversation before they all followed him inside the house.

'Where are the other arrests being made?'

'Naples, Paris and safe houses on the route they use.'

'Anywhere in the UK?'

'A house in Acton and another in West Sussex, where we should pick up some targets. We're not expecting to find any victims, although you never know with these jobs. And two addresses in Manchester.'

'Were you going to tell me?'

'Only after we'd completed the arrests. Sorry.'

Dane realised the leaks from his office caused this lack of trust and understood the position White was in. He told him how they'd trapped Phelan and about Binks's and Parr's attempt to rent a house in Essex.

'The Parrs made the Italian connection a few years ago and set up the route into Britain. We'd not heard any mention of Binks before his murder, but I'm sure you're right and he was part of the set-up. There's a never-ending supply of human cargo for their filthy business, and we can't keep up. The criminal gang's profits are off the scale and outstrip the drugs trade. The risk is much less with people smuggling, and many of the victims will take their chances if it means a better life for themselves.'

'Do the kids have any say in the matter?' Dane asked.

'No, not really. Some parents sell their children, but they kidnap most of them. Promises of good jobs trick the women and they only realise they've made a dreadful mistake when it's too late. We'll never eradicate it unless we have the resources, but that's the usual refrain from us coppers. As long as they keep the true extent of the problem out of the public eye, the politicians get away with doing nothing.'

'Will you publicise the raids?'

'There should be some coverage, but only for a second on the late news. And as most of this is taking place on mainland Europe, I can't guarantee that much at home.'

'I might be able to do something about that,' Dane replied, thinking about Jane.

There was a shout from the kitchen and the sound of vehicle engines starting in the yard outside.

'Something's happening,' White said and popped out. He returned as all the vehicles roared out of the farmyard.

'They're about to hit the place. They've all gone except for one officer who'll look after us.'

A heavy silence descended over the farmhouse, and they settled down behind the binoculars in the sitting room to watch the excitement. Half an hour later they watched as a Mercedes truck pulled out of the Parr courtyard. It paused at the gate, then turned and headed down the hill towards the nearby village. As it stopped at a T-junction, an armoured police vehicle suddenly appeared and blocked the road as another burst through a hedge behind it.

'Blimey, they don't muck about, do they?' Hayley muttered.

Commandos hauled three men out of the cab and dropped them face down on the ground. It was slick and all over in seconds. They opened the rear doors and released a gaggle of frightened women and children, leading them into the nearby farmyard. More police vehicles skidded to a halt outside the Parr residence disgorging gendarmes who invaded the house. Dane caught a movement by the pool out of the corner of his eye and squinted through the binoculars. He focused in on Dragon as he sprinted across the patio and into the little shed, pulling the door closed behind him.

'Did you see that?' he said to White.

'What?' he replied, and Dane described what he'd seen.

A message was passed to the raiders, and they watched as six officers cautiously approached the shed and surrounded it. Dane remained glued to the binoculars as one commando kicked the door open and another threw a flash-bang pyrotechnic in. They saw the series of explosions and blinding flashes, then seconds later listened to the thunderclaps echoing over the landscape as the lead officer barged in. He reappeared alone and pressed the key to his radio. Moments later, the young officer asked White a question.

'They're saying it's empty.'

'There must be another exit because I saw him go in that way and he hasn't come out. Tell them to check again and be careful.'

The message was transmitted, and the officers returned to the shed. Dane turned his binoculars to the slope below the property, sweeping the ground.

'They have put a cordon in, haven't they?'

'I'm not privy to their plans for the assault, but they must have,' White replied.

Dane caught a flash of something pale against the foliage and searched the area, which was only about a hundred yards from the road. They all heard two distinct pops and recognised them as gunshots coming from below their position. Dane tracked the binoculars right to left, and saw a figure sprint into the scrub below the building they were in.

'Brian, it's Dragon. He's armed and heading up here. Probably looking for a vehicle or somewhere to hide. You'd better tell this young lad to whistle up some support, then prepare to repel boarders.'

White spoke to the gendarme, who radioed for help, then drew his sidearm and watched Dane, who was still peering intently through the binoculars.

'Got you,' he whispered. 'He's coming straight for us.'

They all went into the kitchen where the door was ajar, and the officer took up a position just inside. The rest of them stood back and waited. Dane watched through the window as Dragon burst out of the undergrowth twenty yards from the building and hesitated for a second. He was panting and bathed in sweat and had obviously not realised this property was the police observation point. As he stepped towards the open kitchen door, the gendarme moved through it, covering him with his pistol.

'Levez les mains – ou je tire,' he shouted, his voice shaking.

Dragon stopped dead in his tracks, a look of astonishment on his face that twisted into a snarl as he half turned to his right, his hand going behind his hip. In a flash, he pivoted, bringing up a pistol, and fired twice. Dane winced at the thud of the bullets impacting the cop's body before he crashed into the door frame. Everything seemed to slide into slow motion. As the officer fell, he dropped his SIG Pro pistol, which clattered across the flagstone floor, rebounded off the sink unit and spun in the air before settling in front of Dane. He saw the shock on Hayley's face and the fear on White's as he snatched up the pistol and took a firing position in the doorway.

Dane was protected by the thick farmhouse wall with only his arm extended, the weapon now covering Dragon.

'Drop it…'

The Albanian didn't hesitate before firing a snap shot towards Dane, who felt something slap into his cheek. He flinched and fell back half a pace. By the time he aimed back through the door, Dragon had gone. He slammed the heavy wooden door and shot the old iron bolt.

Hayley and White had propped the French officer up in a chair. He was shaking like a leaf and gasping for breath as he stared at the damage to his ballistic vest.

Hayley glanced up. 'Where is he?'

'I don't know.' He turned to White. 'Get on the radio and tell them Dragon is here and we need back-up fast.'

'You're bleeding,' Hayley said. She grabbed a cloth from the sink and dabbed his cheek. 'You'll live. It's just a scratch.'

'Thanks. Keep your heads down.' Dane checked the pistol. The magazine was full and there was one round in the chamber. He moved to the sitting room window and just caught sight of Dragon walking round the back. Dane moved to the half-glazed side door of the house and watched as Dragon peered into the barn then turn and hesitate, as if unsure what to do next. Dane pulled the door open and shouted.

'Freeze, Dragon. Drop the gun, you can't get away.'

Immediately the Albanian turned and ran, firing four shots wildly behind him, causing Dane to step back before taking aim at the receding back. He didn't fire. Dragon was heading down the hill and away so was no longer a threat. Then he remembered the children riding their horses. Dragon was running in their direction, so he followed. By the time he reached the road, Dragon was fifty yards in front and sprinting hard, not looking behind. As he ran Dane heard the distinctive two-tone wailing of police sirens in the distance and hoped they were the gendarmes returning. Dragon must have heard them as well because he slowed and darted off the road into dense woodland. Dane too swerved into the trees and saw Dragon thirty yards in front of him. Then he lost sight of his quarry. He slowed, taking a position behind a tree. Complete silence. Dane scanned the undergrowth but couldn't see Dragon. The heat of the afternoon was oppressive. He wiped his brow and his cheek stung as sweat ran into the cut. Two police vehicles sped up the hill towards the farmhouse. Once they'd passed, Dragon burst from his cover and moved downhill. Dane went after him; Dragon was moving more slowly so he could gain ground. Now Dane heard voices shouting from behind him. Dragon turned and spotted Dane and, with a look of fury, fired. Dane was forced to duck and move for cover to his left. His foot hit the crumbling edge of a deep depression, which gave way, sending him tumbling down the slope to land with a thump at the bottom. He'd lost his pistol and frantically scrabbled for it through the long grass and leaf litter. He heard footsteps and turned to find Dragon advancing.

'You've interfered once too often,' he snarled, and lifted his pistol.

There was nothing Dane could do; he was trapped and unarmed. He closed his eyes and waited for the inevitable shock of the bullet. Images of his parents, Robyn and Vicky flashed through his mind's eye and he held his breath. There was a shot, and he flinched, then another followed by a ragged fusillade, but he felt nothing. He opened his eyes as Dragon fell, riddled with shots. Dane looked up and saw three gendarmes and Colonel Paul on the rim of the depression, their weapons at the aim.

*

Dane and Hayley were taken to the main police station in Bergerac, where the investigators took their statements. They spent the night in a comfortable guesthouse and, after a breakfast of coffee and pastries, met Colonel Paul in his office. White held a muted conversation with Paul before informing Dane that a gendarme had been found dead on the road below the farmhouse.

'I suppose that accounts for the shots I heard before I spotted Dragon,' Dane said.

'They're all devastated. Apart from that, the operation was a success. The preliminary interviews have started and the examining magistrate will allow you to talk to them later today,' White said.

It wasn't until late in the afternoon that they were shown into a small room where Neil was waiting, handcuffed to a table. He stared at them with a blank expression.

'I understand the prosecutor has charged you,' Dane said.

'So they've informed me. It's an outrage. I've done nothing wrong. I was just visiting Mrs Parr,' he replied, his voice shaking with indignation. 'Who're you? Are you from the consulate?'

'No, we're British police officers. I'm in charge of the investigation into the murders of Parr, Wilson, Binks, Lowe and Patey.'

'What's that to me?'

'I suspect you're next on the killer's list. Have you any idea why you should be?'

'None whatsoever. It's a tragedy that Colin should die like that, especially after all his public service. I was shocked and saddened to hear about his death. But it has nothing to do with me.'

'Why are you here in France?'

'I've been a friend of the Parr family for many years. I was helping Joyce through her grief.'

'Why did you leave your home so abruptly?'

Neil's head snapped up. 'What do you mean?'

'You left your flat in Chelmsford the same day you arrived back from a trip to Italy.'

'I don't know what you're talking about.'

'It's no good trying to mess me about. I've got you in technicolour CCTV footage in the supermarket and later that afternoon leaving the country. So, why did you?'

Dane watched his expression as he tried to come up with a plausible excuse for his actions.

'Mr Neil, what was your role at the Agnes Brown children's home?'

'Graham employed me on a casual contract to provide remedial lessons to the children. They were all tough kids and not doing too well at school.'

'You're not a qualified teacher, are you?'

'No, but you didn't need to be to do what I was doing for them.'

'How did you know Binks?'

'We'd done similar work together before and he trusted me.'

'And how about Wilson, Lowe and Joiner?'

'They all worked there, and we saw a bit of each other while we carried out our duties.'

'And did you see each other socially?'

'No,' he replied, his face now a deathly pale and a sheen of sweat appearing on his upper lip.

'But you used to spend a great deal of time together, didn't you? All of you in the house in Chelmsford.'

'I have no idea what you're on about.'

'Oh, but you do. Where you and your accomplices abused those children.'

Neil tried to get up, but the handcuffs restrained him. 'How dare you accuse me of this muck? Guard, help me,' he squealed.

'Who's Stephen?'

'Stephen – Stephen who?'

'You were there with him while you were raping Julie Miller and the other children. Stephen, with the smart suits and silk ties and foul taste in pipe tobacco. Where is he?'

238

Neil fell silent and slumped in the chair, face ashen. 'I refuse to say anything more without my solicitor,' he stammered.

'You all abused these poor kids for years, you committed unspeakable acts on them, and now you're going to pay for it. The others are dead, and you are next. Stephen, or whatever his real name is, is also in danger, so I'll ask you again. Who is he and where can I find him? He'll die if you don't tell me.'

'I intend to make an official complaint about your behaviour at the first opportunity,' Neil blustered.

'You'll have to wait until the authorities here have finished with you. On your release, I'll be waiting for you in Britain with another tranche of charges. There's a queue of your victims eager to make statements about what happened to them while they were in your care. They're identifying you and your friends, not that there's many left alive. And if you think a French jail is unpleasant, imagine what it'll be like residing at His Majesty's pleasure convicted of child sex crimes.'

'You're bluffing. You wouldn't come in here making these bizarre allegations unless you were trying it on. Well, I won't fall for that.'

'You misunderstand me. I don't need any admission from you. I have the evidence to charge you with sexual abuse and multiple rapes of boys and girls, and I will do so. If the French choose not to detain you, I'll execute my European arrest warrant and extradite you to Britain. I've come to ask you for information about the smartly dressed, well-spoken man who raped the children with you. I'm asking you to identify him to me so I can prevent his murder. If you're not prepared to help your friend, that's up to you. Goodbye.'

They stood, and Hayley banged on the door. As they waited, Dane ignored Neil, who stared at the tabletop. His whole body was shaking with fear.

Joyce Parr looked pale and her hands shook. This was probably less to do with dread than the fact she'd not had a drink for nearly twenty-four hours, Dane guessed. She wore a prison tracksuit and her usual carefully arranged coiffure was lank and drawn back in a ponytail. She drew deeply on a cigarette, blowing the stream of smoke over her shoulder as if attempting to spare them a face full of nicotine.

'It looks like I'm in the shit,' Joyce said.

'You're in about as deep a pile of it as I've ever seen.'

'What are you after now?'

'The identity of Stephen. He was a friend of your husband's, and they abused children together in Chelmsford.'

'I don't know any of them,' she replied, deadpan.

'Apart from Binks and Neil and Patey.'

'Okay, if you're going to be pedantic, I knew them.'

'I might believe you'd never met Lowe or Joiner, but not Stephen. You know him all right.'

'What's in it for me if I give you what you want?'

'Nothing.'

She looked up, anger flashing in her eyes. 'You've come to me. You need me, so start negotiating.'

'There's no deal on the table. I'd like to find Stephen before the killer does. If you tell me his name and I'm able to prevent another murder, then that might go in your favour. If you don't, and he dies before I can help him, then I'll ensure it goes against you. But I'll find him whatever you do.'

She glared at him while furiously puffing on her cigarette. 'Will they let me serve my sentence in a British jail?'

'It's a possibility, I suppose. Why?'

'The food in here is awful and the other women won't speak to me. At least in dear old Blighty I might get the occasional shag,' she said, then shrieked with laughter.

'Do you know the man I'm looking for?'

'Of course I do, but I'm not telling you who he is,' she sneered. 'He'd never lift a finger to help me. But I'll tell you this for free, Mr Policeman. Be careful, because he's powerful and ruthless, and that's all I'm prepared to say. And now I want to go back to my cell. Try not to slam the door on your pinkies on the way out.'

'That's just about the evillest bitch I've ever had the misfortune to meet. I hope she rots in hell,' Hayley said.

30

You could hear a pin drop in the chief's office when Dane finished his report. Wix appeared stunned as Sobers slowly shook his head. The chief constable looked thoughtfully at Dane and Hayley, and then said, 'I hope you're both okay after your experiences?'

'I'm fine, ma'am,' Hayley replied. 'Although if we can keep the excitement to a minimum for a few days, I'd be grateful.'

Everyone laughed except Wix. 'I think the pair of you should take some time off and we'll refer you to the welfare department, to be on the safe side.'

'I don't want a holiday, thanks,' Hayley said.

'You've both had a traumatic experience,' Wix said. 'We must look after you. As an employer, we're duty-bound to ensure you're not damaged by it all.'

'We did our job, and I'd like to carry on doing it.'

'That is not your decision, Constable.'

'Yes, it is, actually,' Dane shot back. 'We still have work to do. I don't need looking after and nor does Hayley. I'm not bothered by what happened.'

'And that's my point. You should be. Your reaction isn't normal,' Wix said.

Dane held her gaze for a moment. 'Who are you to decide what is or is not normal? You know about my background, training and experience. Dragon was attempting to escape. He'd already shot two people and would have slaughtered us without a second thought. We gave him every opportunity to surrender, but he took a chance and lost. I have all the support I require, and I'll ensure Hayley has as well. But we both want to get back to work.'

'If you're sure, then do that,' the chief constable said and sent them on their way.

As they drove to the incident room, Hayley turned to Dane. 'What's the matter with Wix?'

'Part of it is the inexperienced manager wanting to tick the right box. The rest is her being unable to understand how someone can survive an experience like that without having a mental breakdown,' Dane replied.

'It can't be good for you, though.'

'It isn't, and it will have an effect, but I know where to go to sort that out. And I have my therapist's card in my pocket for you. I strongly advise you to give her a ring.'

'Thanks, boss. I'll take you up on that.'

*

The team had been busy while they'd been away. Another six people had contacted the incident room following the appeal, and Sally described what they'd reported.

'The evidence is getting stronger every day. The head of social services has set up a review of all the other homes in the county and our investigations have come to the notice of some councillors. They're concerned about what this will do to their reputation.'

'That's their lookout,' Dane retorted. 'If they'd done their job properly in the first place, they wouldn't have this issue to confront, would they? How about the church? Has there been any feedback on that side?'

'No, nothing,' Sally replied.

'How are the other enquiries progressing?'

'We're working on the victim statements and we aren't getting much done on the murders. To be honest, there isn't a lot left to do apart from tracking down Stephen and Julie Miller, so we can handle it.'

'How's Vonn?'

'She's been to her doctor who's signed her off sick for a month. I visited her yesterday and she looks dreadful. It turns out she has a pre-existing disorder that's flared up. She is very poorly but in good spirits and fed up to be missing the action.'

'I'll give her a buzz later.'

Hayley had hit a brick wall in her quest to find Julie. 'I've never had a case like this before. I'm normally able to track them down, but this lady doesn't want to be found. There's nothing anywhere about her from the time she ran from the home. She might be dead,

I suppose, but there are no records to support that. If someone had murdered her, there'd be a spare body floating around, and there isn't. There are no outstanding misper reports that refer to her or anyone who fits her description. There are no bank accounts or credit cards that belong to her I can identify.'

'Is it difficult to assume another identity?'

'It's surprisingly easy, especially twenty years ago. I think that's what she did and covered her tracks effectively.'

'Keep looking,' he replied and left her to it.

Dane got changed for a run on the treadmill in the gym, which meant he could concentrate on his thoughts and not on the road ahead. The exercise cleared his head and as he jogged he considered how to identify the man he believed would be the next target of the killer.

He came back to his desk energised and called in Reece Lewin. 'Did the diary ever reappear?'

'No, Phelan must have swiped it.'

'Never mind, it's gone. I want to see the search records from each of the murder scenes, please.'

Dane spent hours poring over what they'd recovered. There was precious little from Parr's home, apart from the contents of the attic. The French had let him have a look round the house in Bergerac, but there'd been nothing there to help him either. He did the same with the others, leaving the contents of Patey's bedsit till last.

Dane still didn't fully understand why he'd been murdered. Yes, he'd raped the girls but that aside, Patey was as much a victim as them. So why did he have to die? There were hundreds of DVDs and CDs and piles of magazines, books and newspapers recovered from Patey's flat.

Dane surveyed the dozen boxes stacked in the corner and, with a sigh, opened the first one and worked his way through its contents. It contained a mixture of local and national papers with many dating back ten years. Dane could see no reason why Patey had kept them, and only gave them a cursory glance.

The next was full of comics and Commando war story booklets. They'd once been popular and Patey had amassed two hundred of them, the oldest dating from the sixties. Those, together with copies of *Beano* and other comic publications from the seventies and eighties, caused Dane to look at it all with a new perspective.

Dane, like everyone else, had assumed that Patey was a slovenly man who hoarded paper and junk. These publications showed he had an excellent reason for hanging on to it all; he was a collector.

As he rummaged through the boxes, a system became clear. The various piles of newspapers all corresponded to a particular period. In the last box he found twenty scrapbooks, all dated, and the earliest begun when Patey lived in the Maldon children's home. Dane flicked through the pages, all filled with newspaper cuttings about footballers and matches. Patey didn't support any specific team, but liked to cut out and save stories about the sport. As he'd got older, Dane saw his fascination changed to crime.

Several small articles mentioning Patey's own early appearances in court for shoplifting had pride of place. There was nothing relating to the rape allegation. A thought occurred to Dane and he turned his attention back to the newspapers and discovered that each pile related to a particular crime.

The biggest group contained stories about the arrest and conviction of Wilson. Dane read each paper cover to cover and discovered many missing pictures, which had been neatly snipped out and carefully pasted into the scrapbooks. There were more collections covering investigations run by Parr, and a story about Binks and his retirement. There were dozens more photographs and clippings relating to other men Dane didn't recognise.

Were these more of Patey's customers, Dane wondered. Had Patey been indulging in a spot of blackmail?

Dane opened the last scrapbook and leafed through it, finding several pictures of Parr, some including Joyce, at black-tie functions. He turned the page and froze at the sight of a black and white press cutting with the Parrs smiling at the camera. Next to them stood a man with a moustache and receding hair. They were all wearing evening dress, but from the left lapel of the stranger's dinner jacket a heavy watch chain ran into the top pocket.

Was this the mysterious Stephen? Dane felt excitement course through him and searched unsuccessfully through all the other papers, trying to identify which one it came from. He called Reece and Sally in and showed them what he'd discovered.

'I'd say this is at least twenty years old,' Sally said.

'Why?'

'Because of the style of the clothes, and Parr looks much younger than when he died. I haven't seen his missus, but she's only in her late forties here.'

Dane studied the picture again and agreed with her. That would mean this picture was taken towards the end of Parr's police service.

*

An hour later, Mrs Morgan led Dane into her front room. Her husband lay on his bed, looking much thinner now.

'I'm sorry to disturb you, but I have an urgent question,' Dane said.

'Ask away. I've nothing else to do at the moment.'

'I wondered if you might recognise the man in this picture with Parr.'

Morgan looked at it. 'Oh yes, I know him,' he whispered, without hesitation and Dane held his breath.

31

'His name is Sir Richard Francis. He's the last of a family of wealthy landed-gentry snobs who once regarded themselves as leaders of the county set. His father was a baronet and a gentle old buffer who turned a blind eye to his only son's escapades. When his father died, Richard Francis inherited an estate of more than a thousand acres of prime farmland and the title. He served as a local councillor for over twenty years. His friends got him onto the police authority by dint of political shenanigans, and that's where I first met him. He's always carried the whiff of trouble about him.'

'You know a lot about him and his background.'

'When you reach the dizzy heights I did, it helps to know who infests the quagmire you need to lower yourself into and understand the politics. Francis was arrogant and incompetent, and we didn't get on. He blocked my application for Chief Constable.'

'Why did he do that?'

'Because I refused to kowtow to him. He's a classic bully and doesn't like people who stand up to him. In the end he fell foul of the expenses scandal. His opponents in the ward scrutinised his record and gave what they found to a local journalist who exposed his fraudulent activities. The establishment wouldn't have survived another lashing by the media, so they let him retire. Since then, he's blown his inheritance on all manner of excesses.'

'Did his name ever come up during your investigation?'

'No, it didn't. But there was at least one man I never identified because of the fear he inspired in all the victims. None of them would even give me a description.'

'The people we're speaking to all describe a strange smell about him and a chain he always wore that went into the top pocket of his jacket.'

'There's an impressive gold hunter watch on the end of that. A twenty-first birthday present from his father, a family heirloom. He habitually smokes a pipe and favours the most appalling tobacco that stinks everywhere out, so it sounds like you've found your man. Well done.'

Dane thanked him and left, hoping he could give him a satisfactory conclusion to the investigation he'd started all those years ago. He needed to get a move on; it was obvious Morgan didn't have long. Dane contacted Hayley and they met at the incident room where they researched the former councillor. It was late afternoon when they arrived at the large shabby Georgian farmhouse set in about two acres of open Essex countryside.

Dane rang the doorbell but received no reply. He wandered around the residence. There was an old stable block, now converted into a garage, which was empty. At the rear, a wide paved patio overlooked the unkempt garden, which must once have been impressive. Someone had recently mown the extensive lawn but left the cuttings on the ground. The overgrown shrubs and a few of the larger trees looked like they'd blow over in a stiff breeze. A delightful view stretched over miles of open countryside that had once belonged to the family. All disposed of by the wastrel son to pay his debts, it turned out. Dane saw lights twinkling from the nearest neighbour, who was at least a mile away.

They waited for nearly two hours before the roar of a powerful engine shattered the evening calm. A bright red E-type Jaguar appeared and stopped outside the front door in a shower of dust and gravel. The man who got out of the driver's seat glared at the strange car and his visitors.

'Are you Sir Richard Francis?' Dane said.

'Yes, that's me. Who the devil are you?'

'I'm Detective Superintendent Dane from Essex Police. I'd like to have a word with you if I may.'

'What about?'

'I believe you might be in considerable danger.'

Francis looked Dane up and down, as if surveying an underling. He was running to fat with receding hair but still had the moustache, while the heavy antique gold chain glinted on his lapel. Apart from his tweed jacket, he wore buff-coloured cavalry twill trousers and brown brogues. Given that his clothes were probably expensive and handmade, he didn't carry them well, looking scruffy and down at heel.

Francis held his hand out and snapped his fingers. 'ID,' he demanded. 'Is she with you?' he grunted, nodding towards Hayley as he inspected Dane's warrant card.

'This is Detective Constable Cross and, yes, she's with me.'

'Come on, then, let's hear what you've got to say.' He led the way into a vast sitting room where he opened tall French windows to let in the cool evening air and waved them towards chairs. Wood panelling and bookcases lined the walls with old, threadbare furniture arranged around an enormous stone fireplace.

Francis took up position in front of the hearth and pulled a pipe and large tobacco pouch from his pocket. He carefully loaded it and lit a match; once it was burning to his satisfaction, he blew a stream of smoke out.

'Right, get on with it,' he barked, standing with his feet apart and hand on hip.

'I'm leading the investigation into the murders of five men in Essex,' Dane said, watching for a reaction.

'Yes, yes, I read the papers. What's it to do with me?'

'We've received information that leads me to believe you're in danger of being attacked and killed by the person responsible.'

Francis puffed and expelled a stream of smoke, the gurgling from the bowl the only sound in the room. He peered into it, and then tamped the tobacco down.

'That sounds unlikely. What makes you think that?'

'Do you recall Detective Chief Superintendent Parr from your time on the police authority?'

He made a show of furrowing his brow and gazing up at the ceiling. 'I bumped into so many plods in those days. It's possible I did, I suppose.'

'Perhaps this will jog your memory,' Dane said, showing him the press cutting.

Francis glanced at the picture and shook his head. 'Those bloody awful receptions and events happened every day. I attended hundreds of them and can't possibly remember everyone I met.'

'How about the Reverend Wilson or Graham Binks?'

'No, those names mean nothing to me.'

'That's a powerful brew you're smoking.'

Francis glanced at his pipe and smiled. 'It's a blend of several strong tobaccos and not for the faint-hearted. I have a useful little man in London who knocks it up for me. I developed the habit at university and could never break it. Probably why I'm still single,' he announced, and laughed.

'Does anyone else smoke that brand of tobacco, to your knowledge?'

'No, it's my own recipe, so to speak. Listen, get to the point, would you? I'm expecting visitors.'

'The reason for this visit is to inform you of a threat to your life. All the victims committed crimes against children. They died because of that involvement and the same person killed them all.'

'So what?'

'You knew them all, and some might even have been your friends. You all used to meet at a house in Chelmsford, where you took an active part in that abuse.'

Francis was about to put the pipe in his mouth but froze. 'I beg your pardon, are you accusing me of something?'

'Yes, I am. I have evidence that associates you with the murdered men and the rape of children. Because of your involvement, you're at risk of being killed yourself.'

Francis's face turned puce, and he pointed the stem of the pipe at Dane. 'Have you any idea who I am? Do you think I'm the sort of person to put up with your bully-boy tactics, eh? You'd better go away before I lose my rag completely, you impertinent shit.'

Dane was about to arrest him when the hairs on his neck stood up. It was as strong a sensation as he'd ever felt and stopped him in his tracks. He spun and walked to the window and stared out, trying to spot the watcher he was sure was there. He scanned the treeline a hundred yards away for any sign. Francis seized on his silence and growled, 'Get out. You're a chancer and I'll be contacting the chief constable about your behaviour.'

'I urge you to come with me, for your own protection,' Dane replied, and then saw it. The sudden movement in the trees, a fleeting shadow, paler than the surrounding undergrowth – but there. Then he realised how they'd been followed.

'You must think I came over on the last banana boat with your friend here. I'm going nowhere, but you are, and you can take your dusky assistant with you.' Francis hustled them out and slammed the door behind them.

Hayley clenched her fists with anger. 'What're you up to? We have more than enough to nick that bastard,' she said, then hurried after Dane to the car.

'You drive,' he stated.

Hayley looked surprised but did what he asked.

'Someone's watching us. Keep going.'

'What? How do you know that?'

'I saw them in the treeline. There's probably a tracker on this car, that's how they've been following us. If we stay here, or they don't see the car leave, or we start blundering around the woods searching, they'll back off for another day and we lose the element of surprise. There's a junction about a mile down the road. As we reach it, slow down and let me out. You go straight back to the incident office but call and put the cavalry on standby. I'll circle round and watch the house. Leave this car there and return but wait about a mile out from the house. Whatever you do, don't come back here until I contact you, all right?'

'Okay, you're the boss.'

Dane pulled the rear seat down and hauled his kitbag in from the boot. He took his suit jacket off and replaced it with a dark fleece.

'We're approaching the junction,' she warned.

'Slow right down and I'll jump out.' Hayley nodded, and as she made the turn, he opened the door and hopped out. His forward momentum sent him sprawling into a ditch, but it was dry, and he landed softly.

As the car disappeared into the evening, Dane got his bearings and waited for his eyesight to adjust to the gathering gloom. He had a mental image of the surrounding countryside from his study of the maps earlier. It didn't take him long to trot the hundred yards to a wood which backed onto the property. He picked his way slowly through the undergrowth, carefully studying his route and the surrounding area, listening out for the suspect. It took him fifteen minutes to reach the edge of the trees, where he took a few moments to survey the vicinity.

After plotting his route to the house, he set off and settled into a small copse sixty yards from the open patio window with a clear line of sight, and watched Francis on the telephone, sitting by the fireplace.

Dane caught his breath and wiped the sweat from his eyes, and then scanned the area again. He had been certain someone was watching while he and Hayley had been in there. But the feeling had subsided and he'd seen no sign of anyone as he approached. Doubt crept into his brain.

The silence was broken by the doorbell. Francis finished his call and disappeared for a minute before returning with three men. He poured them all a drink, and they gathered round a laptop computer on a table. Dane could hear the murmur of conversation with the occasional loud guffaw but no distinct words. They remained riveted to the screen and now and then one of them would point at it and there would be discussion and the nodding of heads.

Dane scrutinised his surroundings looking for any movement, for the person he'd been sure was there. But he didn't spot a thing. He felt his phone vibrate with an incoming text from Hayley. A back-up team was in position and waiting a mile away. An hour after they arrived, Francis's visitors polished off their drinks and wandered out of the sitting room.

Dane listened as car doors slammed and engines started, and then headlights flickered through the trees as they drove away. Francis reappeared in the sitting room alone and settled down near the window with a book and a drink.

Twenty minutes later Francis suddenly looked up and turned, cocking his ear as if listening for something, before getting up and leaving the room.

A minute later Dane heard raised voices then a loud crash, as if someone had knocked over something heavy. It all went quiet and he was about to move when, with a bellow of rage, Francis staggered back into the sitting room with his arms secured behind his back. He was being pushed forward by a small woman dressed in black and carrying a rucksack. When they reached the middle of the room, she delivered a crushing kick to his groin.

Dane heard the thud of the impact and the gurgling cry as Francis toppled face down, writhing in pain. She pulled a rope from her rucksack and tied his hands together before looping it round his ankles.

Dane sent a text message to Hayley and sprinted across the lawn. By the time he reached the patio, she'd secured another length from Francis's throat to his ankles, pulling it tight so his heels were within inches of the back of his head. His eyes bulged with fear as she stuffed a rag into his mouth. Dane ran onto the patio and slipped on a patch of moss, which sent him sprawling. His knee crashed into the doorframe, smashing a pane of glass and causing him to cry out in pain.

The woman spun round like a cat, a razor-sharp Stanley knife in her hand, ready to repel any attack. She was slim, with long dark hair tied in a ponytail, and brown eyes.

Dane was dumbfounded to find Vonn Clyde standing defiantly in front of him.

As he hauled himself painfully to his feet, she leapt behind the prostrate Francis and held the blade against the rope. 'Stay there, or I'll cut it.'

'Hello, Julie. I've been looking everywhere for you.'

Her eyes flew wide with shock. 'That's not my name anymore.'

'Maybe not, but right now I'll stick with Julie.'

32

They stared at each other, the small woman holding the blade to the rope, ready to murder again, and the police officer rooted to the spot, desperately wanting to rub his throbbing knee.

'If you move, I'll cut it and he'll die,' she snapped.

'Okay, I'm staying here,' Dane replied, putting his hands out in front of him. 'Don't do anything you might regret.' He waited as she stared back at him.

'Now, what are we going to do? I guess you'll want to escape, but I can't let you kill him.'

'Why not? He deserves it.'

'I understand why you've been taking your revenge, but it's the wrong thing to do.'

'What other option did I have? A court would never convict them,' she said bitterly.

'I don't agree. In fact, I intend putting this creature away for a long time. Gareth Neil is sitting in a French prison with Joyce Parr. When the French courts have finished with them, I'll be waiting to lock Neil up for what he did to you and Gerry and Steph. I came here this evening to arrest him,' Dane replied, nodding to Francis.

'Why didn't you?'

'Because I wanted to stop you from making any more mistakes. Let's just say I left you a tethered goat, and you took the bait. But this one deserves to be in a jail cell and that's where he's going.' Dane shifted his weight to ease the pain in his knee.

She tensed. 'I told you, don't move.'

'You should have come forward with your evidence.'

'What would be the point? When I tried to do something before, this animal raped me – again – and – again.' She punctuated every word with a savage kick to his ribs.

'Why now? What made you decide to do this after all these years? You'll ruin your life and they'll send you down for the rest of it.'

'I doubt that,' she replied, and grasping the top of her hair, yanked the wig off.

Dane gasped at the shock of seeing the few straggly wisps remaining on her otherwise bald pate, and the grey, sickly pallor of her skin. He observed how much weight she'd lost since he'd last seen her.

'They would all have spent years in prison. That's real justice for all the victims.'

'Not long enough. They'd be free while they left me with this,' she snarled, pointing to her head. 'So, I handed out some rough justice.'

'But murdering them solves nothing. They escape with a few seconds of terror and pain when they should suffer in their cells as convicted child molesters.'

'I nearly came to you, and it would have been you because you're the only person who ever showed any understanding. But I needed to see these scumbags snivelling and crawling on the floor. Begging me not to kill them. I enjoyed watching them gasping for their last breaths. I made sure they understood who their executioner was. And that's what was going to happen to this one. The worst of them all. What he did to me and the other kids is beyond comprehension, with never an ounce of pity.'

She kicked Francis again. He groaned behind the gag, his eyes bulging in terror.

'While I understand your hatred, this must stop now. You can't kill him,' Dane said.

'At least I tried.'

'I've got to arrest you.'

She laughed. 'You can only do that if you catch me first.'

'I'd rather you released him and came quietly. He's going nowhere and there's more than enough to charge him with what he did to you all.'

She shrugged. 'The lawyers will line up to get him off. They'll say we're all liars and not to be trusted. Why should we go through all that? It isn't fair. He should be the one suffering.'

'I'll make it my business to ensure he pays for what he did. Of course they'll defend him, but we're already building a formidable case against him. They won't be able to keep him out of prison.'

'I believe you mean that, but you're stalling me. I expect they'll be here soon, and I don't intend to die in jail.' They both heard the crunch of tyres on the gravel outside the house. 'Time to move.'

'I'll be looking for you, Julie Miller,' Dane replied.

She smiled and sliced through the rope. Like a coiled spring being released, Francis's legs tried to straighten, incxorably tightening the noose around his throat. She picked up her rucksack, darted through the patio door and disappeared into the night.

Dane leapt forward to support Francis, then remembered his last experience and hobbled to the kitchen where he found a carving knife. By the time he returned Francis had stopped struggling. Dane cut the rope and flipped him onto his back, frantically trying to work the noose free. It took too long, but he managed it and when Hayley and two uniform police officers burst in, they discovered him pounding away on the comatose man's chest.

'Call an ambulance and help me,' Dane bellowed.

The paramedics arrived and relieved the exhausted Dane. As they lifted Francis onto a stretcher twenty minutes later, one of them turned to him.

'You saved his life.'

'Good,' Dane replied with grim determination. 'I don't want him dying yet. He's got a date with me.'

'Who was it?' Hayley asked as he slumped into the sagging settee.

'That was too close for comfort. It was Julie Miller. At least she didn't hit me this time. She legged it across the fields.'

More officers arrived and secured the property. They fanned out and while Dane waited for a search warrant to arrive, a huge manhunt swung into action. The force helicopter circled the surrounding countryside for hours, shining its searchlight down as dozens of police officers trudged through the countryside. A dog tracked the suspect's scent to a small lane a mile away where the trail went cold.

Dane told Hayley what had happened since he'd jumped out of the car but left out the real identity of the killer. He hadn't planned to do that, but once he started the lie, he found it easier to keep it going.

Wix and Sobers arrived, and he briefed them while showing them round the old house. In a converted room that had once accommodated servants a sophisticated computer was set up alongside another enormous collection of photographs and videos.

'Let's see him get out of this one,' Dane muttered, as he looked at the lines of photo albums.

'Would you recognise her again?' Wix asked.

'I won't forget her in a hurry.'

The fugitive evaded all attempts to find her, and Wix called off the search at daybreak. Pauline Rose, with her specialists and forensic scientists, gathered the evidence Dane needed to deal with Francis, who was now under guard in the hospital.

Dane got home after lunch the following day and rang Vicky. When they said their goodbyes, he settled on the bed and closed his eyes. He'd lied to her about the night's events. He could never admit to her, or anyone else, that he had deliberately allowed a murderer to go free.

But he would not give Vonn up. She'd suffered far too much pain, and he didn't see why she should suffer any more in what little time she had left. No one would forgive him if they found out, and he wondered for a few seconds if he wasn't being a hypocrite. Dane dismissed the thought, knowing he would continue the deception and deal with the feelings of guilt alone.

*

The investigation carried on as Hayley redoubled her efforts to track down Julie Miller. Sally and the rest of the investigation team concentrated on building a rock-solid case. The hospital released Francis into police custody four days later. His lawyers made strenuous representations to the chief constable to remove Dane from the investigation.

When that didn't work, they sought to persuade the courts to render the search and seizure of all the material from the house declared unlawful, which failed as well.

Jane Mitchell had followed Dane around scribbling copious notes. She stood with him as the jailer led Francis from his cell to the custody officer, who handed him over to the interviewing officers. As they passed in the corridor Francis glared at Dane with undisguised hatred.

Bob Soanes, who'd recently arrived to replace Phelan, was co-ordinating the interviews from the viewing room. Dane and Jane joined him and together they watched as Francis refused to answer questions.

Jane was excited about the material she'd gathered and hoped her next stop, with a firearms unit, would be as much fun. When they arrived back at the incident room, they found Sally visibly upset.

'What's wrong?'

'The welfare department just informed me that Vonn Clyde was admitted to Bute Hospice last night. She's in the advanced stages of cervical cancer and not expected to live for more than a week. She's asked for you to visit her. You can go anytime.'

'Oh, no. How awful,' Jane exclaimed, with her hand over her mouth, all her excitement evaporating in an instant. 'The poor thing, she was so lively, and never stopped bloody working. Please give her my best wishes.'

*

The sight of Vonn lying in the bed with only a single catheter pumping palliative care shocked Dane to the core. She looked skeletal, and he knew she'd given up.

'I'm so sorry to see you like this, Vonn. Is there anything you need?'

She studied him with her trademark intense stare. 'Why didn't you turn me in?'

Dane sat beside the bed and gazed out of the window for a few moments before turning to face her. 'A dose of guilt, perhaps. I missed the chance to help you when I found you hiding in Basildon all those years ago. Instead, I took you back to that home and left you in their hands.'

'I wanted to tell you then about what was going on, but I didn't completely trust you. It was my fault for thinking I could sort it out myself and by the time I realised my mistake, it was too late. So please don't blame yourself.'

'I should have done more. You're not a danger to anyone now and I won't make things any more difficult than they already are. It would serve no purpose, and only give Francis and Neil some wriggle room. Your secret is safe with me, provided you promise not to kill again.'

'Scout's honour,' she replied and tried to laugh, but it caused a grimace of pain. 'I owe you an explanation.'

'Yes, you do.'

'Once I got away from that place and the social workers, I travelled around for a few months and found my feet. I used a couple of different names and did a few odd jobs in bars and restaurants before I settled down and picked up an education. The medical problems started when they diagnosed me with genital warts on my seventeenth birthday. I've suffered a never-ending succession of issues ever since. The doctors and nurses would lecture me about my perceived loose lifestyle and treated me like I was a tart working the streets. Because of what happened, I've never enjoyed a proper relationship with anyone and there's only ever been me. Once I created my new identity, I got on with what I hoped would be the next phase of my life and moved to the West Country.'

'Why there?'

'Because it's a nice place to live. I joined the Met a few years later.'

'How did you get through the vetting?'

'My identity is watertight, and the Met are useless at checking up on people. I'd make a complaint if I had time,' she smiled. 'It's only my name that's false. All the qualifications are real. I obviously said nothing about my previous history, and they never asked, so I got away with it. I loved the job, but I gained a reputation for being an antisocial cow and saw no reason to prove any different. I was on plain-clothes observations in Borough Market when Steph tapped me on the shoulder. She didn't realise what I was doing and invited me round for a meal and told me what she'd been up to. I liked her husband. She's done well for herself.'

'Yes, she has, and they've taken Gerry under their wing.'

'Good, I'm glad. Poor old Gerry, that Binks was evil. Anyway, Steph mentioned about Wilson being locked up. I'd not heard about that, so I did some research into him and the others. I intended to expose them all. But I bottled it. I couldn't face going against them again. They'd beaten me the first time round. And, if I went public, my history would come out and I'd lose my job. They'd quashed everything I ever said and painted me as an attention-seeker and an untrustworthy witness. If I came forward and made my allegations after lying to get in the police, they'd twist it against me. So, I gave up and got on with my career.'

'What drove you to change your mind?'

'It started with a problem bloke on my CID team. A right muppet who fancied me and tried it on. I told him I wasn't interested and he didn't like it, so started spreading all sorts of rumours about me. He had a gang of mates who were out-and-out bullies, and they thought no one would dare go against them. I did, and what I said brought a world of trouble down on my head, with senior officers threatening me with all sorts. My own chief superintendent ordered me to drop it all because it made his division look bad, and I wouldn't get away with doing that to him. I recorded our chat and then complained about him as well. After he accused me of lying, I produced the tape. They sacked him, which sent my popularity ratings even lower. Wix took me under her wing and when she got her promotion, suggested I apply for Essex. I had to think long and hard about that because it meant I might run into people who'd remember me. Parr, for instance, or you.'

'I'd never have recognised you. Well, I didn't, did I.'

'When Wix gave me the posting to your team, I nearly turned it down. I'm glad I took the chance because once we'd met and you obviously had no recollection of me, I loved it. It helped to be involved in investigating my own crimes, of course.' She let out a short grunting laugh.

'You'd already started killing them by then, hadn't you?'

'Yes, I had.'

'Why?'

'I'd fallen ill again. My doctor diagnosed cervical cancer and I'm certain the stress of the problems with the Met caused it. I was already on long-term sick leave, so I said nothing about the diagnosis or the chemo.'

'But surely your boss visited you?'

'You're kidding. I had no visits from anyone from the job for more than a year. Wix kept in contact, but only by phone. So, it was easy to hide my secret from everyone. I'd already passed the medical for Essex and once the discipline hearings ended, they let the transfer go through. The doctor informed me the cancer was inoperable and terminal on the day I officially joined Essex. So, I devoted what time I had left to sort them out. I took the law into my own hands and killed them. They deserved it and now I'm happy to die because I settled the score for what they did to me and all the others they brutalised. Wilson told me where Parr lived. I enjoyed killing Parr the most. He recognised me as soon as he opened that door. The look on his face when I zapped him with the Taser and tied him up was priceless. When he realised he was about to die, the real coward came out. He struggled and pleaded for mercy, like he made me do. I watched him. I looked him straight in the eyes as he died. He wasn't so cocky then.'

'Why did you kill Patey?'

'Because he caught sight of me, and the idiot would never keep his stupid gob shut.'

Dane threw his hands up. 'You were behind me in the cell block. That's where he saw you.'

'Yes, that nearly ruined everything. I accidentally walked into his eyeline. I put my finger to my lips and nipped out of the way.'

'I wondered what he'd seen. But did you have to kill him?'

'That was his fault. When Wix cancelled the surveillance, I popped round to his flat and suggested he clear off. But he tried to blackmail me and get me into bed. "How about a quick one, for old time's sake," he said. Not a clever idea and the last mistake of his wretched, insignificant existence. I put him out of my misery. If he hadn't been so stupid, he'd still be alive. He was as much a victim as I am. Binks wet himself before I even tied him up and Lowe came within an ace of overpowering me. I was getting weaker, so I had to whack him with the Taser. I'm sorry I hit you, but I'd used so much power on Lowe there wasn't enough left in the Taser to knock you over, so I had to use the bottle. You nearly got me there, a few moments earlier and you would've seen me.'

'When would you have stopped?'

'Once I'd killed them all. I didn't know Francis's full name or where to find him, and none of the others would give him up. Working with you helped me, and I even considered visiting Parr's wife until you found out about the surveillance on her place. So, I followed you.'

'I knew someone was there. I found the tracker by the way.'

She managed a weak smile. 'Modern technology. I kept tabs on you and Hayley without even leaving my house. I had to go sick because I was really getting worse and didn't want to be part of the interviews with the other victims. They might have recognised me. When I tracked you to that house, I knew you'd found him. So, I dosed myself up to the eyeballs and got there in time to see you talking to him. I recognised him immediately and couldn't believe my luck when you left him there. I watched the vehicle drive away on my phone and thought I was clear. When he was downstairs with his visitors, I broke in and took the pictures he had of me and then I jumped him after they'd gone. But for you, he'd be dead.'

They fell silent. Dane noticed her squirm as a pulse of pain coursed through her. How sad she should end her life like this, to be so matter-of-fact about the murder of five men.

'What about Gareth Neil?'

'I missed him at his flat, but you can't win 'em all. I'm not that bothered about him. It was Francis I really wanted, the worst of the lot, some things he did to us beggars belief. He would've killed someone, for the thrill, if he thought he'd get away with it. One night, a few weeks after I'd complained to the police about Patey, he strangled me with his tie. I regained consciousness in my bedroom at the home. Steph told me that Parr only just stopped him from doing me in. She fell silent for a moment. 'Listen, I've always been on my own, and I'll die alone. Would you do me another favour, please?'

'That depends what it is.'

'Take care of my funeral and give my few possessions to charity.' She leant over and pulled an envelope from her bedside cabinet. 'It's all arranged, and the details are in here. I'd feel happier if you'd sort it out for me.'

'I'll do that for you, Vonn.'

She smiled her thanks; the effort of talking had worn her out. 'There's no evidence to link me with any of the scenes. I've destroyed all the pictures of me they kept. That was all I took from them, apart from their lives, of course. So, there's nothing left to incriminate me. Thank you for not arresting me.'

'I'm sorry it has to be like this.'

She managed a wan smile. 'That's life.'

*

The investigation into the activities of Francis gathered pace. They completed the interviews and Dane watched as Francis was brought before the custody officer and charged with multiple counts of rape and other sexual assaults. The lawyers complained about the lack of bail and threatened all sorts of legal ramifications, but Dane knew it was all bluster. For all his prominent position in society, Francis was now regarded as a pariah. Sally and her team continued to speak to more victims of abuse and had a list of thirty people. Many identified Francis as their abuser.

Dane sat opposite Wix as she read his update on the investigations. 'Still no sign of Miller, I see,' Wix said.

'No, I expect she's resumed her false identity which is too good to break.'

'So, we have a serial killer on the loose and no way of finding her?'

'I wouldn't go that far; she'll slip up one day.'

'But when? And at what cost? This is all your fault. If you'd done your job properly and put a cordon around that house before rushing in like a reckless amateur, we could have arrested her. This is another example of your maverick, I-know-better-than-anyone-else attitude. No risk assessment, no planning or thought and totally unprofessional. This is your final warning. Any more of your crass behaviour and you'll be out on your ear. So, buck your ideas up, Dane, because I'll be watching you. Now get out.'

'Yes, ma'am.' *I asked for that.*

He'd just got back to his car when his phone rang. It was the hospice informing him Vonn had died peacefully in her sleep. Dane felt desperately sad and hoped she found peace in death because life had denied her any.

Rest in peace, Julie.

His mood lifted the following morning when he received a call from Laura Hobbs. 'Hello. Is everything all right?'

'Yes, I wanted to thank you for everything. Christopher and I are leaving Witness Protection tomorrow.'

'Where are you going?'

'We're being taken in by new foster parents in Suffolk. We went up there last week and it's brill.'

'I'm pleased to hear that. How is Christopher?'

'He's still a prat but I'm glad we'll be together.'

'So am I. Good luck, Laura.'

*

On the morning of Vonn's funeral, Vicky drove them to the crematorium. As she parked, Dane received a call from Brian White.

'Gareth Neil was murdered in prison last night.'

'Do they know who did it?' Dane replied.

'Yes, one of the Italians we captured from the van stabbed him.'

'What about Joyce Parr?'

'We've placed her in solitary confinement for her own safety.'

'Do you think she'll talk now?'

'Who knows? I'll keep you posted,' White said.

Vonn Clyde had no family and few friends, so her funeral was a relatively quiet affair. The office attended *en masse,* sad at the loss of one of their own. Wix looked sombre as she read a eulogy. As everyone filed out, Dane stood alone by her coffin. He felt someone beside him and turned to find Hayley.

'Nice service,' she said.

'Yes, I suppose it was.'

Hayley shifted on the spot.

'What is it?'

'I found her.'

'Who?'

'Julie Miller. I've identified her,' she whispered, moving closer.

'Ah.'

'It's an interesting story, and it's been a useful exercise for me to discover how she did it so effectively. She took extraordinary measures to cover her tracks, and it was only a stroke of pure luck that I found her. No one else knows who she became, and they never will now.'

'What have you done?' Dane said, glancing at her inscrutable face.

'I was a bit careless and pressed a delete button by accident. Sorry about that. So, what should I do, boss?'

'You don't need me to tell you what you should do with that information. I won't ask you to protect me or lie for me.'

Dane heard Hayley offer a quiet prayer over the coffin. Then she turned to her boss again.

'I understand why you did it, and I'd like to think I'd have the courage to do the same. The only people who will ever know are me and you because I'm not going to say anything. Vonn suffered enough. She fought all her life and deserves to be remembered as a good copper and nothing else.'

'I'd agree with you there.'

'That's settled, then. Come on, I'm gasping for a smoke.'

The End.

Printed in Great Britain
by Amazon